THE PROBLEM AT
THE ORPHANAGE

Broken Beach Publishing, New York

Library of Congress Control Number: 2022906693

Trade Paperback ISBN: 979-8-9863307-0-9
eBook ISBN: 979-8-9863307-1-6

FOR MOM AND DAD

Also by David Biesty

The Outcast Missing Someone

THE PROBLEM AT THE ORPHANAGE

DAVID BIESTY

1

Artie has been off the thruway for over an hour. The twists in the road and the occasional glimpse of fall colors in the trees slow his progress.

–You will be late.

He tries to keep the car at the posted forty-five-mile-per-hour speed limit for this country road, but his cautiousness forces his foot up a minuscule distance from the accelerator pedal at each bend and double curve that he must transit. The sedan—a hybrid with NYS government plates—is new to him. He had tried to set the cruise control speed specification to the exact speed limit. But even if he had been successful, his tapping of the brake upon approaching a curve would cancel it, and he could not remember how to resume the automation feature. Involuntarily, his face keeps inching closer and closer to the windshield as his foot moves higher and higher off the gas pedal.

–Late, late, late. No doubt, this is a big project for you; had to take it. Messing it up. Phone nav told you it would take less time but couldn't speed. Department car has its tracking on. That's what they said. That's what was written in those forms you signed and initialed at the bottom of each page. "Just sign it and go, like everybody else," that pretty woman at the motor pool desk told you. You had to read it, had to go through fifteen pages of lawyer stuff. The car tracks everywhere you go, every speed on every road, GPS, E-ZPass tolls, gas usage, weather conditions, seat belt. You couldn't speed, couldn't take turns too fast, don't overaccelerate, create a PIN for the gas card. Don't return it with less than three-quarters of a tank of gas. Who to call in an emergency. Slowing? Resume cruising speed. Slowing? Force your back into the seat and keep your hands at four o'clock and eight o'clock.

But then a bend, an ess, a double ess. He finds himself with his face over his two hands at twelve o'clock and his right foot off the accelerator, covering the brake—losing time.

Across the vale that the road winds through, he spots a tree whose leaves have begun to turn. Summer recently ended, but up here the nights are starting to get cold, sometimes to the forties. Downstate, lower in altitude, with the warm Atlantic water nearby, the change to fall would come much later. He turns the AC temperature lower, noticing the country-road driving he's unaccustomed to is making him sweat. He wonders if running the AC in a hybrid auto could spike his gasoline usage and throw up red flags at the motor pool office.

–You have no idea how much more gas this car will use with the air conditioner running.

A large tractor trailer rumbles past, moving in the opposite direction. The displaced air pushes his car over, the right wheels going onto the shoulder. The tires reverberate on the uneven surface. He overcompensates with the small steering wheel, sending the car's left wheels across the double yellow lines. He adjusts calmly, with no cars ahead, back into his proper lane.

The radio is static. He is unsure of the controls and turns it off rather than be distracted trying to learn how to get a clear station.

He finds himself hunched over the steering wheel again with hands at twelve o'clock. He sits back.

–It will be fine. You'll be a little late, that's all. They're the ones that have to explain themselves to you.

He rolls his shoulders against the seat with pressure in order to get comfortable and maybe get the knots out of his tensed deltoids. He moves his hands back to the four and eight position that he newly learned in his safe driver's course—online.

Another tree with the hint of fall color ahead. It stands out on the slope of his side of the road, high and to the right. Orange and yellow among green.

–Pretty tree. You should be enjoying this scenic drive. It's a big change from flat Long Island.

He loses sight of the vibrant colors when the hillside—below the tree—steepens where it appears to have been dug out for the road. He develops a fondness for that particular tree. After passing it, he daringly cranes his neck back to see if he can spot his tree. The view from the rear of the small car is restricted, and nothing can be observed above ten feet, blocked by the ceiling of the car.

"Turn right," his phone navigation tells him. His relaxation disappears as he strains his eyes trying to discern a place to turn in the palisade of trees. He pushes his glasses back.

–You needed more of a lead. Nothing here. Looks like a mailbox ahead.

"Turn right."

He does full brake. Tires grate. He overshoots the narrow turnoff. He releases the brake and slowly proceeds forward, looking for a safe place to make a U-turn.

–You can't see too far in either direction, a very bad spot to get stuck parallel to the flow of traffic. You have an accident in your future.

He drives a mile and stops on the shoulder, just past another crushed-basalt driveway. He double-checks for cars, then backs up the driveway before pulling out, headed back to the proper turnoff.

"Make a U-turn when it is safe," his navigation system tells him.

"You know I already did," he scolds the app.

"Turn left."

And he does, into the driveway. Artie notices a sign buried in foliage, seven feet up—Orphanary for Foundling Girls. It is more than ten feet in from the road.

–Orphanary for Foundling Girls. You would think they didn't want you to find it. And looks like the top part of the sign was sawn off.

Artie's car creeps slowly, crunching up the steep, uneven, finely crushed aggregate roadway—trees on each side, wide enough for one car with the occasional siding for passing vehicles. Artie Alston feels relief, and his shoulders untense as the narrow passage of forest breaks to reveal the school. The path flattens, becomes perfectly smooth concrete. A SLOW! WATCH FOR CHILDREN sign greets him.

–That's responsible.

The sun is illuminating the trees, and light comes back to him as he enters the clearing of the campus. Low greenery with mums set in flower beds gives him a welcome, homey feeling. The first building—to his right and slightly downhill—is immediately accessible from the original crushed aggregate road. It appears historic, not properly maintained and free of landscaping. It is coarse brick, two stories with a tower on the right side.

–Looks unused.

A modern garage door can be seen on the side. The road bends left beyond a green lawn and brings him to a modern four-story school building. Its veneer is shining in tall glass with dark, faux wood panels.

–Like a modern office building.

Some young men are out front adding fresh mulch to the flower beds on each side of the stairs. He pulls to a stop.

–Nice mums. Where do you park around here?

He calls to a worker wearing brown coveralls, "Excuse me, young man."

"Yes, sir," he answers, moving closer. He approaches the car, holding a rake with both hands to the side, away from his body and Artie.

"Could you tell me where to park? I have a meeting. I'm a little late actually. Is this the correct building for Miss Hunt?"

The young man looks around.

"She's the president, I believe."

"Headmistress? Yeah, you can leave this car right there. Go up these stairs. Someone at the desk can help."

"Thank you. Are you sure I'm allowed to park here?"

"If you're going to Headmistress, sure."

Artie turns the car off after shutting the window and exits. "Your crew is doing a beautiful job on this landscaping."

"No crew team here."

"I mean you and the other workers."

"I'm a student."

"Very nice. I see you take great pride in your school's appearance."

The young man winces and gets back to evening his mulch with the rake that he grips tightly.

–He's a boy. That must be the school crest on the chest of his gardening uniform. Gardening club is such a fun activity.

Artie bounds up the short flight of stairs, his legs happy to be unwound from the car. He passes through the first set of automatic, glass doors, a foyer with a mosaic tile floor and then a second set of doors.

–No lock, no security: you must note this.

Nobody is here. A still hallway extends to either side. He heads toward the OFFICE OF THE HEADMISTRESS sign.

He knocks as he walks into the large reception area.

–Smile.

"Hello."

"Hello back at cha," a smartly dressed secretary says to him from behind a mostly empty desk.

"I'm Artie Alston from the State Education Department."

The woman stands. She has a long, pink, high-waisted skirt that is covering a good deal of her white blouse—two buttons undone, showing a little cleavage. Her hair is pulled back from her face and stands high from a black headband.

–Like the sixties.

She is moving a mint around in her mouth. She extends her right arm to him, palm down, wrist flexed.

–Could she expect me to kiss the back of her hand?

Artie awkwardly attempts a handshake.

"I'm Sandi. Nice to meet cha."

"Yes, nice to meet you. Not everyone is happy to get a visit from…" He does air quotes. "The State."

"Oh, I like that thing you did with your fingers." She copies his air quotes.

"Yes."

–Does she not know what that is? Why are you smiling?

She smiles back and holds her hands together near her waist and rolls her shoulders left and right.

"I have an appointment."

A blank stare comes back at him.

"With President Gabrielle Hunt."

"Oh, Headmistress. Super. Right to the top for you. Not many people get in straight away to see the grand, exalted wizard without a stop with a teacher."

Artie waits for direction.

–*Wizard of Oz* reference, you hope.

"You know, peek behind the curtain like the movie. 'We're off to visit the wizard.'"

"Yes, yes. Would you direct me to her office or let her know I'm here?" He rises up on his toes and relaxes back on his heels.

Sandi walks out from behind her large desk and past Artie to the door he entered from. There, a speaker is on the wall—a round, screened hole with a metal plate around it holding two toggle switches. "Headmistress, there is a man, a nice-looking man," she says, holding one of the switches down.

–You can't let that flattery take hold, totally inappropriate.

"He's from the State. He has an appointment."

"He should come in," streams through, garbled.

"This way," Sandi says to Artie and leads him back past her desk to an open door that is closer to her workspace than the antiquated intercom.

"Thank you," he tells Sandi.

She smiles back but follows him in. "Headmistress, this is Mr. Artie Alston from the State." She turns to Artie. "Oh, I forgot to do the thing with the fingers."

"Terrific, Sandi," the woman behind the desk says while looking down into a small mirror and applying eyeliner. The room is large, with wood paneling—a lighter shade of oak. The white ceiling is high and coffered in a darker wood. The walls have bookshelves but few books. Instead, many pictures of what could be the school grounds and staff are in tilting picture frames. The desk is modern, with a pane of glass over the wood top, and has a desk pad with leather edges. A large, paper calendar—greatly marked up—is visible. "Hello, Mr. Arthur Alston from the State. I will be just another second."

Sandi leaves, and Headmistress continues framing her eyes.

"It's actually Artie. Please call me Artie."

"Artie," she says indifferently, still looking down to her mirror. She also wears a white blouse. She is curvy but large. Her cleavage strains up and out of the open top of her blouse as she breathes. Artie notices.

–No wedding ring.

"Yes. My father is Arthur. My mother didn't want two of us, so my name is actually Artie. It's not a nickname."

Headmistress finishes, looks up at Artie but then goes back to looking down. She takes her time, indifferently and noisily putting away her cosmetics. When she is finished, she looks up at Artie and scoots her chair closer under the desk.

–She is pretty, though not your type. A lot of perfume. The females here get a lot dressier than in your office.

Her hair makes him think of the Farrah style that was popular once. She laces her fingers together and places her forearms onto the desk. She leans in on her forearms, and her breasts surge from contacting them, rising into the opening of her shirt. "Well, I am Headmistress Gabrielle Hunt."

Headmistress extends her hand, palm down, flexed down, as Sandi did.

–Is this a thing? Seems old-fashioned.

Artie reaches out and awkwardly shakes her loose hand. "I know my superiors let you know about this a bit back ago. It seems the state audit required by law has lapsed some time ago."

–You sound ridiculous, repeating yourself.

"That is, someone noticed, and it's so far past in the past."

–Ugh.

"You could say expired, that an in-person, focused survey became necessary."

"Please sit down, Mr. Alston." She exhales and relaxes her shoulders, sitting back. Her breasts move down from the shirt opening as if deflating slightly.

Artie, noting there is no chair in front of the desk, scans the room. "Should I retrieve one of the chairs from by the door?" he asks while walking back the way he came after spotting some sturdy wooden chairs by the entrance.

"That would be fine. I prefer the students to stand in front of the desk if they get sent to me. Not at attention, mind you, but smartly. I think it helps instill respect, and that encourages them to keep their time here in line with the school's priorities."

Artie grasps the chair and is surprised by how heavy it is. He bends his knees and back and adjusts his grip. While looking down through the chair slats, he notices the wood on the walls is peeling where it meets the molding.

–Faux wood panels or glaze?

He hefts the chair, bends his knees some more, lifts and carries it to the desk. It drops with a ringing clump that echoes in the high-ceilinged area.

"Don't you have some clipboard or expanding file case with papers for me to sign?"

Artie sits, adjusts his glasses and blows out a deep breath through tight lips. "We have all I need. That is, we need, since the State ED works with schools, together. Everything is accessible on my phone or laptop, which is in the car, but I have spent some time with the file already."

"And what department are you with…"

"Artie, please call me Artie."

"Artie. Education Department?"

"Yes."

"I am trying to recall who we deal with over there." She again leans her breasts onto her forearms, causing them to rise. Artie stares.

–Look somewhere else. She's not your type.

Headmistress gets up and rounds the desk, moving toward the door. She has a skirt on that ends above the knee.

–Seems a little short for work. How old do you think she is?

The skirt is tight around her large backside, which pushes out with every step in her three-inch, stylish heels. At the side of the door, she leans into the molding and calls into the outer office. "Sandi."

Artie looks over his shoulder at Headmistress' ass and sees Sandi arrive at the doorway. "Yes, Headmistress."

"Do you know who is our point person with the State?"

"Besides Mr. Alston?" she asks.

"Mr. Alston is with me now."

"That's fine. Do you need tea?"

"Yes. We'll have tea. Then can you check our filings. Just what's in the office. You don't have to go all the way down to the records room. Mr. Alston doesn't need to be here all day."

–Was that meant for you?

"I am actually going to be on this for a while," Artie says, straining his neck to see both women.

"Ahem," Headmistress clears her throat.

"Do you need anything else?" Sandi asks.

"That is all."

Sandi disappears as Headmistress starts back to her desk.

"Just the tea, please, Sandi." She sits.

"I am unable to find a K-12 cert for your school. If you have your copy, we could wrap this up pretty quickly."

Headmistress resumes her position with her breast on her desked forearms. Each breath causes rising and deflating that Artie struggles to avoid looking at. "My files are all in order. This facility is considered one of the most successful in the state. We have incredible success with these young women. Success that even children in well-off, parented households do not rise to. Paperwork isn't an issue. The girls are the issue."

"The students," Artie says to take his eyes off her breasts and find her eyes.

"Of course I am talking about students. That is our emphasis, not paperwork, forms, filings, what have you." She sits back, giving Artie's attention a break from the flooding and ebbing tides. "I am recalling our original charter for this entire facility was with the Division of

Youth as a home for orphaned girls. A lot has changed since then. Those would be paper records, old files, not on your phone."

"Yes," Artie says meekly. "But we can't have a lapse. Education has to have some oversight. This is a school as well."

"This sounds more like an interagency issue than an issue with this school." She crosses her arms, moving her breasts up into her blouse opening.

–You can't take this as unprofessional behavior. You can't react. She's not even your type.

Artie takes a deep breath. Headmistress notices. He lets it out slowly, his lips almost together. A low whistle can be heard. He's embarrassed by how she is affecting him. "I believe…" He pauses again for a breath. "I believe we are all on the children's side. We are a team for them. The State, that is, the Office of Children and Family Services, which was the Department of Youth but was changed in the eighties, and the Education Department are working with you. We provide resources for your boarding, education establishment."

"Do you mean money, Mr. Artie?"

"Yes. The ED directly funds this institution, and not through the county, because of the situation, special situation. Is that correct, that this school does not report to the county's board of education?"

"No, sir. We don't. We have girls from all over the state, some even from out of state. The county is not involved. As for your resources, as you call it, that funding is weak. We could not elevate these girls, these family-less girls, with only the money the government sends us, some of which is pass-through money from the federal government's department of education. We mostly run on human capital here."

Artie cannot understand how this became confrontational. "We only want to do our focused survey and let you get back to teaching, taking care of these students. The State has a right to these records."

"Well, I don't see why you don't just get them from Youth Services or whatever you call it. We are plugging away, and I think you could accomplish this better if you went up to Renssalaer. I mean, if they have the records, then in my view, the State has the records. You work for the State, so you have them."

"I will contact them, and hopefully this will go smoothly."

"Of course it will. We have people up in Albany and New York City."

Sandi comes in with a large mug of tea for each of them, a plate with lemon wedges and a porcelain creamer. The mugs and plate have the school emblem glazed on them. She leaves as Artie pours some milk into his tea, watching it turn a gray hue. "Is this cream?"

"That would be almond milk substitute. You don't have a nut allergy, do you?"

"No. Thanks for the warning." Artie tastes his tea while Headmistress squeezes a lemon wedge above hers. He regrets not choosing the lemon.

"We don't have many real milk products. Hormones. We want to limit that for the girls. Puberty is tough enough. We do have real ice cream. I don't believe the faux ice creams are near as good, and if you treat yourself, it's fine once in a while. In fact, tonight is sundae night. We even have some real whipped cream that our chef, Donna, makes herself. Local cow, no hormones, she tells me."

"That's nice, sundae night."

"You can come, of course. I don't know how long it is you will be around."

Artie notices some stress was removed from the room with the dessert talk. "I was hoping to see the campus, get acquainted with the area—lay of the land, so to speak. Maybe someone could show me around while Sandi pursues the filings."

Headmistress stands and comes right to Artie. Before he can stand, she is right next to him, her breasts at eye level. As he begins to rise, he notices he has the start of an erection. He plops back in his seat, turns from her and coughs, trying to buy some time and ease his new stressor. "I'll be right with you." He bends further forward, covering his mouth and clearing his throat.

"It wasn't the tea, I hope."

"No. I'll have another sip."

She goes toward the door.

He takes a big gulp of tea, which is almost too hot to bear, but it helps his lower situation. He stands. "I am right behind you."

Out in the front office, Sandi is at her desk, idle.

Headmistress says, "You can bring your tea or leave it on Sandi's desk."

"I'll take that," Sandi says.

Artie hands her the mug. She puts it down on a plate and gives him a wave.

–She's not doing a paperwork search.

He walks alongside Headmistress to the opposite side of the building and into an empty gym. "Not much here. We do not have enough girls to sponsor extramural sports. Dance aerobics and Zumba are favorites."

"This is a nice facility."

–No seating?

"This building is from the nineties. All the classrooms and day cafeteria. That's lunch and breakfast." She pauses. "But not in that order."

Artie chuckles along with her as she leads him up a switchback flight of stairs to the second floor. Initially he is lagging, with his face level with her sizable rump, then noticeably, awkwardly, he speeds to a position beside her. They walk into the cafeteria. The room has individual chairs—not benches—and neat tables. It looks freshly mopped, and beyond, he can see a gleaming, stainless-steel kitchen with young men in whites cleaning. The two go out to the hall again.

"Also, we have some offices on this floor. Classrooms upstairs," she says, reentering the stairway through the doors. On the next level, while they stroll the corridor, Headmistress says, "This and the fourth floor are the same, older girls up higher. All the labs, but the same layouts. Let's go down."

Artie stops at a classroom and peers into the door glass.

—A clean, sleek layout.

Then he continues following Headmistress. She stops at the elevator and presses the call button. "Two elevators. We let the seniors use it and faculty and any girls with conditions requiring its use." They enter the elevator, and Headmistress presses the M button.

—A lot of mirrors.

Artie checks his look at the back and each side of the elevator car. He secures his glasses with an index finger.

When they exit the building, Headmistress asks, "Would you like to continue the tour of the campus?"

"Yes," Artie says, finding himself enjoying Headmistress' company more than he would have predicted when he first met her.

Headmistress pulls a radio from her designer handbag and after a squelch says, "Doc Washington, pick up."

"Yes, Headmistress."

"Do you have a golf cart available, a nice one for a guest tour?"

"Of course. You can have mine. Do you need me to drive you?"

"Anyone is fine. We are outside the Saints' building."

"On the way."

Headmistress returns the radio to her bag. "We could walk. But I don't have those shoes now," she says and turns sideways to Artie, kicking up and back one high-heeled shoe, showing off to Artie. "It goes with my bag." She remains that way, inviting a reply. "I think they do, anyway."

"They do go well," Artie says finally, and she returns her foot to the paving stones.

—That EEO, sexual harassment training has you on edge. Relax.

"I see the cart coming now," Headmistress says with an underhand, palm-open swing of her arm toward the old building Artie saw on entry.

"Is that the original school building?" Artie asks, nodding his head at it.

"I believe it was. It is the Butt."

"Butt?"

"B.U.T.T. We say Butt: barracks, utility, tools and transport. We could see it, if you like. No classrooms though. It's been landmarked. Our capital budget came up a little short to redo the interior. No one wants to change the exterior, historical and all that."

The new-looking golf cart pulls up. Jorgie is driving. He has his rake beside him, handle up. He stands and grabs the rake from where it's secured to the outside of the golf cart, holding it tightly while he hustles around to Artie and Headmistress. "Good afternoon, Headmistress."

"Good afternoon, Jorgie. This is Mr. Alston from the State."

"Hello, sir. Doc Washington said you needed a driver for the tour."

"Yes," Headmistress says. "Mr. Alston will sit up front with you, so he has the best view. I'll take the rear."

Jorgie steps aside and holds out a hand to help Headmistress up onto the back step, and he keeps her hand until she is settled on the rear-facing seat with a noticeable drop in the back of the cart. In one motion, Headmistress crosses her legs, releases Jorgie's hand and turns, angled toward the front passenger seat. She lightly kicks up and down one of her designer heels, the back slipping out and resetting.

–She has shapely legs for a woman of her size. You have to stop looking.

Artie climbs aboard. Jorgie resumes his position behind the steering wheel. Then he clips his rake to the outside of the cart.

"Nice and easy, Jorgie. I'm not going to fasten my seat belt."

"Yes, Headmistress." The cart accelerates smoothly around the right side of the Saints' building, along a walking path and slightly uphill.

"The Cousin's please, Jorgie."

"Yes, Headmistress."

"The building there, to the right, is the arts center."

Artie turns back to look at Headmistress. She has sunglasses on now. Artie looks down to avoid looking right into the eyes that he can't find behind the dark lenses and winds up glancing at her chest.

"Official name is Saint Germain Cousin's Building."

Artie looks back to the front at the building. It is also new, one story, brick with faux shutters framing the windows and a high, steeply pitched roof, evoking a modernized, old church. Jorgie gently stops the cart in front of the building.

Headmistress, pointing to the landscaping, says, "Jorgie, convey to Doc Washington: he should have these flower beds cleaned out."

"Yes, Headmistress." Jorgie moves to the back of the cart to assist Headmistress, who is patiently waiting for his hand. "I could get started on it now, while you are inside."

"That is not necessary. I don't want you filthy for the remainder of the tour."

"Yes, Headmistress."

Artie and Headmistress walk up the three steps. "Very polite young man," Artie says.

"They all seem that way. I know for a fact they are not all gentlemanly when superiors aren't around." Headmistress stops at the door, waiting for Artie to open it.

"Oh!" he exclaims and opens the door for Headmistress. She waits again at the next set of doors, and he repeats.

They enter an open, airy room. Artie looks up at the high ceiling with exposed, finished wood beams. There are girls at tables in different sections. A female teacher comes toward them. "Good afternoon, Headmistress," she greets them. She is thin and also in a skirt and blouse.

"Good afternoon. Miss Richmond, this is Mr. Alston from the State. I am giving him a tour."

Glenda Richmond holds out her hand, high and palm down.

–Another one.

"I'm glad you came to see us," she says.

Artie gently shakes her soft hand. "Very nice room for creativity," he says, purposely being complimentary.

"Yes, open creativity time we call this. Limit on screen time."

"Difficult to do now, isn't it?"

"I think most girls like the break. All in the big room it gets to be a positive peer pressure."

"And you seem very positive."

Headmistress leads Artie through double doors, into a similar room but with older girls—clustered at different tables, with lighted mirrors and open, tiered tray cases—applying large amounts of cosmetics. Some girls are at dress form mannequins.

–No adult present?

"Good afternoon, Headmistress," one girl standing at a clothed dress form says, and the rest follow her lead greeting Headmistress.

"Good afternoon, young ladies. This is Mr. Alston. We are just showing off to him. Continue your good work." She turns and leads Artie out a side door. "These young women in there are sharp. Fashion eyes in all of them."

–An eye for fashion?

"A good deal of makeup on some of the students," Artie says as they follow a path to the front of the building.

"This is the time for them to experiment. Unsupervised, as I am sure you noticed."

"I did."

"We have more formal cosmetology classes. Part of our self-image programs we have for the young ladies. We find that when left alone to try to find their best looks, they make mistakes. Overapplication being the most obvious and common with those who are new to the field. Discovering colors, hues, shading, depth: all come from mistakes. And they feel freer to make them there, together. They critique each other. I won't lie, some can be cruel, but they learn to phrase it more supportively. And then they improve in the more structured class-room, self-image instruction. We teach them to dress their faces for a business meeting or job interview just as we do with apparel."

Artie nods along, his hands clasped behind his back, head down, eyes furtively glancing alternatively at Headmistress' legs and cleavage, straining not to turn his head.

"We get quite a few donations from high-end design houses for the ladies' graduation. Pantsuits too. Some of the graduates take to those more than others."

"I'm sure graduation must be an especially difficult time here."

"I do miss some of these fine, young women."

"I meant for the students. They have to leave this beautiful cam-pus, with no family to go to who could support them through their university years."

"We let them stay for a year or two in the graduate dorm section on breaks. It's small. They go to their college dorms. Our young women have a one hundred percent acceptance rate to universities. But can come back on breaks. They are quite changed when they do. Outside influences, that's why eventually it has to end. Some have relatives to go to. Foster care helps until twenty-one. But then a very cold split." They are back at the golf cart. "Jorgie," Headmistress says, holding out her hand for assistance. Jorgie leans his rake against the golf cart and complies. "We should go by the athletic fields and Adjutor's, that's our aquatics center. Then to the Joes'."

Jorgie says, "Yes, Headmistress," and climbs into his seat.

Artie gets in and, after they start moving, turns back and asks, "I saw the students had those bags for the makeup. Theirs or the school's?"

"Their personal train case, or lifestyle case as some call it now. The school supplies it. No sharing. They actually have to maintain it. There are a lot of items to keep track of. Teaches personal responsibility."

"I see."

–Somewhat.

"Those are the soccer and ball fields back that way. Waiting for the stadium lights to be installed next spring, maybe summer, so we can extend recreation time. We only have those two low stands," Headmistress says, motioning her arm laterally across the length of the athletic fields at the trilevel metal stands that are each fifteen yards long. "No family to come watch the girls. It would be tough to play another school and have family here, rooting for our opponents. The cheerleading spirit squad helps take the edge off of it all. This is the Adjutor's, our aquatics center," she continues with the guided tour. "The outdoor pool. A recreation pool; it has a slide, some fun for the girls in summer. Sun and fun. That was drained already. The fall nights up here make for some cold pool water. When did we drain the pool, Jorgie?"

"That was right after Labor Day, Headmistress. Doc Washington and I did it. Took two days for all the water to drain out. And then we winterized it, drained all the piping and added some pool-safe antifreeze, removed some jets and other parts. It's all locked up."

"You see the fence?" Headmistress asks Artie.

"Yes, I do."

"Yeah, don't want any of the girls in there. Could take quite a tumble into the empty pool." They get out of the golf cart. "We had a deer in the pool one summer. Jorgie, that was before your time, wasn't it?" Jorgie nods yes. "Doc Washington and another boy were on the sides trying to get the deer to swim toward the stairs. They thought he couldn't climb out with the hooves off of the bottom and was—being a dumb animal—unable to find the stair." Artie and Headmistress walk up a few steps, leaving Jorgie at the cart, and make a right, along a tall, one-story building. They reach a gate with a heavy padlock. "We can't go in. I don't have the key, but really, it's just an empty pool."

–Nice setup.

Artie looks around the neat sundeck with chaise lounge chairs stacked in a corner and tables and chairs beside them. A slide is on the far side of the pool, at the deep end. Headmistress is already walking back toward the doors of the Adjutor's, where Artie catches up with her.

"Anyway, they splash the water in front of it and get it headed to the stairs and out of the pool. And the beast just leaps that big fence like we would step over a log. Beautiful, the way it moved. Scared of Doc Washington and all the ruckus but so graceful. And off into the woods in a snap."

Headmistress waits by the double glass doors for Artie to open them.

"Allow me," he says, sort of being sarcastic but still willing.

"Thank you." Through another door that Artie obliges her on, and they are in a lobby. A glass wall on the left shows a twenty-five-meter pool with swim lanes marked off. "There is the indoor lap pool. Not open now. Need proper personnel. All the girls take swimming. No diving. Couldn't get the pool deep enough for a diving board: the mountain rock limited that. Plus safety considerations. We do an open swim every other weekend and holiday weekends. Locker rooms in front; access outdoor and indoor pools from them. Very convenient. Not enough girls for a swim team. A company comes once in a while to check it. Some sort of certification. You don't require that for your report, do you?"

"No. Beautiful facility."

–A lot of money for all this.

"Off to the two Joes' then." They walk out and get in the golf cart.

"This Doc Washington, what is his doctorate in?"

"No." Headmistress clucks giggly. "He is called that because he is so good with the grass. No, he isn't academic faculty. He does a great job with the foundling boys in the career path."

"I see." They get back on the golf cart and drive to the two dormitories.

Headmistress gets out of the golf cart and stands in front of the flowered courtyard between two three-story brick buildings. "Such a shame, the flowers are at the end of their season. But it was a little long this year really. We should be grateful for that."

"Yes."

"On your right is Upper Joe's. Named after Saint Joseph. The dining hall for evening meals is there. And on our left is Lower Joe's. Lower being lower classes. I should say grades. They are not low class at all." She smiles and looks at Artie, waiting for him to say something.

"Beautiful campus, simply beautiful."

–Almost too pretty. Hiding?

"Would you like to go in?"

"Yes."

"Let's see Lower Joe's. This dortoir is grade K to eight. A proctor on every floor."

Artie and Headmistress enter the unlocked lobby and pass through another set of doors. "What is the security here? We just walk into these buildings, especially the dormitory. Seems unsafe."

"We have a security company: SecureThrust. I do not like the name. You can guess why. We contract with them. If you came by yourself, these doors wouldn't open. You are on camera, facial recognition," she says chirpily. "Maybe I should have warned you. The company monitors the facility. They have you, your car. They monitor the girls. If a door won't open for them, they can use their phone app or the security pad." Headmistress opens the door back to the small lobby and points to a black rectangle on the wall that looks like a plain piece of glass. Artie steps through the doorway and looks skeptically. "Look up above the door."

Artie does and sees a small camera. "Very intricate."

"Yes."

Artie goes back in, and they walk down a hall. "This security company is on-site?"

"No. No personnel here. They link with the police. Also fire. It has run smoothly. Seemingly nothing happens though. I can't think of a thing we needed them for. Oh! Someone burnt some food in the Saints' cafeteria. We had police and fire come. They aired it out though. Smoke detectors alerted them before anyone even reacted down there. But no security issue. People worry undesirables from the girls' former times would come and stalk them or something. But hasn't happened. Security team is aware and proactively checks social media. Some girls have restraining orders against their deplorables. The company monitors for that."

–That's incredible.

"Very, very advanced, almost Big Brother."

"They give us a steep discount because we are a charitable institution. Someone on their board has a deep affection for our work. Love our women in STEM program." They come to the end of the hallway, having passed many solid doors. "This last room is empty. I can show you in. I can't allow you to see an occupied room."

"Good policy." Artie steps into the room Headmistress has opened. He is surprised to see only one, neat bed, no mattress. It is spacious with a bureau, a dresser with lighted mirror, as well as a desk and bookshelf. "Very spacious. Only one student in this size room?"

"Yes," Headmistress says, waiting for Artie to exit. "We have excess rooms, in case of some urgent, unplanned need."

"There certainly is plenty of need." He lingers, looking around.

"That is a pipeline issue. We don't address that here."

Artie opens the door to his left. There is a bathroom with designer tile halfway up the wall, a shower with a glass door, a pedestal sink and another lighted mirror. "An en suite!"

–Better tone it down. Professional.

"Sorry. I was expecting something more like my old college dorm."

"Yes. The rooms are nice. We would obviously provide the mattress and bedding, but we would not keep or store old ones in the rooms. We have a contract with the local dealer. They can get us a quality mattress in a day. Very understanding people, know how hard it can be on the girls when they are, seemingly, here suddenly."

–Is that a full-size bed?

Artie steps out of the room. "Nice facility."

"We had a tall girl once who needed a longer mattress. Special XL Full. But we forgot to order the bedding for that size. Took a bit to get her settled. Although she said it was the nicest bed she had ever slept in, even with her feet hanging over the edge, sticking out of the comforter."

Headmistress takes out her cell phone. "Hello, Lana," she says into her phone. And then to Artie, "She knew we were in. Security." Back to her phone. "I am walking to your office. Come meet Mr. Alston from the State."

Lana steps out from a doorway beyond where they had entered the building. Artie waves awkwardly.

–Another well-dressed woman.

"Lana Stanley, this is Mr. Alston. We are showing Mr. Alston, who represents the State, our fine establishment."

"Nice to meet you," Lana says and holds out her hand to Artie.

–Another one.

Artie shakes gracelessly. "Nice to be here."

"Do you have any questions about the dormitories?"

"Just what is the protocol of supervision?"

"Simply, we proctors are residents. One on each floor. The other faculty, they spell us on vacations. Even Headmistress has done some nights away from the chancellor's lodgings."

"Excellent."

"Spells." Headmistress giggles. "Artie will think we are witches."
Artie smiles quizzically. "Relief is a better term."

"And do the students have a difficult time cleaning and other
committee work?"

"Well, it's all shipshape," Lana says with a wide sweep of her open
hand.

–Like a game show model and made-up enough to be one. Pretty
enough too.

"We have a private company," Headmistress says. "For certain
buildings, we contract out the cleaning. The two Joes' included. We
needed an all-female cleaning staff so the girls wouldn't be uncomfortable. Common areas, cleaned daily except Sunday, during class
time, and twice weekly the dormitory rooms. All while the girls are in
class. We discourage them from coming back to their dortoir during
school hours. And besides the remote security, we have a supervisor
from the school here when the cleaning company is working."

"Security in the halls?"

"The hallways, yes, not the rooms," Lana says.

"Icky," Headmistress adds. "The two floors above are the same as
this. Do you need to see them?"

"No."

"We'll go then," Headmistress says.

"Nice to have you at our little school," Lana says to Artie as he
waves goodbye and follows Headmistress out.

As they climb into the golf cart, Headmistress says, "Most of the
staff refers to this institution as a school. Better for the girls not to
be constantly reminded they are at a displaced childhood assemblage.
Mr. Alston, dinner will be served pretty soon. That's in the Upper
Joe's, right there," she says, pointing across the open-ended courtyard.
"Would you like to join us and see that building then? I have some
work in the office."

"That would be nice," Artie says as they pull away.

–Would love to see what the food is like.

Headmistress picks up her phone and sends a text. "I had Sandi notify dining that we have a guest tonight."

"Not too late for new arrangements, I hope?"

"No, of course. Jorgie, I need to get back to the Saints'. I'll check if Sandi made progress. That's the campus, oh, except the chapel."

"And the monastre," Jorgie adds but then looks forward, head down, as if he should have known to keep quiet. "Ma'am, Headmistress. I'll bring you straight back."

–Monastery?

"If Jorgie wouldn't mind, I could drive past the chapel and maybe the monastery. If that's all right with you, Headmistress?"

–Headmistress? Can't believe you're saying it.

Jorgie drives around to the front of the Saints' building. He stops and gets out, moving around to once again assist Headmistress. "Very well," she says only to Artie. "Dinner is in less than an hour." She pauses and looks sternly at Jorgie. "Jorgie. You will take care of Mr. Alston. Back to Upper Joe's in time for dining. I will convey your mission to Doc Washington. He will let them-of-the-decline know that you will stop in at their compound."

"Yes, Headmistress. I have to take Mr. Alston back to the Butt to get on a side-by-side."

"Yes, the cleanest one. See you soon, Mr. Alston," Headmistress says and walks away.

Artie stares and catches himself.

–Proper, proper; you are representing your department.

2

So this state Mister was staring at Headmistress' ass: she's an elegant woman and should be respected. But they were a similar age, I guessed. I wanted to take my rake and crack him across the back of the head with the handle for being improper. That would get me back in juvie. Couldn't get stubborn: they're adults. No way I wanted out of here before June. Nicest people.

I floored the accelerator pedal and cut the wheel sharp, hoping to catch Mister State off guard, maybe upset him a little, but he took it in stride.

"Nice golf cart. Do you play golf?" he asked.

"Nah. I've been to some courses—school related. They don't have carts like these. Not for public to use. Private clubs, I've seen pictures of real nice golf carts that the wealthy members own at some clubs. Even have AC."

"How is that school related?" he asked, staring right at the side of my face. His head was a little too close to be talking right at my ear. I kept looking straight ahead at the path.

"Greenkeeper. My career path, my future. Golf courses are beautiful to work at. Outdoor work I prefer."

"Why not a college track?" he asked, still turned to face my ear, all rude.

"Never considered it. I didn't have much, no school before I came. High school here was a dream for me. Elevation and area were enough mathematically for me. I never did good in no numberals much. Readin' level was subpar."

"You had a difficult time."

Mister State wanted to hear my story, and I didn't want to tell, so I said, "Par. That's a good golf term." We were approaching the chapel. "This place is locked up. Reverend Mathis does Sunday service only. People go in other times. Have to go to the office at Saints' and get the key. They give it out, if you want to pray."

"Doesn't the school have the modern security features here?" he asked suspiciously.

"I don't know what that is. There's a key. Sometimes Headmistress comes in end of day. I drop her off, and she says good night, says her prayers I guess, and then follows that path to her lodgings." I nodded toward the chancellor's house. He turned and looked across the sloped lawn broken by a flower-lined path connecting the buildings.

"A well-appointed home," Mister State said.

"She is well-favored."

He gave me a double take. Then he got out of the cart, walked up to the entrance of the chapel and tried to look through the dark panes of glass where the double doors met. He grasped the brass handle of one, then the other, trying to open them.

"I told you it'd be locked."

He turned back and looked at me but did not come down the steps.

"We could have gotten the key from Saints'."

He tried to peer beyond the darkened glass again.

"We could ride back over and get the key."

He didn't answer and started back to me.

"Sort of have to go back that way to trade the golf cart anyways."

"I guess it's only a chapel," he said unconvincingly and got back in his seat.

I told him, "If you still want to go to the monastre, we have to go to the Butt for the side-by-side UTV. Too rough a ride for the cart."

"I would like to see it."

I hit the accelerator, aiming for the Butt. When we pulled up to the open garage doors, Doc was standing next to the UTV—the new one with the enclosed cab but with the doors off. Headmistress must have called ahead and told Doc to have someone get it ready.

"Hello, there," Doc yelled as I stopped. He went right to Mister State. I grabbed my rake and went into the garage and stowed my tool.

When I returned, Mister State said, "You do a great job on the grounds. Everything is pristine."

"Thank you. We have a sharp crew," Doc added, noticing I was beside him.

"Sir, here is the key to your golf cart."

"It's the school's golf cart, Jorgie," Doc said to Mister State. "Mr. Alston's telling me you are doing a fine job of showing him around. Good boy."

"Headmistress doing the showin'. I mostly just drivin' them."

"Very well. See that you get out of the side-by-side down at the club," he said and handed me the key. "Nice and easy when you go off path. No joyriding."

"Yes, sir."

"I am sure Jorgie will take good care of me," Mister State said. "I wonder, Doc. Okay to call you Doc?" Doc nodded agreeably. "Do you have the filings for students like Jorgie here, in the greenkeeper track? Would that be also with the main office?"

"Students?" Doc paused.

He was collecting his thoughts, like always. "A man of few words chooses them wisely," I heard him tell Headmistress one time.

"No papers here. I couldn't approve them being handed over to anyone, anyone at all."

Mister nodded, like he was mirroring Doc from a moment ago. "I assure you the New York State ED has authority to view, even take copies of transcripts, even relevant medical files. We have the students' best interests in mind. That is our daily task."

"Students?" Doc considered. I climbed into the driver's seat. "All that is through the main office."

"Yes, yes, of course. I asked you because it started to seem like there were two different paths students here take: vocational or university prep."

"Vocation? Like a religious calling?"

"No. I meant like career," Mister said.

"You enjoy your tour," Doc said, turned his back to us and walked to the garage. Mister State sat next to me.

I started it up but then remembered what Headmistress ordered me to do when I got here. "I'll just be a minute, Mister," I said. "I forgot to tell Doc Washington about the task Headmistress wanted me to confer to him."

"No rush," Mister said, friendly like.

I hustled into the garage, past the rows of tool lockers and the other vehicles. I patted Doc's newly shined-up Ford Mustang before knocking on the glass of his office door. "Sir," I said to his back.

He had been taking the upper shirt-half of his coveralls off. He had a green T-shirt on. He turned and nodded at me to continue.

"Headmistress wanted to convey to you that the flower beds at the Cousin's need to be cleaned out."

He lit a cigarette. "Thank you, Jorgie. Let me know what that state nerd is looking at. He's up to something." He sat down and gave a slight wave of his cigarette toward the door, letting me know I should go.

"Yes, sir," I said low, not knowing if it was my place to do such a thing. I went out to the side-by-side, pondering on how I was stuck between too much authority, and I didn't like it.

When I got back to the driver's seat, I said aloud, "This is a nice ride."

"Yes," said Mister.

"Oh, I was tellin' myself. I haven't driven this new one yet. These are nice in winter, I bet, when the doors are on and you got heat. No joke the open cabs. Heated seats too."

He nodded, and we took off, full throttle.

3

Here come my Jay with some old dude planted in the seat of his
four-by go-kart. I smile at Jay, makin' sure he'll stop even though he's
got some old dude tellin' him where to go. Jay speeds up the go-kart
and then hits the brakes hard, wrenches the wheel and makes that
machine slide a little closer to me. His face all calm, like he has been
practicin' that move, like he's a drift racer. Old dude holdin' on for life,
like he might mess his high-water pants that show his argyles too
much. He got his outboard hand up high, white-knuckling the roll bar.
I smooth my uniform down and throw my shoulders back to make
good posture like Headmistress told us, "First impression every time."

Jay comes out and around the go-kart to me. He goes to the far,
uphill side of the path on the dirt so he doesn't seem too much shorter
than me. "Hi, Veronica." He has his hands down by the sides of his
legs, wipin' them clean on his work onesie. Probably hopin' to touch
my hair or something. "Do you need a hand?"

I smile. "No, Jay. Headmistress says you aren't supposed to be doin'
my things for me anyway."

"Can I hold your train case for you while we talk?"

I pass it over to him. The old dude is gettin' out of the go-kart. "Your best friend is comin' to check on us."

"Headmistress has asked me to give him a tour. He's from the State."

"Mister, are you going to shut this place down?" I ask old dude as he approaches.

"Good evening, Miss…"

"Mr. Alston, this is Veronica. She's going to be the valer victorian."

"Stop it, Jay. You don't know that."

Old dude's not even as tall as me.

"Nice to meet you. I will not be shutting down the school. I am doing a focused survey to assure all parties, the students, the faculty and the New York State Education Department, that this institution is doing its best."

"Are you saying I'm in an institution?" I tease the old dude. I push my hair back from the right side of my face and give him a big smile and a laugh. Jay stares over at the dude thinkin' how he got so friendly with me. I got Jay jealous, like always.

"Nothing pejorative. It seems like a fine place, beautiful facilities."

"Jay takes real good care of his place."

Jay looks to the ground but is smilin'. Old dude looks at Jay and seems to pick up on what's going on.

"So you are a senior, Veronica?"

"Yes. My last year here."

"Do you have a favorite class? Or area of study?"

"I like fashion."

"Do you have a university in mind?"

"Parsons. I would love to go there."

"A very different place. Country campus like this to New York City can be a difficult acclimatization."

"I spent time in foster homes in cities. I had been in two homes in

Albany, and that's the state capital. Well, you are from the government, so I guess you know that."

"Yes. I didn't mean to discourage you. I am sure you will flourish there, and I wish you the best." He turns to Jay. "Jorgie, we should continue with the facility survey. It will be dark on the way back, looks like."

"I ain't worried about that," he say extempore. Old dude waits a moment and then goes and sits in the go-kart, hopin' to move Jay along, but my Jay has got his attention all on me. We move a little farther away. "I hope you don't go to New York. I ain't gonna see you."

"I told you I got to go to college. University, as that dude calls it. I'll see you. They got golf courses down there. Richest place there is, the city. They got everything. You be a greenkeeper. I'll design plus fours."

He looks down, kickin' the grass, lightly first but then more aggressively. "I don't know. I said I would never go back to the city."

I would probably never see him again postgraduation, but he got me things.

"I was pretty messed up there. Headmistress saved me."

"I know all that, you told me plenty. Are you gonna get me some cigs soon?"

"I don't know. I might see Brother Dom now. Headin' down there with Mister."

"Get some spinach too."

"I don't like you smokin' cannabis."

"Not up to you, now is it? Brother Dum is gonna be plenty unhappy when he sees that state dude." I pause to let it sink in. "You believe that," I swear to him.

Jay starts back to the go-kart.

"Bye, Jay."

Jay turns back suddenly, smilin' like he can kiss me goodbye when he hands me back my case. Old dude say, "Time to go. Nice meeting you, Veronica."

Old dude seems to be eyein' my knee-highs, so I ignore him. Last thing I need is another pervy oldster touchin' on me.

"Isn't she beautiful, Mr. Alston?" I hear my Jay askin' State Dude as I walk away.

4

My intonation will be broken. Words will fly at me: coarse, vulgar words.

"Look at his guy," the barbarian will say to all. "Fuckin' mess."

I will rise and hold my hand up to stop them. "Ease your spirit. Ease your mind. Let loose some of these earthly cares."

"This guy's got blood all over his goddamn face." The barbarian's serenity will be easily upset—as it often is. The mop attendant from the cadets will be with him. They will have a guest. He will be slung, cross-like, across their shoulders, his glasses askew.

"Namaste," I will greet them. Blood will be on this familiar man's head: dried but with a stream of fresh red trickling down from his hairline, very uncomfortably under his glasses and across his eye with the occasional drop falling from his lashes.

"Shit storm wortha' snow out there. You gotta see what the other guy looks like, right, kiddo?" The barbarian will disquiet me with his slang. "You gotta move it and help us get this fucker some first aid."

"You should've saw. Brother Dom went out in that blizzard. Car was crumpled on the passenger side and front," the mop cadet—wearing his blue, short-sleeve coveralls with a white, long-sleeve thermal underneath—will say of the barbarian. "He went up that hill, through the trees—it's almost full dark—toward the civilians' road. Snow to his knees and still fallin' convulsively with wind gusts rocking him."

"Fucking foot out there already," the barbarian will interrupt, calming, trying to catch his breath. He will not be exaggerating, only his usual manner in which he would describe something as banal as baking. His breathing will have a slight, whistle-like wheeze. I will notice the wetness of the barbarian's robes as well as the jeans he wears underneath them.

"Then he gets to the car that's careened like a hundred yards downhill and into a tree. And he heaves at the door, then pulls this man out. Mister's head is bloody like you see and floppin' around. Brother Dom gets the body hitched over his shoulder and starts descending the slope. It's a bear. I head up, leaving the mop, and meet them halfway down. Fortunate it was downhill when we were draggin' Mister. Not the reverse. Mister starts comin' around, asking us where he is."

"Says he knows the kid from the school but can't be sure. 'I know you. I know you.' He's muttering like a big, fat baby," the barbarian will say.

"I have seen him up at the school facility with Headmistress. Mr. Alston. She hates him. We were here, remember?"

I will nod.

"Anyway, are you going to get the fuck out of our way?"

"Please, Master Kyle, we want to get him to the infirmary."

"Yeah. We gotta get this guy's inner calm set up right, but first we gotta fix his skull."

"Peace," I will say and step aside, breaking my hands apart and showily gesturing with open palm for them to pass, though not having really been blocking them in the first place. I will follow, hands together at my lips, dipping my head to the brothers I pass who are unsure if this is worth upsetting their evening prayer. It will be, as always, rare to have an outsider, but this will be an exigent situation that cannot be ignored. A life in need is a life indeed, as the great ones had always taught.

Inside the Bangoro Industrials Infirmary the patient will be plopped onto a low-backed swivel-top stool. His outer garment will be removed. The barbarian and mop cadet will work quickly and with surprising coordination. They will clean his wound. The mop cadet will quickly hand the barbarian gauze and a saline water bottle. The barbarian will punch a hole in the cap and spray the sterile water into the laceration, cleaning away the dried blood and foreign material.

"OWW," the patient will yell, wincing.

"Ain't got no painkillers here. Not allowed. Former users. You gotta suck it up," the barbarian will say. He will pull a safety razor from the first aid kit and drag it up from the man's hairline toward the acme of his skull. The hair will pull away, showing the fullness of the gash caused by the car crash. My face will wince, though I try to avoid it. The barbarian will be unmoved by the gore. "Fuckin' ripper you got." He will shave another vertical line, parallel to the gash, exposing clear skin all around, taking no particular care to avoid reinjuring the wound area. The patient will seem to be in a trance, his pain dulled by the barbarian's roughness or from shock. The barbarian will squirt, with high velocity, the sanitized water, pushing away the newly shaved hairs and the remainder of the drying blood. He will jet the solution directly into the wound, the fluid reddening as if to cause bleeding again. He will push down, not lightly, with the gauze onto the wound, moving the patient's head back but then buckling down, his back arching. "Gotta do it. Gotta be done."

The barbarian will fish through the kit. "Here we go. Ain't as much a beauty as stitched, but it'll hold. You wasn't no beauty to start with." He will pull the Steri-Strips out of the kit. "Kiddo! Two fingers each side. Push in and clamp this gash tight, side to side." He will gesture with index and middle fingers of each hand, holding them parallel to the top of the man's skull, jabbing them to touch each other. "Like this. You know what I'm aimin' at."

I will contemplate why he asks all this of the mop cadet and not me. He will think as always that I am a bit of a priss. He will never see passivity as a strength. He, a savage indifferent to the patient's moment, will not because of gore shirk from the task he had been inured to.

The teen will push the jagged, starting-to-proud flesh at the edges to abut roughly.

"You gotta hold it. Gonna be slippery."

The boy will struggle with the task.

"Let it go. Let'er go." He will dab the flesh again, wiping down to the face that still has dried blood on it. He will hand the boy the Steri-Strips.

"Do I need gloves for this? The blood could..." the boy will ask the barbarian, totally ignoring me—his senior.

"The blood ain't gonna catch you nothin'. Put the strap on when I get it together. We go top down." The barbarian will go behind the patient and start with his index fingers holding the juicy sides together. "Right under there."

The boy will place the strip and lightly tap each side secure with his fingers. The barbarian will add his middle fingers and hold the next section closed without removing the fingers he started with. They will continue on until the wound looks remarkably improved.

"Good job, kiddo." The barbarian will unkit some gauze, cover the dressed wound and excessively wrap the head, covering the strip of missing hair. "Kiddo, you did so good, this guy's not gonna need a doctor. All's he'll need is a barber to fix that hair." He will laugh lightly at his own joke and cause the mop cadet to smile.

"Friend, what shall we call you?" I will ask, while the barbarian cleans the face.

"Artie."

"Artie. I remember. Do you know you were in a car accident? There is a snowstorm right now. Was anyone else there? Anyone who could have been injured?"

"I was by myself. I was attempting to beat the storm, get down to the thruway. I didn't want to get stuck staying overnight."

"Apologies. We do not have any aspirin for you, nor anything stronger."

"There's some ex-druggies convalescing up here," the barbarian will blurt.

"That's not important now," I will say. "Friend, these two saved you. This is Brother Dom. He went out first and pulled you from your car. Then this apprentice—you said you might know him—helped get you inside and dress your wound."

"Thank you. Water?"

"Your thanks are noted. Young page, would you go to the kitchen and get our new friend a glass of water. Not too cold."

The mop cadet will run off.

"You're lookin' better," the barbarian will say, too loud for the small, antiseptic room. "Do you wanna get your coat off? You don't wanna get sweaty. Won't be able to tell if you're feverish."

"Is the pain great?"

Artie will nod his head up and down, though it makes him wince.

"Let's try something." I will reach down and hold his hands palms up. I will place my thumbs gently but firmly and exert pressure into the area between his thumb's and index finger's metacarpals, squeezing the flesh, pincerlike, beyond his comfort. "Karma. Calm. Serene. Balance." I will repeat, and the barbarian will join in the intonation.

"What?" Artie will say a few times, as if we are conversing.

The mop cadet will return with the water and stand ill at ease, unsure if he should interrupt or allow us to proceed. I will stop the intonation, as will the barbarian, but one syllable too late to be synchronous. I will lightly shake the patient's hands and then gently replace them to his lap. "I hope that made some improvement."

"What were you saying?" he will mumble.

"The compression of the soft oblique arches of the hands is an ancient Mongolian chirologist's distraction from the pain of the flesh."

"What?" Artie will say.

"Ice," the barbarian will clamor and push past the mop cadet to the refrigerator. "We got these squooshy ice bags for to cut down the bruising." He will pull one from the freezer, wrap it in a small towel and place it on Artie's head. "More gauze, kiddo. The roll."

The mop cadet will comply and wrap the ice pack on top of the already heavily bandaged head.

"Hold your end tight." The barbarian will wrangle his thumb out from under the bandage, where it was temporarily—like all things of earth—caught. They will knot the end back on itself, completing a tower of bandage.

"Artie, friend," I will say. "Please adjourn with us to a prayer room. You will be more comfortable. There is no leaving tonight. I think even Jorgie will not be able to make it back the short distance to his school via the four-by-four."

Jorgie will nod approvingly.

"We have no phone, so when Jorgie returns tomorrow, he will call for a tow truck, and we can assess your condition."

"What?" Artie will respond. "Who? I can't understand."

The barbarian will roughly grab him by his well-padded head and look into his ears while tugging the bandage up. "Ears look okay, but you can never tell. Concussed, I'd bet."

"Peace," I will say to the barbarian.

"Right, brother, right. I can't say no gamblin' stuff," the barbarian will say, bending to front his face too closely to the patient's. "We got people addicted to that kinda thing here too."

"Peace," I will gently remind the barbarian.

"Right, right, TMI info. Don't pay no attention to that, kiddo."

"We shall proceed with our welcoming this blessedly karma-laden person to the Dragon AI prayer room. The room is empty, and I trust it has been kept serene and appropriate for any wonder of life."

"I keep it on the schedule," the mop cadet will reply.

I will gesture with my hand to the door, and the barbarian and mop cadet will get ahold of one upper arm each and assist the patient to his feet. They will start to move toward the door.

"Peace, please do not forget the guest's outer garment," I will say while slowly nodding at it.

The barbarian will extend his free hand and pull it along with him, the jacket dragging partly on the shining floors. At the Dragon AI room, all will be in order. The pastel colors will make it perfect for someone unaccustomed to monastery life and ailing from a brush with karma or maybe even the afterlife. The two aiders will lay the patient on the cushioned platform and wriggle a pillow under his head.

"Ain't got no blankie in here," the barbarian will say, grab a sheet and cover the patient. "I'll leave your jacket next to you, but I don't think you're gonna need it." He will turn to me. "I don't know if letting this dude sleep now is a good move. If he's got the bruise on the brain...could be bad."

"Mother Nature has made a statement. Who are we to protest? Natural Law is. The patient's course is set and not by us." They will look at me with less reverence than the ancients themselves would garner, confused by my wisdom. "Brother, your look makes known to me that you should return to your prayers and dwell on the thoughts of predeterminate law, acceptance and kinship."

He will start nodding in the short motions his state of near necklessness allows.

"And you." I will focus my attention on the mop cadet. "Revered in your place as all who adhere to their status in this and each other path, perhaps you should return to those duties."

"Yes, Master Kyle, sir," he will say.

"Peace."

"I gotta get back to the side door and make sure no one dashed off with my mop and bucket gear," he will say while hurrying along, unnecessarily nervous about the theft of his mop.

"Yo! Kiddo," the barbarian will yell after him, breaking monastery standards.

"Peace," I will begin to say, but he proceeds loudly.

"You done great!"

The mop cadet will not turn back.

"I gotta get back to my prayers," the barbarian will say to me and shuffle off with his stubby-torso-rocking walk.

I will return my pressed-together hands to my lips, bow my head to Artie Alston and leave him to contemplate.

5

I left Veronica behind. She didn't seem to care for Mister State. He gripped tight when I floored it and quick turned, kicking the back wheels out on the slide. There was a little bump there I hadn't seen. Believed Mister might fly out of the UTV, his ass bounced so high off the leather. "I ride it a little hard," I said loud to him over the sound of acceleration.

"I like it," Mister yelled back. "As long as I stay on!" He laughed a little before I turned my eyes forward.

We raced across the smooth grass toward the forest edge with me having took him for his word that he was okay with the cooling air blowing past us. I didn't want trouble, but he didn't seem the type to lie to me and set me up for a talking-to from Doc.

"More fun than driving that sedan," Mister told me when I stopped.

"Yeah, this new side-by-side machine, I wish I could take it with me when I graduate."

"I bet."

"Probably get one, you know, at the course I get to workin' at."

"Someday. You probably start at the bottom."

"Huh?"

"Well," he stated, uncomfortable. "I don't mean bottom, bottom. You would be under a head greenkeeper. I just assume…they get the best cart."

"Yeah. You are probably right." He might have been jerking me around. "I'd prefer to work at a woodland course over links. I believe they're prettier. And a desert course, I wouldn't know what to do there. See this part here." I stood, leaning forward and pointing down the gravel trail. "It is steep, and gravel slips at this decline. So I promised, it's seat belts on, every time." I sat and buckled up. "And I gotta ask you, too. This side-by-side ain't got roll bars for no reason."

"I will. I will." He complied.

"I'm going low." I switched the UTV to full four-by-four, low-crawl mode. "And we're goin' down." I started forward, knowing the most jostle was right there going over from level to steep. "We'll be fine, that was the worst part. I do this all times, more than once a day some days." We bounced along and slid a little, now and then. It felt like the back wheels wanted to pass the front on the side, and it took some gravel with it. Mister handled it fine but held on tight.

"Why don't they grade and pave this?"

"These monastre types, they like alone. Nature. They can talk for hours about it. Separate from society."

Mister nodded.

"They had big plans. I could show you."

"Sure, if it won't take too long."

"Not at all. It's on this path. Maybe two hops over. Here it is, actually." I stopped the UTV on a mostly solid, less declined area with a tree two inches in front of me. "You see that trunk right there I'm nosing?" I got out.

"Yes." He stood stiffly.

"We call that the emergency brake."

He smiled. He got it.

"It could slide. Probably not right in this spot. This is one of the more level parkin' spots on the trail. Not that people park here: only up and down. Some places the side-by-side could start down without the wheels even turnin'. Nose a tree up or tie it off. I don't know if you saw the winch up front."

"I didn't. I do feel I am in good hands. You seem to know all about this four-wheeler and this trail."

"I guess." We started walking, perpendicular to the slope. "I certainly been up and down this more than any them monastre types. They don't leave. Not at all, I believe. Here it is."

"Tracks. Parallel tracks. Were they building a train?"

"A funicular. That's what Doc Washington told me. The two cars are over there. Down the hill a little, you can just make them out."

Mister moved his head around trying to see through the density.

"They're tipped over. Wood almost all rotted, metal skeleton remains. Forest is takin' it back. Learned about that in program. Slowly the forest would take back a lot of golf courses. Not the desert ones. The sand might take them."

"I can make them out."

"They were stuck side by side there at the passing. The track widened, split there. One went up, one down, with a cable connecting them. Passing is at midpoint, and they split and then come back to the single tracks."

"Interesting. I see the track at my feet. Do you know why it was abandoned?"

"Doc Washington gave me two reasons. One was that the hired company was shitheads—his words. They could build it. Couldn't get it to run. Not a lot of funicular companies to choose from. Doc Washington said they should have got Walt Disney, but I don't know if it was serious. Two: people would come from all over to see it. Even though it is private, private property, they came. Some came to see it bein' built. Some came to see it run or ride it. They were all

45

disappointed. Hardly ran, Doc Washington said. The previous Master, before Master Kyle, saw one in Pittsburgh. Believed it would help them visualize separation from our physical society."

"That's quite the story. Would have been something to see."

"That was the problem. No good for monastre types who want to forget the world."

"I guess it is hard to forget the world when the world won't forget you."

I noted to myself his words and to ask Brother Dom or Master Kyle about them, maybe Veronica. Mister seemed pretty smart.

"Let's resume the trip."

We got buckled back into the UTV, and after backing clear of my emergency brake, I resumed descent. Soon we saw the widening of the monastre grounds and its main building.

"Beautiful woodwork," Mister said while he stared up at the two-story, plus attic building. He twisted his body forward, turning to get a better look clear of the UTV's top.

"Looks like they brought it from China."

"Maybe Tibet," Mister corrected me. "Is this the whole of the monastery?"

"Yeah. This building and that small garage over there, tucked into woods where we passed. That's where they store hand tools. There's a bunch of acres. They tend a good-size garden, greenhouse. See it from the other side." I stopped by the steps to the entrance. We got out and walked. "That's cook's side-by-side. He has it up at the Butt, parks up there. He works with Chef Donna. Six days a week, comes down and makes dinner. We help him bring stuff down with the side-by-side. Food and provisions. They get UPS, FedEx, Mail. Zippy. Oven-Ready-Go. Doc Washington said he had to tell them try and get it all together. Told them forget Sundays. They don't seem to care or have control of it."

"Can't they ascend? Seems odd."

"They don't leave. Never. Do everything through Doc Washington."

"Do family members visit?"

"I believe not." I opened the eight-foot-tall, six-foot-wide, wooden door that moved slowly, silently.

"Let me feel. This door is six inches thick." He rubbed his hand across the carved design. "Is someone's face concealed in this geometric pattern?" I shrugged. He pushed. "It moves so easily. And quiet."

"As long as you don't push too fast. Nothin' fast down here at the monastre." We went in, and he pulled the door closed. "We wait here. Master Kyle will be along. No telling when. He is a patient man."

"The inside is very different from the outside. Fluorescent lighting. Very corporate, modern and sanitized."

"Very. Everyone keeps neat. Plus school has some staff operating down here. Doc Washington has to check the boiler regularly. Although he has a computer program that monitors it and warns him. They got alarms, smoke detectors, full sprinkler system. No AC though."

Master Kyle opened the interior door with the little chicken wire glass. "Namaste." He swept his hand out broadly, the wide sleeves of his robe waving as he extended for a handshake. Mister shook with him. Master Kyle put his hands together by his lips, turned to me and bowed his head slightly. I returned like Brother Dom had shown me. "Artie," he said back to Mister. "I was expecting you."

"Yes. Artie Alston, State Education Department."

"I am Master Kyle. Temporary cornerstone of this house."

"Nice to meet you."

Master Kyle nodded to Mister like he did to me. Mister tried to imitate.

"Is the permanent cornerstone away?"

"Nothing is permanent. These mountains are crumbling and flattening right before us. We are a jiff. Time an illusion."

"Oh. I was told this is school property. The ED is doing a focused survey of the school. So, for the report, I had to see what is going on."

"This is nature's property. This is nature's air we are breathing."

"Yes. What is this, in brief?"

"We are a house for men who have given goodbye to the physical world. We pray for those others that they may find the divine. All our works are for the general good of the world."

"And you interact with the school?"

"Not really. All the information is in the school office. Rent, fees. We pay through the school. But we are physically separate."

"I saw that on the ride down. Do you have another title?"

"Magisterium. Kachina. Most call me Master Kyle."

"Is there a board that oversees this tax-exempted, charitable institution? I'm assuming."

"Chairman of the board is another title I do not promote. It is a legal defining of me. But no one is really of charge in this world. No person. We go as fate dictates. And this is where my awareness is now. We can do a walk-through."

Master Kyle opened the door to the main hallway, and they went in. I followed, thinking things were getting testy. We went past some prayer rooms that were open and empty. Then Master Kyle turned up the wide main stair and brought Mister to the second-floor dining hall. I knew it was their one-meal-a-day time. Most of the brothers were eating quietly. It looked like broccoli, shrimp, rice and some cut-up fruit for tonight. Blue-ice-flavor sportsade was the drink. I saw a bus tray with plates at the end of the first low table. I grabbed it and carried it past Mister to the kitchen window. He seemed surprised.

Master Kyle told Mister, "It's good to see our youngest be so useful. Idle hands and all."

On my return to the pair, I spotted Brother Dom. His back was to Mister and Master Kyle. He pointed up to the sky with his left index finger, following the pointed path with his eyes toward the heavens.

Mister seemed to note that also. "Very austere," he said. "It must take getting used to: sitting on the floor."

"The humble mind not. If the mind is humble, the body will be."

Mister looked away from Master Kyle. He didn't seem to know what to say. Like Master Kyle schooled him, and Master Kyle had a ton of sayings like that.

"Okay," Mister said. Just like that and walked out of the room.

We followed. He stopped in front of an open room.

When Master Kyle—walking slowly as always—and I caught up, I saw Brother Carey lying on the room's center mat. He was on his back, barely breathing, like always.

Master Kyle whispered to Mister. "This is the SecureThrust prayer room. Please speak with gentleness. Brother Carey is attempting synchronicity with the universe. He has been successful for some time. He was our shaman and root doctor before this accomplishment. He hasn't been replaced."

"He hasn't got up in months," I said low to Mister.

He turned and started down the stair. He went directly to the foyer.

When Master Kyle and I caught up, Mister was standing still, staring at the entrance door.

Master Kyle spoke first. "Would you like to see the Key Deer Energy Greenhouse?"

"Not necessary."

"I hope you are satisfied with our good work."

"Did you, the brothers, make this door?"

"No. It was donated. The Grouse Pharma Door of Harmony."

"It must have been some project to build this place. Get the materials down the hill."

"I believe nature was parted for the build and replanted for the silence when complete."

"Activity level pretty low here?"

"It is not the actual physical exertion that counts toward one's progress, nor the nature of the task, but by the spirit of faith with which it is undertaken." Master Kyle threw another rock of Eastern wisdom at Mister. And Mister didn't like it.

"Yes, anyway. It seems a lifestyle of self-denial."

"Personal effects can have a personnel affect."

"Well then. As long as there is no interaction between the students and this institution, I suppose the State is not involved. To be clear, the students do not come for religious instruction, is that correct?"

"Correct. We see this apprentice and two others. I am fairly sure. They come down with Doc Washington with supplies and do facilities work under his direct supervision."

"Part of the greenkeeper track," I said.

"Very well," Mister said and started to pull on the big door he admired so much.

"How is your head?" Master Kyle asked him.

"My head?" Mister aggravatedly replied and turned back.

Master Kyle moved close to him and placed his palm at Mister's hairline. "I remember you hit your head. I hope it heals well."

Mister had enough. He pulled off, adjusted and resettled his glasses. "I don't think we have met. And my head..." He started pulling on the door again.

I moved past them to lead Mister out.

"It's only a new memory to be made," Master Kyle said.

I did my bye to him and closed the door. Mister was already in the machine.

I sat in the driver's seat and buckled up. "Ride back can be rough too," I told Mister, pointing to his safety belt.

"Certainly," he said and complied.

"Slide backwards a little, couple of times. Can't go too fast or the side-by-side's tires will slip and just start shooting gravel behind."

When I started it up, the headlights came on. We pulled away and hit the incline.

"Will you be going to the dining hall?" he asked.

"Only to bring you in. I got supper at the Butt."

"I didn't want to make you late for dinner. You must be hungry. Long day for you. Thank you for taking time out to show me around."

"Most welcome. That Master Kyle, he sure is wise. Knows all about that spirituality. He quotes all them Buddha, Confucius sayings. We don't learn that stuff up at the orphanary. That last one was Xavier."

"He was quoting Saint Francis Xavier? A Catholic missionary, I'm fairly sure."

I looked at him but then turned back to the path, not wanting to be disrespectful about it. He didn't know half as much as Master Kyle.

"Jorgie, I am from the government. I am here to help. The men at the monastery are there for their own reasons. I am suspicious of that. You should be too. I only tell you this with your best interest in mind."

"I don't know about all that. Wasn't Xavier a missionary to the East? Them at the monastre are syncretic."

"Did the guy with shabby baseball cap tell you about syncretism?" We hit the steepest section, and Mister rocked back a little. Even with a little more gas in crawl mode, the UTV slowed. "He motioned to you. Was that a signal? When he pointed?"

I was a little worried; if he picked up on it, then Master Kyle must have. "All glory to God. He pointed to the heavens, showin' the way."

"Oh. Who was he?"

"Brother Dom. Brother Dominic." The incline lessened. I couldn't relax, with the questions and the off-roading. "He's a nice guy. No one else up there is much friendly to me."

"Sometimes, people like that notice, and they do it for their own reasons."

"I don't believe that about him," I said and shook my head. "No.

He's the only friendly one. He's the only one that is friendly to Doc Washington too. They have quite the affinity when Doc Washington comes down. No one else. Master Kyle, he's just businesslike with Doc Washington. Imparting wisdom and listing deficiencies." We approached the top. "Hold a bit tighter. I'll give the machine a touch extra gas to get over the lip of the trail. It'll rock a little."

Mister held tight, and we did a little flop and then we were on the smooth, near-flat grass. It was mostly dark, and the landscape lighting was on.

I didn't zoom off. Mister liked it before, and I didn't want to seem too buddy-buddy. He was suspicious. Didn't want to, but I believed I would have to tell Brother Dom about him noticing the secret sign—that he wanted me to pick him up tonight for adventuring, as he called his drinking and whoring at the town gin mill. Redirect, as Brother Dom would have said. He knew a lot of legal terminology, but he said he wasn't a lawyer in his previous awareness. "You know, Master Kyle can see the future."

"Could you stop for a moment, Jorgie?"

I let my foot off the gas. We rolled to a gentle stop, and I killed the motor. I gave him my full attention like I figured he wanted.

"This is what I was trying to say before. You need to be suspicious of things people say. No one knows the future."

"He doesn't know it—the future—he feels things. I should be suspicious of you also then, by your logic."

"You are right. Be wary of us both."

I started her up and drove toward the Butt, giving the UTV more fuel and enjoying the speed. I glanced over at Mister State. He had a hand gripped to the roll bar and a smile on his face. When we got out at the Butt, I told him, "I'll take your advice. I was ponderin' how I should listen to a man who tells me to be wary of what he says. It's a dilemma I got to set my mind on. Or not. When people are nice to you, you want to believe."

"Trust, but verify, they used to say. Power is often misused."

"All right, I gotta go switch the keys back for the golf cart to run you up to the Joes'."

"I'll come in with you," he said and followed me to Doc's office.

6

Artie notices the odor and then the gas pump to the right side of the raised garage door as he follows Jorgie into the open interior of the Butt.

–Numerous off-road vehicles. And a nice car. All kept very neat, for a garage.

Artie stops outside the glass-walled office. Jorgie switches keys out from a cabinet on the back wall. "Doc Washington checks the keys all times. This is his office. That's his muscle car there."

"Nice. He seems to trust you. Speaks well of you."

"Yeah." Jorgie closes the office door. "I gotta go upstairs. Tell him we are switchin' back to the golf cart. Then I'll run you up to the Joes'."

"I'll take a walk up with you. See how it is. That way I will have seen the entirety of the complex."

"I believe it's simple. Stairs this way."

Artie follows Jorgie across the garage floor, and he admires the orderliness of the tool chests and pegboards full of wrenches and other mechanic's tools. "A very organized shop."

"Yeah, now with everything put back and no bangin' or compressors firing, it's kinda peaceful, relaxing."

At the top of the stairs, Artie hears the clamor of boys interacting coming from his left. To the right, through an open doorway, he sees a dim room with two rows of beds against each long wall. The beds have metal frames; each has a tightly made mattress with a single pillow and a white sheet-top folded down over a woolen blanket.

–Looks like army surplus.

"Chow room—the Kit—is this way," Jorgie says. "Sounds like everyone is eatin' something tasty."

Artie peers straight ahead into a poorly lit, tidy office. There is an organized, dark-wood desk facing the door with a window behind it. A high-backed, plush office chair is tucked in under the desk. Along each side of the room, there is a long table with plywood dividers creating narrow, individual cubbies with a computer in each. A plastic folding chair is in front of each station. The walls are painted white and have large pictures of green landscapes. The worn wood floor creaks as his steps follow Jorgie to the left and into the kitchen/dining room.

–An upstairs office and a downstairs office?

Artie spots Doc Washington immediately. Doc Washington guffaws and then smiles at a boy standing over his near-finished dinner plate, telling another boy he wouldn't know a curveball from a changeup if it hit him in the ass. The boys are on both sides of a long Formica table in straight-back, vinyl-upholstered chairs. There is a small TV in the corner of the room permanently mounted to the wall. Doc Washington notices Artie, and his face goes to serious. "Gentlemen, gentlemen," he booms between open-mouthed chews, and the boys quiet and sit. Jorgie snatches a hamburger bun from a bowl in the center of the table. "We have a visitor. Best manners for Mr. Alston from the State."

"Education Department," Artie announces to all. He notices the boys are all dressed neatly in school-initialed polo shirts and khakis. "It is great to meet you all."

Jorgie says, "I switched out the keys. We are goin' up to the Joes'. Mister has the Headmistress waitin' to have dinner."

"I'm sure she's not waiting, Jorgie."

A boy snickers at Doc Washington's comment.

Doc Washington leans his head to the side, giving the youngster a stern look. "We have a guest, I said."

"Is this the entirety of the greenkeeper career path, here?"

A different boy chuckles.

–I count fifteen. Jorgie makes sixteen.

"These are all the boys at the school," Doc Washington answers. "There aren't any K through eight boys."

"You keep a neat operation. Must be difficult in such an old building."

"It's an all-pitch-in situation. Works well enough for most things in life. Cleaning is like pooping: stinks when you do it, stinks more if you don't."

–Pooping?

"Ah. Good teamwork lesson. Is that sloppy joes? I haven't had that in quite a long time. Used to love when my mother made it for supper—no vegetables."

"No mothers here," a tall boy across from Artie says.

"I didn't mean anything by it," Artie says apologetically.

–Unprofessional of you. Remember these boys' situation. Don't baldly try to fit in.

"Swaine, that's enough," Doc Washington scolds. "Mr. Alston didn't mean it like that. You know it. Don't play martyr." Doc Washington looks away from the boy and grins at Artie through his sauce-laden moustache, his teeth reddened. "Good boys, one and all. The road to manhood is long."

"Yes, they seem well on their way. Especially, as Mr. Swaine has newly reminded me, a tough start for these terrific young men. I see a fully equipped kitchen there. Do you cook in it? Or staff cooking?"

Doc Washington looks back over at the commercial kitchen appliances, which look all in order. "More heating up than cooking."

"Chef Donna drops off trays for us," Jorgie says. He looks at Doc Washington for approval.

"Go on, Jorgie, you're giving the tour." He takes another bite.

"She gets trays down to us, like these here sloppy joes. Got more in the oven I bet, always plenty. Good lumps today: chickens salad wraps. She's a real good cook. Hate it when she goes on vacation." The boys erupt into shouts and boos.

"Now, now, gentlemen." The boys' cries ebb at Doc Washington's urging. "She's a good cook. Popular here, more than at the Joes'. She knows what these boys like, is all they're getting at. They all like pizza night. But not too many pizza nights."

Artie smiles at the good-natured boisterousness.

"Better get up to the Joes' if you don't want to go right to dessert. Jorgie didn't drive too hard for you, did he? It's real off-road going down there to the club."

–A fun ride. The club?

"Not at all, very cautious. A very jovial scene I am leaving."

"As long as they clean up, and they do, I don't mind. It can be a ton of fun."

"Yes."

–Don't jealously compare this to your only-childhood. Leave it.

"All of this reminds me fondly of my college fraternity house. I was in a frat. What you have seems to be an enjoyment of a similar sense of fellowship. Good to see." Artie looks directly at Doc Washington. "They called me AA at the frat. Which are my initials. And all had an insider's laugh because of the Alcoholics Anonymous connection. But it was ironic because I rarely drank."

The boys are quiet.

–Way to take the air out of the room.

"I'll be going then. Thanks for allowing Jorgie to chauffeur me to the Headmistress."

"Good night," they say in unison.

Artie notices Doc Washington chimes right along with them.

Jorgie grabs another hamburger roll, reaching over the shoulder of another boy. "'Scuse my lean, Swaine."

Swaine rolls his tall, thin frame back into Jorgie. "Fly on me?"

Artie follows Jorgie down and outside to the golf cart they were in earlier. Jorgie munches on his plain dry roll. Artie smells the gasoline again.

"Will you eat at the Joes' with me?" Artie asks.

"Nah. I'll come back."

"Sorry I am making you eat late. I see you are hungry, making do with a plain hamburger bun."

"I like 'em. I'm hungry, but I'll get plenty when I get back. Won't have to do cleanup. Not if I take my time anyways." He smiles at Artie as they climb in the cart.

"I see how eating all together like that can be fun for a young man. Even under the difficult circumstances."

Jorgie begins driving at a reduced pace, holding the steering wheel and the half a bun he still has with the same hand. "Circumstances?"

"Yes. The entire foster care or foster home situation you have here."

"The orphanary?"

"Yes, and the situations—all different, I am sure—that brought you and your peers. A unique environment to grow up in."

"Seems okay. I read lots of books and movies about orphans. Doesn't seem so unique. James Bond, Bruce Wayne, Annie."

"Washington Carver. Alexander Hamilton. Eleanor Roosevelt."

"Yeah, you know your history. So there's nothin' perfect about being spoiled by kindness or material things. I tell Veronica that. She's the girl we stopped to talk to."

"Yes, I remember."

–He seems to have a real crush on her.

"No. Who would want champagne every night? A pop tastes sweeter if you only have one a day. *Coddled* is the word I was searchin' the back of my mind for. You don't do no one a kindness by coddling them. You could ruin a child with comfort. You miss a lot of adventure. Adventure, that's hard to come by. People pushed out into the world get all that. No. It isn't kindness to spoil a kid. It's cruel."

–Sounds rehearsed.

They arrive at the entrance to the Joes'. Jorgie stops the cart, and the motor goes quiet.

"I have enjoyed talking with you, Jorgie. You seem determined. A determined young man making the best of the situation."

Jorgie gets up and starts walking to the stairs. "I don't believe it's a situation. Only thing, I'll be sad to graduate. But I'll know how to do a day's work."

"I'll follow you up."

Artie distractedly follows Jorgie, his mind running through the many ways the monastery will make his report trying.

–Numerous problems could arise in documenting such unusual conditions. A new age, Eastern-type monastery. How to describe it in official terms? A real monkey wrench.

They go through double doors, and they are in the dining hall.

–More wood paneling, but highly polished here.

Artie sees knives, forks, plates and can hear polite conversation. All the girls (in school-crested blazers) and faculty appear, to Artie, to be sitting and eating at once.

"This way to Headmistress' table. I see she has an empty seat right next to her. Must be for you."

–Looks like a delicious prime rib, roasted brussels sprouts and mashed potatoes.

"Evening, Headmistress," Jorgie says and motions for Artie to sit in the open, high-backed chair. "I got Mister back in one piece."

"Thanks for joining us, Artie," Headmistress says. "We do have a strict seven p.m. start time. Extracurriculars have plenty of time this way. We had to begin. But your main course will be right out. You missed the salad appetizer."

"Thank you," Artie says, sitting. He watches the waitstaff, all female in waist-length white jackets, scurry about.

"Jorgie, you should know better than to come into the Saint Isidore's Dining Hall in your filthy work clothes."

"Sorry, Headmistress. We were a little behind."

Artie speaks up to defend Jorgie. "I was the one who made it a rush job to get here. Jorgie has done a great job seeing me around."

"Very well. Jorgie, you are dismissed."

"Thank you, Jorgie," Artie says as a plate of food is centered in front of him with a quarter turn for presentation.

"You're welcome, Mister," Jorgie says and starts out, his head turning to try inconspicuously to survey the room.

–Must be trying to spot Veronica.

Artie puts his napkin on his lap.

–You only do this in restaurants. Seems very fancy. You never put a napkin on your lap when you eat at home.

"I hope Jorgie didn't pester you too much. He can try *so* hard to please everyone. Thinks he can come into the dining hall wearing coveralls. For the life of me."

"Not at all." Artie takes a bite of his prime rib. "This is delicious. I see you all eat at the same time, like West Point."

"We eat a little late," Headmistress says. "Like some Europeans. If we eat early, the girls get a little snacky. A good figure is part of self-esteem and helps one look professional."

Artie keeps enjoying his beef as she talks.

"You may have noticed the cut of prime rib is on the small side.

Maybe you have gotten a bigger one there. A queen cut, I have heard it called."

Artie tries his brussels sprouts and after swallowing says, "I can't help but comment on the stark difference between this and the scene at the Butt. It is quite stark."

"The boys?" Lana Stanley asks from Artie's other side.

"Yes. They are eating warmed up trays of sloppy joes. I like sloppy joes, but it appears a meal like that could be made from the leftovers of this delight. Is every night likewise?"

"These girls deserve every extra they get," Headmistress says. "What they have been through! And we are trying to get them to appreciate their self-worth. So when they graduate and are in wider society, they expect to be treated with dignity. Here we strive for STEM excellence. This must be nourished. The STEM fields need women, and we believe we are an important part of that pipeline."

"I wouldn't deny these students anything you can provide them. I applaud it. But not all the students are present. The kitchen eating space the boys have is bare bones compared to this and, just like their sleeping quarters, over a garage. With tools, engines and fuel odors."

Headmistress puts her elbows up on the table, leans forward and entwines her fingers.

–Here we go again with the heaving cleavage. You be professional.

"The foundlings love staying there. They think they are living like firemen. What boy wouldn't want that?"

–Young men.

"They are on a different career path. The Butt is the place for that. They don't complain."

"Have they been encouraged to choose college preparatory academics?" Artie asks.

Headmistress takes a deep distracting breath. "They can choose their own way. These girls excel, daily. Science, technology, engineering make up all important facets of their education and taught in a way that each girl can learn at their own pace."

–Did she forget mathematics? She couldn't have meant cosmetics.

"As well as classics like history and English language arts and foreign language."

"Generally," Lana adds—to Artie's relief as the tension is building, "the young women students arrive here more academically advanced. Unfortunately, most of those boys were, before arriving, taking shop classes in juvenile detention facilities. Even though they don't call them that. Some from backgrounds where they were more likely to be involved in crime—I mean victims as well as lawbreaking—than graduate high school. We don't only take the easy cases."

"And," Headmistress says, holding her head up high, "I am proud of those foundlings. There's nothing wrong with what they are trying to master."

"I didn't mean to imply there was."

"Someone has to mop up the labs at the end of the day. Good honest work." She returns to her food, and Artie follows.

"And," Headmistress starts again after pushing her plate back a few inches, which causes a waiter to appear and remove it, "I like Jorgie. It's good to see our youngest be so useful. Idle hands and all."

–That sound familiar to you?

"I saw him bus a tray at the monastery."

Headmistress takes a heaving breath.

–Better hope you didn't get Jorgie into a fix.

Headmistress resumes. "If he wants to be a greenkeeper, I will encourage it. This school believes in individualism. Our Lord made us all different. And I am not shamed to believe it is bragging to say this staff, this committed staff, does a fantastic job. Without much help from the government. The hard work is never done."

–Does she mean finished? Or does she mean no one does hard work?

"I am sure you can find some errors. But we are endeavoring to make this the best facility it can be. If you expect perfection…expect to be disappointed."

"This is a focused survey the New York State Education Department has me conducting. I am so far impressed. I do not know why, except for the amount of time that has gone by since your last review, that there should be such exceptions taken."

Headmistress leans back into her chair. "I feel this is more than that. I heard you spoke to one of our female students. You should have cleared that with the office first. I wouldn't want one of our girls to be intimidated by an unfamiliar man interrogating her."

–Veronica certainly wasn't intimidated by you.

"I…"

–Don't blame this on Jorgie stopping for his crush. Not fair to him.

"I had a casual conversation with a student I was passing in the course of the tour. I was encouraging her college aspirations. Only impressing on her how graduation from university will open doors for her. When you are a university graduate, the world is your oyster."

"But what if she were allergic to shellfish?"

"And not everyone gets a pearl," Lana says, nodding.

–How did you get to this point?

"This orphanage is a boon for these students." Artie gulps down his mouthful. "I only expect the highest level of reporting from what I can see now."

"We refer to the orphanage as a Displaced Child Assemblage. Orphanage sounds offensive. Like these girls were abandoned, and our Lord never abandons one of his children. DCA, that's a less offensive term."

–Why the big change? Did she call someone about this survey I am doing? Less cooperative.

Doc Washington, now wearing a white dress shirt and khakis, comes to the table and sits in front of Artie, immediately to his left.

"How is everyone this evening?" he asks, smiling. A place setting is brought by the waitstaff.

–Is he eating again?

"I am well," Artie says, still eating. "I haven't had a piece of beef this perfectly cooked in a long time."

"We are well, Doc Washington," Headmistress says. "The boys enjoyed their evening meal, I'm sure?"

"Very much so," he answers. "Mr. Alston commented to me about how much fun it was. Said it reminded him of his college days."

–You said frat. Thought he might provide a respite.

"I was telling him the same," Headmistress says, wiping crumbs from the blouse atop her breasts. She smooths her blouse and eyes Artie.

"You have some appetite," Artie says to Doc Washington as a plate with dinner is put in front of him. "Didn't I see you eating with the lads at the Butt?"

"I had a little down there. Enjoyed it too. Fresh air makes one hungry. I see you are enjoying it. Probably the fresh air. You must normally be tied to a desk for work."

"Yes, I am. The dinner is very tasty. Maybe the additional fresh air, it has turned me extra hungry; that and the hour."

–Was it a show, him eating at the Butt? Do the boys know he eats here?

"These meals together serve as a casual but effective daily faculty meeting," Headmistress says. "Doc Washington is fulfilling a requirement."

"I guess all this food is just my cross to bear." Doc Washington blurts a single syllable laugh.

"Doc Washington, your manners."

"My apologies, Headmistress. I should not casually mention our Lord like that."

"It's a common expression," Artie says.

"Not at this table."

"No, ma'am."

–You can't get anyone on your side.

"That reminds me of another point. This institution has, besides the rent-paying monks down the hill, a chapel. I need to assure my superiors that there is no pressure of any kind on the students toward one religion or another."

"There is no requirement, implied or overt, to attend services," Headmistress says. "As for that religion." She does an air quote with one hand. Artie pushes his plate back, having finished, and his plate is removed. "Those men—hill dwellers to me—I do not even consider them religious. New age hooey. Neo-Eastern nonsense. Not Christian men."

"Shouldn't be an issue that you have," Artie says. "Which religion they choose to practice, or more aptly, amalgam of religions they practice. As long as separate from the education at the school."

"Some of them monks, or whatever, look more like goodfellows." Headmistress touches an index finger to the side of her nose.

"What are you implying?" Artie asks.

–This could completely wreck your report.

"No, no," Doc Washington says, eyeing Artie. "All on the up and up. They are all religious men. Well educated. They are spiritual," he says after turning his persuasiveness to Headmistress. "They don't worship our Lord, but I believe them to be spiritual."

"What about this rash accusation?" Artie asks Doc Washington directly.

"Oh, no. If Headmistress doesn't mind my plainness?" He waits for Headmistress, who nods for him to proceed. "Those men chose to go there. Many successful careers were left behind to follow their calling. And I know Headmistress doesn't approve of them turning away from our Lord, but they do worship nature and respect it. Which I know Headmistress is a great supporter of."

"Fine line," Headmistress says, "between wiccan and protector of nature."

"They cover most of the bases," Doc Washington continues. "But all suspicions should be allayed by the security company. They cannot come—the school insists—without background checks, including fingerprints."

"I would never have allowed anything else," Headmistress adds.

A bowl of ice cream is placed in front of Artie and then the others. He notices the girls getting up with their bowls and forming an orderly queue. "That is most reassuring. I am quite relieved to hear it."

–Thank goodness.

"I told you this was sundae night," Headmistress says, seeming completely composed.

–Is she good now because of dessert or my assurance?

"You can go to the fixins bar anytime. Guests do not have to proceed along the usual routine."

"Thank you, this is wonderful."

"We only do vanilla on sundae night. I hope that's okay."

"Oh, it's tasty. I'll go up in a minute," Artie says, noticing the easy-to-spot (because of her height) Veronica at the toppings table.

–You better not get near her, in case she starts a conversation and gives cause for Headmistress to intervene.

"Doc Washington," Headmistress says, "I believe it is sundae night at the Butt as well. Would you assure Artie the foundling boys have their needs met?"

"Oh sure, they even get to scoop their own flavor."

"Are they unsupervised now?" Artie asks.

"I have my number two, Swaine, in charge when I am not directly supervising. Gotta let them breathe."

–You stick with the plain vanilla. Too much food as it is.

Headmistress and some of the other faculty stand and go to the dessert bar. Lana dips her napkin in her water glass and, after standing, holds the moistened tip toward Artie. "You have a smudge by your hairline, left side," she says. Artie accepts and wipes his forehead. Lana follows Headmistress.

"Thank you," Artie says after her.

Doc Washington finishes chewing, puts his utensils down and dabs his lips. He points his napkin briefly at Artie's clean forehead. "Probably from riding the machine. I hope you'll do a real kindness to those boys when you do your reporting," he says while checking that none of the women are within earshot. "Don't force the hand that makes the school take their masculinity from them. It's bad enough as it is. They don't need to be mollycoddled; I tell them that myself. Let them have their boys-will-be-boys. Keeps them gentlemen around the girls. And believe me, these kids' backgrounds, you don't want to frustrate them and keep them on a leash. The end of that leash'll be awful hard to hold."

"I won't compromise the report. You have nothing to fear from an honest survey of this establishment."

"I am glad to hear it. We'll keep this to ourselves."

–You can't agree to that.

Headmistress and the others return. "Do you enjoy fresh blueberries, Artie? I believe they are locally sourced."

Artie takes a half spoonful of ice cream and says, "I'll stick with plain, really just a taste. Feeling full."

"They liven up the bowl, the colors. I think they are a superfood as well."

"Antioxidants," Lana adds, nodding enthusiastically.

"I wanted to ask about the chapel."

"Wonderful place," Headmistress says. "Beautiful. I find it quieting when I go alone to pray. It's a little small. Not that we fill it for Reverend Mathis. But I miss the grand space of a more formal cathedral."

"I noticed quite a bit of gold in the chapel when I peeked through the window," Artie says.

"Well, I didn't know you were inspecting the chapel," Headmistress answers. "Yes. We have a lot of gold leaf. Doc Washington had a gilder come. He also showed the foundling boys in the trades path how to apply the gilding. More than ten years ago. We have been fortunate also with donations for the ornamentation. Most items were given directly to the school for use in the chapel. The school did not purchase them."

Doc Washington's eyes dart back and forth between Headmistress and Artie, but he doesn't speak.

"Can I be reassured—from the sufficient seating—that the students are not coerced to attend?"

"No," Lana says enthusiastically, turning her head side to side. "Never forced."

"I wish more did attend," Headmistress says. "I feel church once a week would help some of these girls to forget their past. Forgiveness, Reverend Mathis was recently telling the few of them that were there last weekend: the forgiveness that our Lord taught is for the forgiver as well as the trespasser."

"Do the boys attend?"

"No," Lana says.

"I don't go, myself," Doc Washington admits. "Headmistress says I would be a better influence on the boys if I went, but—"

"This great tempest is upon you," Headmistress says.

–Overreaction?

"Yes. I believe in the Lord, but I do not tolerate well the Reverend Mathis. Always with Jonah and the whale. Headmistress and I have discussed it. We put it aside."

"That's often the best," Artie says. "Religion can be a difficult topic."

"Sometimes I can agree with Doc Washington. Reverend Mathis does spend an inordinate amount of time in the Old Testament, which is a little outmoded and smitey for me. But I...believe the Reverend is a learned man when it comes to our Lord. Belief in God is all we ask."

"And a nice honorarium for the Reverend," Doc Washington says and receives a sour look from Headmistress.

"I hope the school accepts not believing as well."

Artie waits through a few seconds of silence. When he starts to add something, Headmistress says, "Is it okay to ask if you believe?"

"Well, professionally, I would not bring it up. I am required to remain neutral."

"Doesn't religious freedom allow one to express their religion?"

"In another situation."

"I think—and I do say think, not believe—that it is egomaniacal to presume there isn't a god, that humans are the acme. And that we should be kind to each other for no reason other than we are not Neanderthals. I mean Neanderthals in the figurative sense."

–Is she an intelligent design theorist? You should go.

"I have a long drive. I won't be able to finish this ice cream. Thank you for a delicious meal and an informative day." Artie stands. "If I eat any more, I will be too sleepy to make it home."

"Would you like coffee?" Headmistress asks.

–She seems so friendly and polite now; can really swing back fast.

"I can't stay. Long ride."

"To-go cup?" Headmistress waves over a waiter and requests a coffee to go. "Milk, Artie, sugar?"

–You can't have that faux milk again.

"Black would be best."

The waiter leaves.

"Doc Washington, if you don't mind, would you show our guest to the men's room? And see him to his car?"

"Of course," Doc Washington says through his napkin as he wipes his mouth and stands, noisily pushing his chair with the back of his knees.

"That's unnecessary."

A waiter hands Artie an insulated, hard plastic, covered travel mug of coffee with the school emblem on it. "Thank you. Thank you to everyone. I can see myself out."

"I've got the golf cart, and I am going back to the Butt," Doc Washington says. "You don't want to stumble in the dark getting back to the car. Bear attack and all."

"Really?"

Everyone has a chuckle. "No. It could happen. Security would alert us if one came out of the woods. And we would round up the girls until it passed. Plenty of deer come on the campus."

"Hell on the flowers," Headmistress says. She stands and holds her hand out to Artie, who lightly shakes it. "It was nice to have met you."

–She sounds like she isn't expecting you back.

"Yes, very nice to meet all of you. I'll be sure and call before I return."

Headmistress smiles painfully and watches Artie follow Doc Washington out.

7

I slipped into the side door of the monastre, the one right near the janitorial closet. I spotted Brother Dom's commodities tucked to the side of the closet, then dragged out the microfiber-pad broom with fringe and started down the hall, catching the dust bunnies at the wall edge. Brother Dom had told me to always look busy, that way no one will ask why I'm there. He's been right so far, as these types spend most of their day motionless and don't want to have to do the chores themselves. I shot back down the hall to where I began so as it won't look suspicious with one side full of blowing dust bunnies and the other side clean. No sign of anyone. Then I got to the stairs. I skipped the steps and gave the landing a swipe. I did the second-floor hallway. Brother Dom was in the dining hall. He made eye contact with me. I finished the hallway and did a once-around the empty Elementroy Industrials residence room.

I wasn't happy that I didn't see much of Veronica on my way out of Upper Joe's. She was acting like she didn't see me trying to catch her eye, talking to Posenica. They would talk all times now. Posenica and me had a deal, a promise, that we wouldn't talk about our days when we were fostermates. Not to each other, not to nobody. But I still had to ponder: As she got close to Veronica, would she spill? Posenica and I hardly talked now that we had the deal. She had asked for it. That was when I first came, after a stint, and bumped into her while I was cleaning out the Cousin's cellar of old arts and crafts. All I knew how to do when I got here was lug trash.

Posenica was already matriculated a year or so. She looked much improved, made-up, hair pristine and her uniform all neat, not like I was used to seeing her. A year made a big difference. Easy to see that day why she didn't want no one, not a trash lugger, talking about the way things were. "I'm boxing in the next round," she said. "I ain't got no time to mind the punches I took in the first." She was awfully smart, like Veronica.

I was sweeping the stair on my way down when Brother Dom—already in his adventuring clothes—passed me. He kept his head down and didn't say a word to me. He only hummed his manta. I skipped the last few steps and glided the broom down the hall, watching Brother Dom go into the closet, grab the cooler and go out the side door. I put the broom back without shaking it out like I was supposed to, then grabbed the two sacks and tarp they were under. I followed Brother Dom out. The self-closing door was quiet as always.

Brother Dom was on the quad, cooler already bungeed tight on the back. "C'mon, kiddo," he said when he saw me—not putting effort into secrecy like I was doing.

"Worked like a charm," I said and strapped the sacks in, near the cooler: they barely fit.

"Always does, kiddo. Jorgie, those guys are either praying, concentrating, meditating, invocating or could all be sleeping."

I put my helmet on. "Wish you'd wear one of these. Doc Washington real strict about it with these four-by-fours. These that ain't got roll bars and seat belts like a side-by-side."

"I'm fine. It's a nothin' trip. Besides, I got the best chauffeur around, the best off-roader the world ever seen."

I sat in front of him, grabbed the handlebars, squeezed the hand brake and started her up.

"Hey, and Kyle told me I did something in the snow, so that means I'll live into the winter."

"He sure knows stuff. But I bet he would tell you to wear a helmet."

"Well he ain't gonna know to tell me. We got that, right?"

"Yeah, we got that. All right."

I pulled away, light on the accelerator, only twisting my wrist enough to get us moving. I got to the woodland edge and drove along it, kept the headlights on low. I saw the gap and turned into the woods. I knew the trail, but we still needed to go slow; never could tell what was going to be jutting out on such a narrow path. Kept along that route, parallel to the main road. We could hear and see the headlights of a car pass every couple of minutes. I turned the headlights off when we got to the incline that went up to the main road. I stood on the foot pegs, watched and listened.

"You are the most cautious teenager I ever did meet. Ever."

When I was sure it was clear, I hit gas, then sat as Brother Dom grasped his hands together in front of me, so he wouldn't fall off the back. We tipped. I leaned my weight forward, and the four-by-four rumbled up and over the incline, out of the roadside ditch, and we were on the shoulder. More gas as we were level, and wanted to do as little time on the road as possible. Brother Dom released his grip on his other hand that he had around me. I saw the Old Bavarian Inn ahead, at the curve. I double-checked both directions: no cars coming, only one moving away, headed to town. We crossed the road. It was actually easier to do at dark because of the headlight beams of approaching cars. You wouldn't get that warning in daylight. Also there was a streetlight here because of the curve, the exiting and entering traffic of the bar, and it was at the edge of town. The streetlights picked up again a mile down in town proper.

I pulled the quad to a stop at the entrance to the worn clapboard, two-story former home that was now a bar with two apartments on the top floor. Brother Dom hopped off. There were a few vehicles in the parking lot. Music and crowd noise were low. "You gonna come out with a beer for me, Brother Dom?"

"Yeah, kiddo. Wait around back." He threw me his jacket. He sported black jeans, black T-shirt and gold chain, like usual, and those funny sandals the monks wore right into the winter. "Don't lose it." He went up the crooked wood steps to the porch and then inside, yelling, "Norm!"

I drove the quad around to the rear and parked it. The door was open, and beyond the screen I could hear Manny in the kitchen hustling, clanking pans and plates.

Brother Dom came out, allowing the screen door to slap closed noisily behind him. "Here's your nightcap." He handed me an import and a near-empty pack of cigarettes.

I opened the beer by slapping the cap edge down onto the side of the step and pocketed the smokes for Veronica, who I would try to catch sometime tomorrow.

"Just that one, kiddo. You're the designated driver." Brother Dom went back in. I heard him yelling at Manny. "Outta my way, Boyardee!" Not sure Manny liked it, but Brother Dom liked to say him and Manny were tight. Manny took it to get through his shift.

After I finished my beer and the kitchen noise quieted, I went in. "Hi, Manny."

"Hi, Jorgie."

"Dinner rush over?"

"Yeah. Slow tonight." Manny went back to tending the grill while also drying and shelving some plates from the steaming commercial dishwasher.

Frank came in through the bi-swing doors.

"Hey, boss," I said, trying to act cool, like I belonged in the kitchen. I never knew how he would take me sitting there. All tight with me one night, pissed just to have me hanging in the backyard other times. I believe he half hated Brother Dom. Dom rubbed him the wrong way. He took it out on me. Then Brother Dom would smooth it over again for next time. Dom needed his respite, which meant drinking, smoking and whoring with Terri.

"Good to see you, Jorgie. Working hard or hardly working?"

"A lot goin' on today. Can I get a piece of that bacoln! Hungry as hell."

"Manny, you got any bacon for hungry, hungry Jorgie?"

"I... so I was 'bout to plate this bacon cheeseburger deluxe. But I could make some more."

"No," Frank said. "Give him a piece off the burger." Frank went back out to the dining room.

Manny plated the bacon cheeseburger deluxe and fries and put it under the heat lamps next to a fish and chips order for Zoie to bring out.

I went and lifted the bun off the top and slid out a strip of fried beauty. I placed the bun back and bit. "Hmm. Manny, you got a magic touch when it comes to bacoln!"

"Fryin' bacon ain't magic. Pig is just good. That's all there is to it."

I sat on the beat-up wood barstool that was to the side of the screen door, my back against the wall. I was getting hot and knew not to get sweaty because the temperature would keep dropping and the ride back on the quad would be tough. If it was warm on the way down to town and I forgot my gloves, the ride back with the cold, night air pouring over the exposed skin could hurt hands to stone.

Frank came back in. He grabbed a dish towel and wiped his hands, heading toward me. "Let's talk outside, Jorgie," he said, then

I followed him out to the quad. He went right to the cooler. I took the bungee cords off, and he opened the cooler top. "What did we score?"

"Lamb chops, sea bass. Two ten-pound potatoes under that tarp."

Frank pulled two vacuum-plastic-wrapped racks of baby lamb chops out and another twelve-pound bag of frozen fillets. "Not bad. I need steak. Until ski season, these locals don't eat much lamb and seafood. Except fried crab and shrimp."

"Got shrimp last time."

"Yeah, the shrimp moved. But steak, I get a better markup. Some tenderloins. Porterhouse. You ever hear of a tomahawk chop?"

"Like Florida State football? Or wrestlin'?"

"It's a steak on a big bone. Looks like a tomahawk. Tomahawk steak."

"They don't eat no cow at the monastre."

"Get it from the school."

"I couldn't take nothin' from those poor orphan girls. They need to eat healthy. Headmistress says the only chance they got in life is us looking out for them. Some of them girls been through a long road, bad things. Drug-addicted, abuser parents or one's ain't there at all."

"Yeah, we all know the sob story. You're an orphan too, aren't you?"

"Yeah, that's why I can't take from them."

"They work you hard. They ain't treating you fair. You'll see when you turn eighteen and you are out."

"Those girls have a good diet. They need all that. Headmistress wants the best for them."

"What about you? Did you ever taste one of those porterhouses? I heard those teachers talking about *tender* when they stop in here to check out the ski patrol types."

"Nah. We got them Salisbury steaks. Mushroom gravy poured all over top too. And lots of."

"Probably ground up scraps scavenged from what the top tier

didn't finish. Did you ever see a meat grinder in their kitchen when you were scrubbing?"

"Yeah. Cleaned it myself. A fine job of it too."

"Well, I'll let you put it all together for yourself."

"I know how to take apart and put back together that grinder."

Zoie poked her head out from the screen door. "Hi, sugar," she said to me and then quickly to Frank, "Boss, table five wants to talk to you about their vodka."

"Fuckin' aye. Jorgie, bring those potatoes in with me."

I grabbed a bag in each hand and followed him.

He turned back to me just before we went in. "I'll tell you. You get some steaks, good steaks. I'll pay you without Dom. Me and you on that deal."

"Brother Dom won't like that."

"You're not following me."

"I'm right behind you, but I can't take from the school. I'll get you more shrimp."

We stepped inside. I stowed the potatoes while Frank briefly went into the walk-in before returning to the dining area.

Zoie stepped outside, pulling a cigarette from her apron. I followed her and sat on a weathered bench. "How you doin', sweetie? You getting enough sleep? You're seventeen and you got bags starting under your eyes."

"I like to be active."

Zoie lit up. She was older, midforties, a little overweight: she carried that at her waist, but her legs were nice. Always sported a skirt and her hair always done up. Except when Department of Health came; then she dashed it into a hair net or something. She kept that handy in her apron.

"Ain't you tired? Why don't you come over to the employee lounge?" I said, tapping on the beat-up bench seat next to me. "You on your feet the whole day and night."

Zoie dragged on her cigarette. "Cause, sweetie, if I sit now, I won't get up. I got open checks. Soon as I get my last tip, I sit. I love that car seat after a shift. Are they taking good care of you at the school?"

"Yes."

"How about that monastery? Those creepy men keepin' away from you?"

"They don't do nothin' like that. They good people. They don't like the material world, that's all. They pray for everybody."

"They pray for you? And me?"

"I believe just everybody in general."

"What about this loser inside that's got you drivin' him around. He prayin' for you?"

"He sure is. He's got his demons. He's here to work them out."

"He sure does got demons. Only reason a man like that would go to a monastery is…"

"I don't…"

"Is none of my business. What else is new in your school?"

"I was asked by Headmistress to give a tour today. Some bigwig from the State, all over campus and even down the hill to the monastre."

"Bigwig from the State?"

"Yeah. Headmistress tryin' to play it cool, but I see she was worried. Charmin' him a little too much."

"And this State guy wanted to see the monastery?"

"Yeah."

"Sure he wasn't lookin' for dum-dum in there?" She waved her cig back at the door.

"Brother Dom's all right. He told me if I can't get settled after graduation, he'll get me a spot there with him." A rat scurried around the front of the garbage dumpster that stood away from the restaurant. We didn't react to it.

"You don't have to go very far just to wind up here. Besides, I bet he says lots of things. I think you don't belong there any more than he does. But for different reasons."

"I spotted Veronica walkin' alone. I stopped and introduced Mr. Alston from the State to her. Told her about how Headmistress asked me to give the tour."

"Make her see you in a good light?"

"I guess. I worry about Veronica. She smokes and…" I looked at Zoie's cig, still lit and near the end. She took another drag, then stubbed it out and flicked it toward the dumpster. "I don't care you smoke them cigabutts." She frowned. "I mean, I do care, but you are an adult. You do what you want. You don't mind by what I believe."

Zoie turned to head back to the kitchen. She stopped and then came and sat next to me. She put an arm around me heavily. "Jorgie," she said. "You have to stop thinkin' people don't mind you. You've been through a lot. I know you never told me no details, but you didn't get in this situation—one most kids like you…especially nice, good kids like you—all by yourself. I know. I seen stuff too when I was young." She took out her cigarette pack and handed it to me. "To show you that I mind you, that I hear you. I quit. Take 'em." I did. She pulled me over tighter, but roughly and quickly released me and stood.

"You don't have to."

She reached into her apron and pulled out her lighter. "Take this too, so you know I mean it. Give 'em to Veronica Von Villeneney, whatever her name is, the one with the flat-pressed, long hair and perfect manicure you are always talking about. If you want, or throw them away if you don't want her to have them. This job will suck a little more."

"You can't go cold turkey."

"Manny! I quit smokin'," she yelled to the screen door. He called out to her, but I couldn't understand. To me she said, "I'll do it, just to show you, you got people to mind you, and when time at that school is up, you remember that. People gotta mind Jorgie." She went inside, turned and faced me while gently closing the door.

Frank came out right after, before I could grasp anything about what happened. "What's she talking for?" he asked me and handed me one of his two open beers.

I took a sip. "Smokin'."

"Don't listen to her. You shouldn't smoke. Now I got work. Cooled off, huh? Do you think you can get me some french fries and fresh mozzarella? Chicken cutlets I'll take too." I nodded. "I told Dom already, but not about the steaks, that the school food thing is between you and me." He clanked my beer with his and went inside.

I moved around to the side of the building under a window where I could hear the revelry, Brother Dom's voice the loudest of all. After my beer I went to the back and lay down on the quad awhile: my head on Brother Dom's coat in the cargo rack, butt on the seat and boots up on the handlebars.

I walked back to the woods and peed, then went into the kitchen. Manny smoked, sitting on a stool, sipping a light beer. "Temperature dropping?"

"Yeah, startin' to. That, and I am tired, makin' me feel cold."

"Have some coffee."

I got up and poured half a cup.

"One hour to go, hopefully no more dinner orders."

"Does Frank let you hang in the bar after the orders are done?" I found my chair.

"No. I gotta clock out. He lets me chill back here, as long as I pay for the beer, half price—employee discount." Manny got up and put on the tiny TV that was on top of the glass-door refrigerator. "Yankees." He sat slumped, looking as tired as I felt. "Your boy already got Terri upstairs. You might get off work early. He's crazy. He had a swing and a miss at Zoie, I think. Terri didn't like that one bit, like Zoie would steal her business. Zoie don't put up with Dom's shit, not for a sec. She's real suspicious of him. Don't abide him a lick. Are you suspicious of him?"

"No. He gets me a break from that place. I know what it is. Why suspect anything?"

"Well, he ain't got no money, no real vow of poverty up there, but they ain't paying him to pray. What's he giving Terri for his ride?"

"He gets me some medical marijuana—for Veronica. Probably gives Terri some too."

Manny contemplated the TV. "She sold me some. I didn't know if I should tell you. I guess that's where she got it from. You and me in the same boat: can't say nothing. These guys don't care about their secrets when it comes to me and you. Who are we going to blab to?"

"People got their own thing. Not hurting no one."

"Accessory to distribution. You be careful. If you are driving that dude when he's holding enough to buy off Terri, and the troopers pull you over, it might be enough to put you away. You think you can flip and blame Dom? He'll bury you. That I know."

"We ain't on the road for much of the ride, mostly trail. Anyways, I ain't got no license to drive on the roads, only private property. They can get me hauled in anytime they want."

He minded the TV for a few minutes, then finished his beer. "I'm going in there for another one," he said, pointing to the double doors with the empty bottle. "I'll get you one, but you gotta pay me. I nab it half price. I'll tell Frank I'm drinking both."

"Nah. You get me all worried about driving but getting me elastic."

He went through the door and left me alone. I finished the coffee, washed my mug and put it away. Manny didn't come back in.

Finally, Brother Dom returned all happy. He kicked one door open, then the other. "Let's ride, muchacho!" he yelled like always when his games were over. We walked out the back to the quad. He put his coat on, and we buttoned up. The temperature had continued to drop.

"Did Zoie get home?"

"Fucking bitch? I don't know. She cold-shoulders me all the time. I didn't see her before I got you."

I started the machine, put the lights on high and pulled away, uphill across the road, headed away from town, looking for the trail turnoff. Brother Dom was talking loudly at my ear—hard to hear even him over the motor and the wind. "Karma-Con! Fucking big idea I had. Money! We get a convention center. We get top yogis. Mats fucking everywhere. You know what I mean? Karma-Con?"

"Karma-Con? Like Comic-Con?" I asked, yelling.

"Karma-Con!"

I spotted the trailhead and slowed to make the turn—big dip as the quad moved down from the road. The whole rig tipped sideways as we left the shoulder. I had to grab Brother Dom's jacket to keep him from flopping out. We steadied and moved slowly through the trees. "Do you mean like Batman and Superman?"

"They can come if they want. Karma-Con! It'll be big, kiddo."

We were quiet until we got to the monastre grounds. When we broke the woodland edge, I kept it slow to reduce engine noise. "Brother Dom, do you believe that guy from the State was lookin' for you? I would feel terrible if I brought him down here for that."

"Why would he look for me?"

"I wanted to ask you for some medical marijuana, for Veronica."

"Your girl Veronica."

"I pondered maybe that could be why."

"Who told you that? He say anything?"

"No. He was inspecting the school. I wasn't sure why he wanted to look around down here."

We stopped by the side entrance. "School owns this land, we rent. Besides, I told you it's medicinal marijuana." We dismounted.

I took my helmet off. "Brother Dom, do you ever get steak at the monastre?"

"No, those guys all Jainists. Or seafood vegan pescatarians. I don't know all the rules. Kyle don't eat any animal. But others eat fish and chicken. Lamb, no veal either. No fish some, only shellfish others. Some dudes on a potato diet. That's why I got you riding me to the OBI. Steak and other flesh." He laughed.

I nodded.

"I'll be right back with a joint for Veronica." He went in through the never-locked side door and returned in a few minutes. The cold was getting to me. "Here you go, kiddo. No worries."

I put the joint into the cigarette pack.

"We have tons of this stuff. I got you. I told you I would get you a spot here if you want. I'm looking out for you." He turned to head back in but stopped and moved closer to me, leaning across the seat of the quad. "You know," he said, concerned. Seemed like he was trying to be sure of his words. "I know you like Veronica, but I think you ain't getting anywhere with her. If you want a ride with Terri, you let me know. I'll arrange it. On me. You gotta suit up though. Town dumpster, that one. Boney bitch. All those drug girls: too fucking skinny." He slapped his big hand twice on my back, then rubbed a circle on it. He paused, took his hand off me and rested both arms across on the cargo rack. His eyes rolled up at me. "I thought I was gonna burp," he said and went inside.

It was a cold ride back to the Butt. I left the machine outside because the garage door was too noisy. I couldn't chance rousing Doc. I had to wake up early though, before him, to put it away, or he would be angry the quad was left outside. I stepped lightly in the door by the stair and went up to the boys' dormitory and crept into my bed.

8

Artie starts his car and takes a deep breath. He watches Doc Washington shoot away in his golf cart, the headlights fading as they move back to the Joes'. Artie is thinking about Headmistress. She has excited him. He pictures her suggestively smoking a cigarette.

–The car is cold. Do you need to let this hybrid warm up?

He adjusts the heat and waves his hands in front of the vents. He starts slowly toward the main road with Headmistress still smoking in front of him, her cleavage swelling with each inhale. Artie can taste the smoke and taste her perfume.

–You're conflating her with your ex.

He grabs his phone, stops the car, finds his ex-wife's number in his favorites and calls. It goes to voicemail. "Dear, I am heading back to my apartment from work upstate. I'll be passing very close to your place. Thought if you weren't doing anything I would stop by. Catch up, have a talk. Call me back if you are interested." He hangs up, plugs his charger in and sets his navigation app for home. He continues his drive.

–You have to wonder if the Big Brother security is monitoring your cell phone while on campus.

He checks to see if his phone joined a Wi-Fi network, but it has not.

As he leaves the pavement, he encounters jostling of the car and the road noise of the crushed basalt. He remembers he never paired his phone to the car.

–If she calls now, you won't be able to take the call, or you'll have to pull over. Why the crushed driveway material? The rest of the roads on campus are so smooth. Don't they want people to know how nice the school is?

Artie pulls onto the state road, and now, being more comfortable because he had previously negotiated the curves and because of the late hour, he goes a little over the speed limit. As he nears the town, he passes a bar. He hears the familiar whirring from Jorgie's monastery tour. He slows and watches his rearview mirror. He sees a four-wheeler—an older kind with handlebars—scoot across the road, toward the bar, under the sole streetlight. The driver has a helmet on.

–Couldn't be Jorgie. Same coveralls; looks like, anyway.

The passenger, on the back, isn't wearing a helmet. Artie loses sight of the pair and then enters the small town. He checks his navigation app, curious as to why it is taking him back a different route than how he came.

–Town of Laffton. All quiet here. Still good travel time expected. A student driving someone to the bar? Probably Washington. He didn't seem like a true educator.

Almost an hour later, Artie's phone dings with a text message. He sees the sign for the thruway entrance.

–Don't check a text while driving. You know it's her. She should have called. You told her you were on the road. She always does it. No calls. Never a call back. Always a text.

Artie pulls over onto the shoulder by the thruway entrance. He puts his hazards on. Checks his phone. 'Cum bye if u want bt not to talk.'

–Can't even get a polite text return.

Police lights suddenly flash behind him. His car interior is illuminated in blue, white and red. He puts his phone in the holder and lowers his window.

A county officer walks over. "Evening, sir," she says.

–Female cop.

"Yes, to you too, a good evening, Officer."

"Is everything all right?"

"Yes, yes."

"I saw the state plates—education. Figured I would make sure you were okay. Odd hour and all."

"I am. Thank you. I am returning home from an assignment. I was at the orphanage school near Laffton."

The police officer doesn't respond.

–Seems less friendly since I brought that up.

"I see you are not familiar with it. New to me also. That's why I went there today."

"Are you on official state business now?"

"Yes. Returning from it anyway. I was assigned this car for the visit. I actually pulled over because I received a text message. I didn't want to text and drive."

The officer doesn't respond.

"It's from my ex-wife."

"Oh, I got one of those too. Ex-husband, that is."

"She wants me to stop by on my way home."

The police officer chuckles. "Well, no way I would take a dangerous text like that driving. I know how it is with the exes. Mine's name is Ben, as in *Ben* up to no good."

"Eggrett, mine."

"You take your time and give me a wave. I'll stay back behind you until you are ready to safely pull into traffic. Not that there is any now. I guess you are getting on the thruway?"

"Yes. Thank you. Is this reportable? They track all the license plate activity. I would have to file an incident action report to my supervisor. A lot of paperwork. I'm willing to do the requirements, but unnecessary if you don't report it."

"No report, nothing here worth pulping trees over. Have a good night."

"Good night. A second or two and I'll be on my way."

–Nice kid. Thought you were in some hot water for a second.

Artie changes the destination in the navigation, then texts his ex back to let her know when she can expect him. He sticks his arm straight out the window and flaps it up and down. The cop car noses out, blocking the lane of traffic. In the rearview mirror, Artie sees the cop wave for him to go. Artie pulls out and bears right for the thruway. He sees the cop kick up dust while pulling a very fast U-turn from the shoulder, and then her emergency lights go off.

Artie drives over the speed limit and arrives at his ex-wife's walk-up apartment—in what looks like a row of trilevel town houses—a couple of minutes ahead of schedule. He goes around a grass divider to the guest parking. She is center row of five buildings in a development. Neither of them had wanted to keep the old house they had shared as a married couple. Artie certainly had been sick of the exterior maintenance. He opted for an apartment; money after alimony didn't allow for much more.

–Eggrett got the better end there, working off the books to hide it from the courts to keep you paying.

Artie climbs the outside stair to the second floor.

–Bet she left the door unlocked.

He turns the knob and walks in. Apprehensive, he leaves the door open behind him. "Dear, I made good time." He sees the couch under the windows, same old beat-up couch from their marital home. A cheap one they bought when they first moved in—mauve pleather that cracked over time. There is a beach towel covering one end, including the arm, with some pillows bulging under it.

–Is that the towel we picked up at that tourist stop in Cape May?

Eggrett comes out from the kitchen, smoking dramatically. Her fingers have their long, painted fingernails pointing straight up, aligned with her metacarpals, the cigarette pinched between her ring and middle fingers. She is thin, with gelled-up, short hair, wearing only a formfitting white T-shirt.

–Those are the heels you like and the false eyelashes. She's even skinnier than last time you saw her.

Artie scrambles to close the front door and then clears his throat as he returns to his position facing his ex. Eggrett stares through Artie's eyes as she walks toward him but then stops and sits on the beach towel laid across the couch. She leans her back into the corner and puts one foot up onto the couch-back cushion, the point of her heel poking the curtains. She takes another drag, and Artie goes to her. He gets down on his knees and plants his face between her thighs. He inhales the lingering scent of shave cream. Headmistress smoking is all that runs through his mind as he performs cunnilingus on his ex. He grinds his crotch against the couch. His heart is racing so fast his head throbs, pulsing outwardly against his skull. He crunches the couch more.

–Don't do it. Hold out for her.

He has lost his control. Eggrett makes breathy sounds and takes another long drag. Artie shudders and ejaculates into his underwear and pants. He pauses pleasuring his ex.

–Damn it.

"Are you going to finish me this time? Or not?"

Artie goes back to what is now a chore. After a few minutes, she shudders and Artie withdraws.

"Same old Artie."

—She enjoys this shaming of you. She holds it over you as a tool to get you to not fight the divorce terms.

Eggrett rises, and Artie enjoys watching her walk away as she imitates a runway model, her cigarette still smoldering in her hand. She goes into the bathroom and closes the door.

Artie picks up the beach towel. "Are those new throw pillows?" he asks the empty room. He notices an uncomfortable squishiness in the groin and all around his underwear.

—Had to be a big one, of course.

He opens his pants and cleans himself as best he can with the towel. Then he wipes the couch seat off with it.

After he straightens out his appearance, including using his fingers to unmuss his hair and neatening the old couch, he brings the beach towel down the hall to Eggrett's laundry closet. He opens the washing machine's lid and sees there are wet clothes slopped at the bottom. He drops the beach towel and takes the wet clothes out—checking for delicates likely to shrink—and places them into the stackable dryer above and turns it on. He starts the small load (hot wash) in the machine, adds detergent (which dribbles out of its container) and then the beach towel. He hefts and shakes the bottle of liquid detergent. He looks around the laundry closet for another. He sees there is none. He tucks the light bottle under an arm, opens his phone's shopping app and orders a new laundry detergent—Eggrett's shipping information is already loaded in the app. He puts the bottle back on the proper shelf upside down.

—She can get another load out of that one.

Artie returns to the living room. He glances about, looking to see if anything looks out of place. He goes to the kitchen and washes his hands. He reaches, without looking, for a paper towel from the rod but only touches the cardboard tube. He goes to the cabinet above the refrigerator, pulls out a fresh roll and places it on the hanging rod after removing and disposing of the used one in the recycling bin under the sink. He then returns to the couch. He picks up one of the throw pillows Eggrett had been reclined on.

–Certainly looks new. You should get some throw pillows.

He rubs his hand along the seat back of the couch, feeling the cracks in the hard material.

–Cracks getting bigger. She should get a new couch, never mind throw pillows. Everything else in here looks newish.

He walks over to the kitchen and looks around to see if all is in order and returns to stand in the center of the living room.

–Guess she's not coming back out. Tired. Would have been nice to stay over. You should have put some music on, maybe stopped for a bottle of wine.

Artie goes to the entry door, opens it, engages the lock, steps out and pulls the door closed. He glances around the exterior of the apartment complex, noticing the dome light of his car is still on.

–Hope that didn't drain the battery.

He grasps the doorknob and tries to turn it, making sure it has locked.

–Very good.

Artie drives home—his crotch uncomfortably moist for the whole drawn-out trip. He falls asleep in his twin bed, wearing the same clothes, entirely exhausted and his thoughts consumed by Headmistress smoking.

9

Artie's tired. And tired of being in the car. His stomach is turning sour from drinking too much coffee before breakfast. He has a bagel with cream cheese to eat at his desk while he rips through work email, as he usually starts his day. He had bought the large coffee for the commute because he got to bed late, but now he has a terrible feeling he may not have time to drop his things at his desk before getting to the bathroom.

     –If you have to bring the bagel into the bathroom, you'll have to toss it in the composting bin. No way to save it. And then what will you eat? Something from the food truck or wait for your a.m. break and rush across Stewart Avenue for something. Shouldn't have had that big prime rib last night, and so late. The emails will be piled up because you were out-of-office yesterday. The replies to your automated out-of-office-today responses (things like "enjoy your day off," even though you weren't off and didn't say you were off—even from people in the same office as you, and those people resend the same email this morning because you were out yesterday when they first sent it) alone will be a hundred.

Artie enters the parking lot and cruises across the first row of spaces to get to the far end and then turn right as he always does. But there is an open spot.

–Well look at you. What a score. Wanda must be out today.

He pulls the state vehicle into the front-row space, the one adjacent to crosshatches and an island with a tree in it that shades the car in the afternoon. The one where you can pull close to the crosshatches on your left, give the car on the passenger side plenty of room and still swing your door out wide with no chance of dinging another car. And right by the entrance to the suburban office building. Only the handicap and expecting mothers' spots are better. The spot Wanda arrives here over an hour early every day to get. And she crosses the busy street to eat a slow breakfast with tea in Panderia, watching cat videos on her phone, and then moseys back across the wide, busy road and is even late some days—just to get this parking spot. And tells all her coworkers about her breakfast routine.

–Plenty of time to drop off at the desk now.

Artie puts the car in park and applies the emergency brake even though the ground is perfectly flat. He gathers his items and turns the car off. In the sideview mirror, he sees a car pull behind him, close, across and blocking him. It stops. It is Wanda's car. He reassesses his items and secures them in his arms. He checks the rearview mirror, and the car is still there between him and the office building's door.

–Is she waving to you?

Artie gets out of his car and stands, still facing away from Wanda's large, old sedan. He closes the door and turns to walk to the building, intent on going around Wanda's car. She has rolled her passenger-side window down and is calling to him and waving.

"Hi, Wanda," Artie says, staying a few feet back from the window and stooping slightly so they can see each other's faces.

"Hi. I had car trouble today," she says across the passenger seat.

"Sorry about that. You made it on time, nevertheless."

"It was a difficult morning."

"I'm sure it was, Wanda."

"My legs hurt today also. I have a doctor's appointment. Right after 5:30 I have to run out."

–Does she expect you to get back in the car and pull out, allowing her to get this primo spot? Is that it? She has some ownership through habit?

"Sorry to hear about the legs." There is an awkward pause. "I'll see you inside," he says and begins to walk around the front of her long-hooded sedan, which jerks forward a bit as he starts to round it.

"Sorry, thought it was in park," Wanda yells.

–She can't be serious.

When Artie finally settles in at his desk with bagel in hand, his stomach quieted and pages of emails in front of him, he can hear Wanda from across the room telling another coworker about her difficult morning and need to get out no later than 5:15 for the doctor.

Artie bites his bagel and logs into his account. He takes a sip of water and chews slowly.

–Morning's the same now. Very different from this point on.

He is in his routine and content. He scans the emails, checking off the easily identifiable, no-read deletes: CCs, BCCs, well wishes, junk (the state email system gets those also), repeats, general office info and rah-rah-team-spirit nonsense.

Artie recalls how when he first began here, he would enter the office like he was walking into a barn-fire smiling—the dread of the parking-lot-to-front-door walk. He would be dazed by ten a.m. Aggravated at the stream of inanity and death by paperwork. But always trying to outwardly display his get-along, we-are-in-this-for-the-children attitude. If it was unproductive and inane, it still had to be done. Some decisions were above him. He learned to accept it and enjoy the work. It beat breaking rocks in the sun or freezing weather. He was comfortable. He had his bagel and water. He could take a mini brain-vacation anytime—eyes open, computer screen set to some busy-looking page, and zone out for a few—then feel refreshed and ready to dive back into the paperwork.

Artie missed the actual paper of paperwork. He preferred it to the electronic paperwork. With real paper there was stacking, straightening, stapling and filing. Walking across the office to show someone something. Going to the copy room to make copies or send a fax—stand around until it was completed. A quick bit of office chitchat. A person from another cubicle coming by to borrow your stapler and then returning it. Weather here, weather there—weather, weather everywhere. Keep your pencils sharp.

When paper was king, there were full cubicle walls. Now the walls are low, only high enough to keep someone from spilling coffee on your desk or to pin up a four-by-six picture. Not high enough to dampen a conversation. Some coworkers' lunch at their desks could be brutal. Eyes on you all day. Electronic paperwork meant sending too many people a copy and never having to get up and move around to complete a task. Where did all the paper go? There was probably some paperwork on that. It was crowding file drawers, jamming industrial shredders and being carted to recycling plants. CD drives piled up in desk drawers. Make sure it gets done. Cover your ass by saving it all, just in case someone asks.

Student and personnel files were kept in the strictest confidence. Student records shredded after twenty years. Another decade or so and they'd be all gone. Better to save the paper. When the office first gradually changed over, people would do the electronic forms, forward and save, but then print and distribute hard copies. Occasionally you would get two of each. When the boss got something he thought everyone should be aware of, you would get an email and hard copy from the originator, and when the boss got around to reading it, he would email and hard copy send it to everyone.

Copy after copy circulating. Multiple layers of supervision signing off on reports. "Change paragraph two and resend." Being sent to Albany, or Washington DC, sometimes overnight. Then the calls: "Who sent this? Why was I sent this?" "Keeping everyone in the loop." And round and round the loop-the-loop it went. Sent into the abyss. Round file material piling up. But you had to be careful; if there was sensitive info, you had to shred-pile it. That's what made the real paper go away: when some inspector general did a spot check on the recycling procedures and found some student info. With a secure email system, there were less worries. Anyone with clearance could request the information now—from the EdCloud—but people rarely did.

He is presently content with it. After being disconcerted yesterday by Headmistress and the other events, this routine is calming. He keeps at his bagel. Artie has come to believe this is a job that needs doing, and he has a knack for it. His frame of mind accepts it. The pay is okay—Eggrett's cut aside. There is a pension to look forward to, as well as good health benefits.

There were some rougher times. When he was on the rocks with Eggrett, he had a chip on his shoulder. Too much of his leave was eaten up by court and lawyer appointments. He became loud. He went to counseling. Not couples counseling. Eggrett was cut and dry. When it was over, they both knew it. Not that he wanted divorce, but he knew she had checked out. Artie was never sure she hadn't cheated on him, but it was a distinct possibility.

Separation left him very lonely. After that, he tried to be chummier with his coworkers, but it sort of backfired. The office was mostly women, and they didn't take to his more outgoing personality. They thought he was loud. Someone complained his voice was too deep. They seemed to like talking about him, not to him.

There was that time he was in some real hot water. If only the cubicle walls had still been up, the unfortunate matter would not have happened. Or the divorce. That's why he has to drive that old heap. Artie was on the phone with his mechanic. He had brought the car in that morning before work because of a rough, grinding noise it was making. He made the mistake of talking loudly to overcome the mechanic's background noise, and he used the shorthand term for transmission. Seemed like the whole office heard him. About half of them complained to both his supervisor, Orange Benton, and the EEO rep in Human Resources (newly renamed from Personnel).

He had to spend some time in training and counseling with the EEO rep. She was pleasant, and Artie didn't really disagree with anything she said. He made his point. She saw the logic of discussing a car problem being perfectly normal, but (and he agreed) in an office setting one had to be aware of word usage, and even though there was no harm meant, and no workers who fit that description were able to hear him say it (Artie even believed it likely there were none in the entire office building), the fact that someone was offended was superior to any other concerns.

Artie's corrective measures were spent during regular work hours talking with the HR EEO rep, watching some informative videos and completing a self-directed lesson. They were no more boring than his usual work activities, and after a week the EEO rep and Orange signed off on his return to full work duties. Artie was relieved. He really had thought he might lose his job because of it. Instead, he lost any closeness with his coworkers but became closer to his supervisor. Orange and Artie were on a first-name basis now. The plaint of his wife leaving him and the divorce proceedings gained him some sympathy. Orange and the EEO rep were both familiar with that type of stressor.

Artie makes notes on yesterday's visit and then sends an email to the relevant county's education office asking them to confirm that they do not have administrative authority over the school.

–Orphanary for Foundling Girls seems even more awkward when putting it in writing.

He plugs the name into the search engine. Nothing relevant appears.

–No social media, no promotion, no school website.

He tries charity rating and crowdfunding sites. Nothing relevant.

–How could they not have a charitable funding stream?

He tries Headmistress' name. Other people's pages come up, but not her. He pulls up the file on the EdCloud intranet. Everything looks in order, if not out of date. He notices the constituted name of the school: Saint Margaret's Foundling Home.

Artie sends another email to the NYS Office of Children and Family Services asking them to confirm their authority over the supervised home and asks for any relevant records.

–Emails out. Wait for emails to return. What's Orange doing?

Artie's supervisor is walking quickly toward him. Because Artie is aware of the myriad health issues Orange has, he is surprised at seeing Orange's listing speed-walk as he turns down the row of cubicles and approaches. He is forward on his toes, head down, his overlong tie swaying like a pendulum.

"We have to proceed to the conference room posthaste," Orange says, passing Artie's desk.

Artie swivels in his chair so his eyes can follow him. Artie's surprise causes him to not absorb the gravity of the situation shown in his supervisor's frenzied actions. Orange turns back and waves dramatically for Artie to follow him. Artie is up but returns to grab his pen and notepad and with quick steps catches Orange as he enters the glass-walled conference room.

"Close the door," Orange says, his breathing slightly strained.

As Artie closes the door, he notices the entire office is watching them, getting up from their desks and forming clusters.

–This counts as a hubbub here. Orange is usually sedate.

"In two minutes, that phone is going to ring," he heaves, pointing to the lone phone on the long table. "You are going to answer. It will be the governor. I'll listen in."

"Is this about yesterday?"

"Yes. I have been instructed to tell you that you are assigned to this school exclusively."

"Is there some unusual activity that has been alleged?"

"I don't know anything like that. She could have a political friend who recommended a student to the school."

"An orphan? It's a supervised home."

"Still," Orange says, looking around the room trying to collect his thoughts. "What do you have so far?"

"I only started yesterday, really. Everything looked fine in person. Maybe a little religious and female centric…forget I said that."

The phone rings. They look at each other.

–Whatever you do, don't call her Governess.

"Good morning," Artie says after he picks up the conference room's sturdy, old phone's handset.

"Mr. Alston, please hold for Governor Kandle."

"Yes." The phone goes quiet. Artie asks Orange, "Do you want to be on speaker?"

Orange shakes his head no while looking down at the table, bent over, resting the weight of his upper body on his clenched fists, knuckles on wood, tie swaying again.

–You've stepped in it.

"Artie Alston?"

"Yes, Governor Kandle. Call me Artie please." Artie recognizes the governor's voice from press conferences on newscasts. He is sure it is her. She has usually given off a friendly reassuring voice of gentlewomanly, confident leadership. He relaxes but then stiffens, noticing Orange is still shaking his downward-facing head, making Artie feel alone in this stressful moment.

"What else would I call you?"

Artie starts to answer, trying to come up with something respectful of her office, but hears the governor say to someone else, "Do we have the right guy for this?" Artie is quiet, unsuccessfully trying to make out what the background reply was to the governor. "Artie!"

"Yes, Governor. I can hear you fine."

"Well, you better hear me. We need you up on your toes for this one. Tiptoes. I's dotted T's slashed. Ahead of the curve. And all of that has to come back to my office first! No press except through the governor's office. You got that?"

"Yes. I wasn't expecting this to be a press issue."

"If we are walking on dirty laundry over there, I want to know about it right away. Before the feds or the press or some local politician who is gunning for my job. But if everything is neat and folded. You know what I mean? On the up and up?"

"Yes."

"Then we don't want to be seen as coming down hard on a charity that's helping orphaned girls. Pressure on me concerning this one."

"It's just standard oversight. The school serves boys and girls."

"Boys? There aren't any boy-touching priests working this place, are there? That whole church/priest thing, we gotta keep an eye on that. That's what the press is jamming down our throats."

"No. It's not a Catholic institution but may have been at one time."

"Because the press is all over that shit. Lawyers too. I don't want to be tied to that. Unless we bring them down for it, tough on crime and all. Protecting the children. And let's not use the term *boys* now. Starting to sound creepy."

"Are you referring to sexual abuse of children?"

"Yeah, priests molesting young boys. Don't you read the news?"

"Any hint of an issue like that, a legal issue, I would have to follow the requirements. Any child abuse, sexual or not, that is an immediate notification to the inspector general and the police."

"Well, my office better be in the loop so we can deny any affiliation beforehand."

"What affiliation?"

"Exactly."

–You have to steer this more positively.

"There aren't many male employees at all. Very few bo…male students. Or residents. Whichever way you would like to refer to them. The girls, females, are mostly in a college preparatory path. From what I can tell so far, they are all doing well. It seems like two different schools, very divided. The males seem to be steered, as I see it, to a more career path."

"We need welders."

Artie pauses and braces for backlash. "There are no welding classes. It seems more janitorial, groundskeeping type of things."

"Who do you report to, Alston?"

"Here, my supervisor is Orange Benton."

Orange stands up straight.

Artie can see the stress on his face. "But as I said, there are other reporting requirements, besides the ones I mentioned before. If there were financial improprieties suspected, I would also be required to alert the New York State attorney general."

"Cal."

"Yes."

"He's a good guy. Short fucker—temper-wise I mean."

"Okay." Artie drags the word out, not sure what his expected reply could be.

"You sound like a good guy, Alston. Next time you're in Albany, we should get together, talk, have coffee."

Artie smiles. "I'm in Albany quite a few times a year actually."

Orange let's out a deep breath after seeing the stress in Artie's face subside.

"Yeah. Well, I'm in New York City a lot also," the governor woofs and hangs up.

Artie keeps the phone to his ear, listening to the repeating tone.

"That ended well, sounds like?" Orange asks Artie hopefully.

"I became too familiar right there at the end. She hung up on me."

Orange sits down and rubs his palms together slowly. Artie sits across from him.

Orange unplugs the phone. "What have we got?"

"Dirty laundry," Artie says. "She wants to know if we're walking on dirty laundry."

"What's that mean?"

"Anything. Corruption, thievery, sexual misconduct, poor conditions for the students."

"Malnutrition?"

"It feels like she was warning me."

"They know you're on thin ice, easily fireable because of your diversity issue."

"That's confidential. They can't know about that."

"I don't believe it. Do you? Explains why they picked you."

"I thought I was doing you a favor by picking up this case."

"They told me to put you on it and not tell you."

"Who?"

"Bradley."

"The head of legal?"

"Yeah." Orange pauses and gets a deep breath in before continuing. "I've met him. Nice enough guy. His underling called me before. You keep your title as scrum leader and all."

"Why wouldn't I?"

"Well, you'll be assigned just to this issue for now. So oversight of only one school is under your pay grade."

"Why would they do this? I could have rubber-stamped it already if I wanted to."

"Not like you, though. They probably knew."

"What's the origination of this?"

"Well, what I can see." Orange takes another deep breath and starts to tap his pen on the desk.

Artie looks out through the glass at the office. Most workers have gone back to their cubicles. Occasionally a head pops up to glance at the conference room.

"Artie, this probably isn't the onset, but some good government group in the city is suing over private schools not providing a solid core education and a lack of government oversight, maybe for political reasons."

"I saw that. Mostly religious schools, if that's what you meant by private."

"We can't identify groups in this case. They are nonpublic schools."

"For political reasons."

"For fairness reasons. Legal had to take a quick roll through all these schools to see where the department stood as the case went forward. This school got flagged because nothing current was available. I heard they tried to kick it over to Office of Children and Family Services. But no way. It's a school also, and the lawsuit is education-related, and here is where we are today."

–This is quicksand.

"Going forward…Artie, I have your back. You are good at this, and that's all you have to worry about."

–No one else got a call from the governor.

"Bright side: you get to keep using the car, and that's twenty-four-seven-use approved. There's not that much work. You get out-of-office time. And there's probably no issues up at that school. You could always drag it out. There's no due date, and nobody's going to want to take it from you."

"Do you think I could do all this and then someone could come in and squash this like nothing happened?"

"It's happened before. Lawsuits take years. Plaintiffs might get dismissed. This school isn't even in the city; might have nothing to do with it."

"Political viewpoint?"

"Could be. Any names up there ring a bell? Sound like they got weight or enemies in Albany?"

"No. I'll keep my ears open."

"You should ask legal what they've got as far as past lawsuits, etc. Maybe some kid sued or was arrested. Shake them up. Let them know you're not going to quietly roll over."

"This school, they have a monastery—a religious institution—on their property. It seems they pay rent to the school. That might be the funding source for the beautiful facilities they have. It's possible someone there has political pull. That might explain things."

"Hmm," Orange says. "Sounds a little conspiratorial. I wouldn't put that in writing unless it's useful. You know, useful for you, CYA-wise."

Artie gets up. "I guess I'll send those emails out. Nothing else to do."

"Nothing to worry about, Artie. If you look too hard at anything, you'll find an issue."

"Are you telling me not to be thorough?"

"Absolutely did not say that. If you think those students are being treated right, then all is well. But if not, we act. As far as who the leadership is connected to or where the money comes from? Not your department."

"I guess if the Regents Exams are good, what difference does it make?"

"Right. We concern ourselves with education. It's not forensic police work."

"That's not reassuring."

Orange gets up to go. He stretches, arching his back. "My opinion? Maybe we could be overthinking this, you know? It's just another school with no real red flags. You're good at your job. Compile the paperwork and then get back to me. See how it looks then. The fact that the governor is interested doesn't make this devious. She's big on women's issues. This is a girls' school. Probably all that's there."

"Not only a girls' school. Other potential headaches."

"Our task is oversight. You don't always get to play the good guy, like you're inclined. Fixing things shouldn't be thought of as an issue. That's the job." Orange starts walking out.

"Unless the governor doesn't want it fixed."

Orange kept walking, pretending not to have heard Artie.

–Got your back until there is a knife in it.

Artie lingers in the conference room. He kills time trying to plug the phone back in, but the wire and terminal connectors are old, and he can't get them to click. He walks back to his cubicle, ignoring his coworkers' stares. He organizes his desk while standing, then looks around to see the curious faces peeking at him. He goes to Orange's office, even though he can see his boss is on the phone, and knocks.

"I'll have to call you back," Orange says into the phone and hangs up. "What's up, Artie?"

"I'm getting a lot of stares," Artie says, staying in the doorway. "That made me question if this is confidential. Like if anyone asks, do I discuss it?"

"All student information is confidential, strictly. You know that."

"Certainly. But not the school, nonstudent, nonemployee information. That is normally open to discussion among my coworkers."

"I guess this is no different."

"Governor Kandle didn't say one way or another."

"Better check with Bradley in legal," Orange says, nodding to convey he is sure of himself. "You keep it between us until legal says otherwise."

"Okay."

"Get it in writing."

"I was going to email them anyway. I will include that question. Maybe they don't even want you in on it."

Orange exhales deeply. "I don't know what you mean by that."

"I was looking out for you."

"You don't have to worry about me. You maybe got yourself rattled. Can't just keep pushing everything around. Legal, me, Child Services, back to you. It will end, and no worries, Artie. Imagine if you had a real problem."

"I'll get to it."

"Do that."

"Maybe after lunch." Artie does a quick double knock on the door trim and walks away slowly, wondering if his supervisor will call him back because lunchtime isn't for a while. Orange leaves him to his slow walk. Artie circles the office floor, seeing what everyone else is doing.

–What are they so busy with that you got slammed with this assignment?

His peers smile suspiciously at him. He nods back and says hi to some, giving them a chance to ask what's going on. None do. Back at his desk, he takes out his phone and plays a game, trying to clear his mind. Then he gets up and leaves early for lunch without telling anyone.

–You're pushing Orange to the limit, but he got you into this. Or maybe not. Either way it seems like you are being given a long leash from the local office.

Artie gets in the state car—conveniently parked very close to the building exit. He goes and buys a big hero at his favorite deli on Front Street that would usually be too far to squeeze into his lunch break. Then he drives to Eisenhower Park to eat and even takes a stroll to help his digestion.

Back at the office building by two, his same parking spot is once again free. He pulls in. Orange and the others give him a once-over when he enters, but no one says anything. He sits at his desk and surveys the room before sending emails out to all the divisions he requires information from.

He calls the main school number and gets Sandi.

"Hi, Sandi. Artie Alston from the State Education Department. I was there yesterday."

"Hi, Artie. We sure enjoyed having you visit with us."

"Thank you," Artie says, surprised at how happy he is to hear her chipper voice. "I had a nice day."

"Oh, good. I hope you had a quick ride home, you having to work and all today."

"It was an interesting ride home, the whole of the day."

"Terrific."

"Is Headmistress Hunt in?"

"No, but she has the Records and Compliance Department hard at work on your request."

"I didn't hear of or see that department."

"Uh-huh."

"Is there someone from that department I could speak to?"

"The cloud."

"Electronic records?"

"I could let Headmistress know you called, and she can get back to you. Oh, here she comes now." Artie can hear Sandi calling to Headmistress. "It's Artie from the State, Headmistress...He's asking about Records and Compliance, you know, the thing you told me to say this morning. Would you care to speak to him?"

–What is she saying?

"He's on the phone right now... You don't really want me to tell him that, do you?"

–What?

"Okay, that sounds better... Artie, Headmistress isn't here, available I mean. She wants me to impart to you that you will have all the electronic records before Friday. Older paper files will be tougher."

"Well, tell her I said thank you."

"You are so nice. You should come up again in a week. We are having a beautiful announcement ceremony. I could send you the details. Headmistress wanted me to invite you, regardless."

"That'd be great."

—She thought of you.

"I do have to return. A few visits are the required minimum."

Somebody says something in the background.

—Is that Headmistress?

Artie is turned on. His face is flush. He pictures Headmistress smoking, a short skirt, sitting—partially reclined—in her chair, behind a clear plastic desk. One red stiletto is propped on the desk, her breast inflating with each inhale of the cigarette.

—You're commingling her and your ex.

"I would like to speak to her," Artie tells Sandi. Artie can hear murmuring.

—She must be doing a better job cupping the phone's receiver. Maybe you shouldn't speak to her. Your feelings are muddled.

"She can speak with you," Sandi says to Artie. "If you don't mind holding."

"I'll hold." Artie pictures Headmistress smoking, in heels and short skirt. This time she is in his cubicle. One foot is up on an open desk drawer. She maintains vicious eye contact with him. Her breasts rise and fall with each inhale. She blows smoke rings. Artie returns her gaze.

He is transfixed, eyes unfocused, toward the window. Minutes go by as his tired, stressed brain enjoys the fantasy.

"On hold a long time, hey, Artie?" Quinn asks as he passes.

Artie shakes his consciousness to respond. "You know how it is. I should have hung up, but now that I've committed so much time, I can't."

"Know it."

–You need a good night's rest.

"Hello, Artie," Sandi says. "Artie, still there?"

"Yeahs, Sandi."

"Did you say yes?"

"I am still holding. Still holding for Headmistress."

"She's not going to be able to speak with you. I forgot about the meeting."

"The meeting?"

"Food vendors and Chef Donna."

"She's busy?"

"Yes. Headmistress wanted me to impart to you that, in the politest way possible, but I don't think I quite have her exact words on the top of my tongue."

"Yes."

–Her ignoring you is making you perspirey. Back to professionalism. Professionalistic. Professionalisticism.

"Artie, still there? You haven't been upset, have you?"

"Uh, I was distracted by something in my office. A lot of educators work on this floor. Apologies. Busy day here also."

"I'm sure. Headmistress also wanted me to impart on you that—and this also she insisted I do in the most polite terms—the school will not allow the documents to be sent electronically. There were second thoughts regarding net security. She is very protective of those girls."

"Students."

"She will have a thumb drive for you on Friday, when you come for the big announcement ceremony."

"I suppose a thumb drive is fine, Friday. I would have liked the first part of the week to go through some things. Organize. Formulate questions."

–You shouldn't worry about the slow pace. Better for you.

"What's the announcement?"

"Oh, you'll have to wait. Men are so impatient."

"I'll be there Friday. You'll email me the details I need?"

"Yes, of course. As soon as I hang up, I'll get to it, and you should see it tomorrow."

"Tomorrow?"

–Let it go.

"Sandi, that is acceptable. Tomorrow. I look forward to your email, arriving tomorrow, and seeing you and Headmistress Friday."

"You have a good night, Artie."

"You as well, Sandi. Oh, Sandi, before you let me go."

–Catch her off guard, maybe.

"Yes, Artie?"

"Is there an Albany connection to the school?"

"Huh?"

"You know, a politician that you are familiar with, for lobbying purposes. Maybe even DC that, you know, advocates for the school's best interests?"

"Nothing like that I've heard of."

"Only asking because they would, maybe, shortcut this for me, for us. Meaning the school and the department."

"I could ask Headmistress."

–Trouble.

"No. No, that's not necessary. No reason to disturb her."

"She's just sitting in her office."

–What? Better end this call. You took a wrong turn.

"It's late in the day. I'll see you Friday."

"You'll see my email tomorrow. Don't forget. And don't forget to RSVP."

They say goodbye.

–It's better you didn't speak with her. You will be composed on Friday.

Artie enters the out-of-office time in his calendar for Friday and then goes to his laptop's map and checks the directions to the school.

He browses the businesses in the town of Laffton, then he expands his map, looking for things to do nearby. He marvels at the size of New York State. He requests directions from Montauk to Buffalo.

—A little over eight hours if you cut through New Jersey and Pennsylvania. Eight and a half if you stay in-state. Big state; how did this school get dumped in your lap?

Artie goes on the New York State Department of Children and Family Services' web page and searches for orphanages to get general information and requirements. Nothing comes up, and he searches supervised homes. Nothing about the school comes up, only links to facilities for children with legal issues.

—Your orphanage seems like an anachronism that should have been disbanded when the State pivoted to all foster care. You have to call Family Services tomorrow. They probably won't email records.

Artie tries searching for the monastery and Master Kyle. He goes back to looking at the map.

—Emails out, inbox emptied. You should head home and see what gets said.

Artie pulls out his phone and checks his personal email and social media. He won't log onto the office's computer for personal things because he worries they will track him. He scans the other cubicles to see who is doing what. He looks toward Orange's office.

—On the phone again. He spends too much time on the phone for you to ever want that job.

Artie goes to the bathroom and then returns to his desk, plops down loudly in his seat and lets loose a loud sigh. He picks up the state car keys and jangles them in his hand.

—Might as well head home.

He logs off, double-checking he is securely signed out. He walks the long way around the array of cubicles, out the door and then to the building's exterior doors. He pauses a minute in the lobby and checks the weather on his phone, wondering if it will rain.

–Will they just let you leave early like this, unchallenged? Maybe tomorrow? Maybe you should go back, finish the last half hour or so? No.

He goes to his conveniently parked state car, gets in, starts it and turns the AC full blast. He notices Wanda's car is in the handicap spot.

–Nerve of her. And you were worried about leaving early.

10

Here come Splain with his muddy work boots and onesie—top down and arms of it tied around his waist—sloppin' his mop around, dirt from his boots makin' things worse. I take my extra towel and cover my legs with it. I spy Jay across the pool, through the office glass. He's in there pretending to do stuff. Keepin' an eye on me I bet, for real. I want him thinkin': I don't want Splain creepin' on Veronica while he pretends to mop. My girl Posenica and I lookin' fine in our racing suits even if Headmistress don't let us sport no bikinis, which everyone knows we could do well. Splain tryin' to find an in, give us a stare-over and talk us up. I know Jay don't like it, and I keep it that way.

"Posenica, what's your boy Splain doin'? Cleanin' or dirtyin'?"

"Swaine is super nice to me. So I don't hate."

"He's playin' undercover janitor or something, like we can't figure he makin' his way over to get his leer on."

"Janitor to the stars, I'd venture," she say through a laugh. "We ain't got no other boys checkin' on us until we get outa here come June. We best enjoy it."

"I got my Jay doin' all he can in the fishbowl, tryin' not to look jealous at this I-need-everything-splained-to-me character encroachin' on us like we don't know his act. Two stunners like us in bathing suits make his dick grow."

"Veronica, you too much. Swaine," Posenica calls out. "Swaine. You got time to come sit with us? We supposed to be swimming now for gym credits but got time for you."

Splain pulls his wheeled mop bucket to the side and leans the mop handle against the wall. He does his heel draggin', slow walk. His wheat-colored work boots undone, the ties draggin' on the tile. He comes and stands over us, way tall. Must like super skinny women because he gravitates Posenica.

I glance at Jay. Posenica got Jay's full attention by callin' out to Splain. I don't know if he could hear us from in there. But whatever pretense he was usin' to watch us while appearing like he was doin' his work, he has dropped: standin' there, lookin' right at us. He's got his onesie zipped to the top, tryin' to look all uniform neat even though the heat set at eighty to keep us barely dressed girls comfy warm.

"Swaine, why you cleaning the pool during gym class?" Posenica ask. She's forty-five degree, back recline in her chaise. One knee up rockin' side to side, slowly. Smile on her face. Sunglasses on, pretendin' she is in Miami grabbin' sun's rays. She's got a paperback on her lap with her thumb holdin' her place in the middle but hasn't read a bit. She had been talkin' and watchin' Splain. Probably too dark to read inside with sunglasses on.

"You look like a Caribbean dream."

"Oh, you sweet. I know I be pretending, but it sure is nice. Hawaii, Tahiti, I get to all them places, due time."

"Do time is what you did before here," I tell her. "We all better, day after day, than where we came."

"Sometimes I miss stuff, though. Like fightin'." Splain rubs his nose with a thumb like he is a boxer. "Up to no good was fun."

"I guess a bunch more no-good was put on me than I put on them. So I don't look back with fondness," Posenica say.

Splain is actin' tough for her, and she don't see it. He acts like he was hard core when out in the weighty world. He was rescued as much as anyone here.

"You look like all good was put on you, to me."

"Splain, you crystalline," I tell him.

He looks at me but then turns his attention back to Posenica. "You gonna have to explain that one to me. I ain't in no AP classes like you two."

"She means you're like fine crystal," Posenica tells him. I laugh. She joins. Splain's smile goes away. "Smile back up, Swaine. We just havin' fun in sun."

"Fun in grow bulbs," I say.

"I'm working. You two havin' the fun."

"Don't be all down, Swaine," Posenica say. "We like conversating with you. I don't want Doc W coming and finding you slacking. Then you get in trouble and blame us."

"I ain't got no trouble with him. He on my back so much, then he be the one gonna have some troubles with me." Splain double taps his fist to his chest.

"Be careful, my Swaine. They rumors Doc W is retired FBI special forces or something. You know that motherfucker got a nine or something."

"I know what he got. He got a locked-up rifle—hunting rifle—in case any bears come."

"Not what I heard."

"I heard same as Posenica. He convince Headmistress he need a rifle to scare off bears, like he gonna shoot it up in the air to run it off. But he's strapped. Ready for anything."

"I got myself ready too. For something—"

"What you got, a bow and arrow?" We could tell Splain didn't like what I said 'cause his face froze up like he was a robot whose battery went dead.

"Swaine, don't be like that. We only funnin' with you. We know you're top dog around here."

"Lapdog anyway." He is not happy with me. Probably mad I covered up when he came over. I see Jay's still payin' attention, so I ain't worried about Splain.

"I gotta get back to work." Splain turns and sees the trail of dirt his boots left on the wet tile.

"You gotta take off your shoes and socks to mop. See." I pull my towel back and show him my feet with toes all perfectly pedicured. Neon pink today. "Not supposed to be on the pool deck with outside shoes."

"My Swaine knows that. He just wanted to say hi to us is all."

"I'm bettin' that wasn't *all*."

Splain takes his boots off. He's sockless. He ties the laces together and hangs his boots over his shoulder and goes back to his bucket. Then he perfunctorily mops up his mess and loudly drags the bucket back toward the office. Mrs. Richmond comes back from wherever she was and goes right to Splain and meets him at the office door.

"Mr. Swaine, you aren't to be cleaning the pool deck while swim class is in session."

"Something spilled, ma'am. I wanted to get it up."

Mrs. Richmond looks toward us. I pull my towel off, and Posenica pretends to be readin' her paperback—still has her sunglasses on. "Were the ladies drinking pop?"

"No, ma'am. I saw somethin'. A puddle, probably pool water. I'll get back to it."

Splain went into the office with Jay. Mrs. Richmond went to her chair and opened her laptop.

"Veronica, you too tough on Swaine. He's gonna snap."

"He's a tall boy. He can handle lots. Besides, I'm providing helpful hints. Maybe you're too sweet on Splain. Maybe that's what's got him wrought. Splain might unfurl and you'd be to blame, killin' him with kindness and all that."

"Like you doin' with your man Jorgie. Look at him now. He don't look cool, calm, collected. Even Mrs. Richmond notice him trancin' behind that glass like it's one-way glass in a cop flick. He knows this ain't no true-crime doc and that we can see him, right?"

Jay is standin' perfectly still, starin' past us, unblinking, hands jammed into the pockets of his onesie, even as Splain goes by behind him. While the office door is open, I can hear all the bangin' around of the mop bucket: Splain not the quiet type. Jay just keep starin'. Mrs. Richmond lookin' over her laptop, eyes flashing back and forth between me and Posenica and Jay. Jay only lookin' at me. I give him a smile and a toe wave. I wink with my left eye that Mrs. Richmond can't see and nod my head toward her so Jay get the idea that we bein' surveilled.

Jay shakes his head and starts talkin' to Splain, but the door has closed, and now we can't hear.

"My Jay, he's just satisfact. I don't mind him lookin' out for me. And you."

Posenica looks up from pretendin' to read. "You'd be better off without that boy when you graduate. He's wrung out, been through it. I wouldn't want to put him through nothin' else too."

"He's cute, some. And I got him figured well enough. Well enough to get us to graduation. Likes you too."

"Not how he likes you. He might be the nicest of them boys, but…"

"Nice boys finish last," I impart to Posenica. I don't care how any of them finish. I'll be finished with them. Mrs. Richmond is back to concentratin' on her laptop, so I open mine and get back to schoolwork.

11

Swaine came banging into the room, finally getting away from Veronica and Posenica. He hated them both, and I had to keep an eye out he didn't treat them badly. Mrs. Richmond must have straightened him out real quick. Veronica smiled at me, and I wanted to get back to doing the pool log, but Swaine went on about shit storms he was bringing.

"See you next Tuesday is all I can say," he said to me, pointing his finger my way.

I walked over to him, by the plant ops door. "Don't mess things up. You bring the shit down on yourself, we all goin' to get it."

"They can't do nothin' hard on me. I seen shit days before."

"Why go back? Go forward. Mrs. Richmond is nice. You'll be banned from workin' over in girls' town. You know that. Then you won't get to talk to Posenica anymore."

"Don't mess with me too, Jorgie. You don't want to see my dreams."

"I'm tryin' to help you."

Swaine was a sweaty mess. I followed him into the plant ops room where all the pool mechanicals were situated. There was a slop sink on the right, and he dumped his mop water in it and then, after putting the bucket and wringer down, wrung out his mop. The smell of chlorine was stronger in here, and now it mixed with whatever cleaning product Swaine aerosolized by dumping and wringing. It made me stand back from the noxiousness. He kept at it unbothered. With the outdoor pool shut down and only the indoor pump running, the noise was tolerable, but you still had to almost yell with the whir echoing off the concrete walls.

"Veronica would be seeing my nightmares if it wasn't for how I feel about you, Jorgie. She hates me. Shits on me. I can sense it."

"No, Swaine. You got her wrong."

"Don't worry, Jorgie. I am going to leave you out of it."

"What? Are you goin' to kill me last?" I joked to break the tension, but he just hung the mop up and then turned the bucket upside down on the hook over the sink for it to dry. "You better calm down."

"I am calm. I'm moving three steps ahead of everyone. I'm in the Doppler pitch. I got warp speed right now. I see it all."

"What are you talkin' about, Swaine?"

"Brother Carey explained it to me," he said, wiping his wet-with-sweat hair over to the side. "Doppler pitch. Time is not a constant. You can use your inner mind. Most people can't, but you can train it to. He's been showing me. Time is waves. It can move fast or slow. It's all about where you sit in the wave. You might think I was talking to you for ten minutes, but for me it might be seconds. That's how it's done. People can't keep up with you once you fully learn it. That's what I'm gonna do."

"When did Brother Carey tell you this stuff? He's down at the monastre achieving synchronicity with the universe, if he hasn't already."

"The other day. But see, you can't understand how it works. It's Doppler. He is experiencing time differently than you and I are experiencing it. He has the Doppler control. Inner mind."

Swaine completely confused me. I could tell he knew what he

was talking about. If Brother Carey taught him something, well, that seemed like a big deal.

Swaine walked across the room to the spare-parts closet that only he and Doc had keys to. He was the number two, as Doc said. That's why he got that key. I got the pool logs because I was better at doing the books, or more likely Swaine wasn't good enough at it.

I followed him over there and stood in the doorway after he unlocked and went in. "Why do you have such a big box of ball bearings?"

"That day will come. I'm prepped?"

"Doc Washington order that many of them?"

"No. I got them materiels."

"Did Master Kyle ever tell you about that Doppler too?"

"Nah, just Brother Carey. Master K says nothing to me. Like I'm not even there with him."

"Kinda like that with me too. Does it seem odd to you that none of them are wise-old-man aged? Like all under sixty?"

Swaine shrugged, reached into a box, pulled out a bottle of blackberry brandy and then took a pull. He offered the bottle to me.

"Nah. Thanks. I got that feelin' trouble comin' from all this talk, and I don't want blackberry on my breath when consequences arise."

"This is legit. For my stomach."

"Swaine, you and I know you stole it from the infirmary. It's for the girls' stomachaches that they—only girls—get. You sunk. That excuse ain't gonna fly."

"I get stomachaches too."

"Not the same."

"Good for goose, good for gandy."

"I hope Doc Washington don't find it."

Swaine took another pull. "I got this place super neat and organized. When he opens the door, it all looks put together, and he don't need to do no searchin'. Besides, I traded one of the girls for it. She stole it."

"What'd you trade?"

"One of the joints you gave me, or maybe one Brother Carey gave me. He said it would help my inner mind, relax me, serenity or something. But I don't like herb, never did. So I traded." He had some more blackberry, then put it in the box of O-rings and pulled the tape back over the top. He stepped out with me and locked the door.

"Who did you trade with?"

"Your girl. Veronica."

"Veronica trading with you?"

"Yeah. You know she likes the herb."

"Maybe. These girls trading everything for everything."

"You look like you're disappointed," Swaine said to me, walking to the short flight of stairs that led to a lower level where the pool mechanicals were. "Grasp, you down there?" he yelled.

"He's down there checking the gauges. Should've been done."

"He got his own bottle hidden in there somewhere."

"He trade with Veronica too?"

"No. With me."

Swaine went quickly down the metal stairs into the pit where the filters, tanks, pumps and chlorinators were. The long hair on top of his head flopped up and down as if he had a hairpiece. The hair on the sides and back had been buzzed short like he had two different haircuts. He moved awkwardly because of his height and the steep, open-tread, metal stairs. I went down after him.

"Grasp," I heard him yell ahead of me as he went around the larger of the filter tanks: the one for the outdoor pool. I caught up to Swaine and Grasp around the back. Grasp was leaning on the back wall with his clipboard tucked under his arm and a blackberry in the other. We were out of sight of anyone who should wander by, but because of the noise, we would never know if someone came looking for us.

"Jorgie," Grasp said as a greeting.

"Killin' time?" I asked him.

"Know it. If I ain't killing time, time's killing me."

"Hey, Grasp, you think Jorgie will rat you out now that he knows where you hid the blackberry?"

"Nah. Jorgie's cool with me."

"Maybe he wanted an invite. Asked me if I was gonna kill him last."

Grasp laughed. "C'mon, Swaine, you know you promised me the same thing last week." They both had a laugh. "Jorgie's an efficiency expert, is all. He likes when things run smooth. The pumps are humming, Jorgie. Gauges all in the green. Just needed a little getaway time."

"I wasn't rushin' no one. Swaine was up there tryin' to make time with Posenica."

"You'll get nowhere with her or any of these other girls."

"I'm goin' somewhere with someone. I'm going to arm up and break this place down if they keep shitting on me. I asked Doc W if I could start an ROTC program for the young men. Get us some rifle practice. Indoctrinate the youngers. Then uprising. We take this place and flip everything around."

"You're bluffin'," I told Swaine.

"I'm prepping. Saving this place. Some people help people by giving food, shelter, immunizing. Some with guns and violence."

"Maybe we start a union," Grasp said, trying to meet Swaine halfway. "All we got going for us is this place, and it would fall apart without efficiency experts like Jorgie here. Place could run forever without me, but lose Jorgie and it's down the toilet for these girls' country club."

"I say it implodes if it don't explode. I got Doc W on the rifle thing. I told him we could be his little militia. Take orders from him and not that Headmistress or Master K."

"That's silly. Headmistress is good to us."

"Better to them girls lazing poolside, pretending it's a class. I gotta get some retal." Swaine walked back around the filter tank toward the smaller one.

Grasp took a pull, then held the blackberry out to me as an of-fer. I shook my head no. Grasp shrugged and had some more. Then he screw-capped it and put the bottle under the tank's base. "Good enough spot," he said.

"Yeah. What's with Swaine?"

"You said it. He got shot down by Posenica. And Veronica gets under his skin all times."

"Seems like more. Like delusioned strategy."

"Got me. I like it here, Jorgie. You do too, right?"

"Yeah. A better life for me."

"Me too. Remember when I first came and I asked if anyone touched you?" I don't answer right away. He re-ponders his question and alters it. "I mean when I asked, did anyone *here* try and touch you?"

"I remember."

"That was big for me."

I nodded in agreement.

"That's why I want to stay. Out there in old world, people always want you. Some pretend they want you in a nice way, but still, that's pretend. Here, it's like they don't want us. Not don't care. Don't want us."

"The grass is always greener where you take care of it," I told him.

Swaine comes back. "Jorgie talking shop again? Grass care? It never ends with him. Jorgie, you get Veronica, and I'll take Posenica and, Grasp, we find a girl for you, a mediocre girl. Mediocre girls are the best. You get yourself a pretty girl, then you wind up wanting to see them more when really my needs are to spread the seed and move on."

I pondered if he was calling Veronica and Posenica mediocre, which seemed far-fetched. "Maybe I talk shop too much, but maybe Grasp don't wanna listen to you talk women all times."

"Probably the saltpeter. They put it in our gravy."

"That's bullshit," I told Swaine.

"Imagine we were having all these orphans? Headmistress go crazy.

Desperate, she starts servicing us herself." Grasp laughed at Swaine's oddness. "That's why there's only a few boys: we're all she can handle."

"They don't put nothin' in our food."

"Jorgie, you're too defensive."

"The drugs you don't want to take, they make you take. The drugs you want to take, they won't let you take. I'm clocked out," Swaine said and went.

"He's just kidding. You take him too seriously."

"Maybe," I told Grasp. "Are you done with that log sheet? I'll put it in the book and wrap it up."

Grasp handed me the clipboard. "I'll hang in back. Shout when you finish, and we'll walk back to the Butt together."

"Ten-four," I said and left him to kill time out of sight.

In the office, I dropped the clipboard on top of the logbook and took a quick glance to see Veronica. She was still in her chaise with Posenica next to her. I looked around the pool area and noted that, again, Mrs. Richmond was not in sight. I kicked my boots off by the heels, leaving them in the office and walked over to the girls.

"Hi, Jay," Veronica said, seemingly happy. I took that as a good sign that Posenica wasn't filling her in on our past.

"Jorgie, how you doin'?" Posenica said, friendly enough, but kept to reading her book.

"Hi. You got Swaine all set up."

"You can't blame us, Jorgie," Veronica said. "We got the goods, don't we?"

"Yeah. You know I believe you're gratuitously pretty. The most beautiful…You too, Posenica. You are pretty," I add to stay on her good graces.

"Uh-huh."

"I don't mean Swaine be like that. He's angry deep in. Talkin' about time travel and the Doppler pitch."

"Ughh," Posenica said and went on reading.

"Splain and his Doppler pitch. Jorgie, let me straighten you. It's called the Doppler effect. And it's got nothing to do with time travel. It's about sound. Sound waves and moving objects."

"He better stick to moppin'," Posenica said, wiggling her head and shoulders. I wasn't sure how she could read doing that and be in our conversation and all.

"He did say somethin' about where you sit in the wave."

Veronica swung her hand back and forth without moving her arm: cut it. I knew how intelligent she was, but nobody knows everything.

"He told me Brother Carey told him. Those brothers are somethin' smart."

"Why they walkin' around in togas if they so smart?" Posenica asked.

"I don't know who this Carey of a brother is, but you go online and look it up if you don't believe." Veronica held up her phone. I let it sit in her open palm. Then she made a click sound and brought it back down, placing it at her side.

"I'll ponder on it. You two believe the chlorine smell is strong?" I was getting some powerful noxiousness.

"I don't notice it any different," Veronica said. Posenica shook her head no, still not looking at me.

"I'll test it." I walked back to the office to grab a test strip to do a quick check. My socks were soaked. Mrs. Richmond was now walking toward me, her flip-flops making their noise.

"Jorgie. Jorgie."

I waited at the office door for her. "Yes, ma'am."

"First Swaine and now you. What's going on?"

"I don't know about Swaine, ma'am. But I wanted to ask if they believed the chlorine odor was unusually intense. Do you? I was grabbin' a test right now."

"Oh, well yes. Maybe it is a bit high."

"No one was in the pool anyways, but I better check."

"Go ahead, please."

I went in and grabbed the strip kit from the desk drawer, then kneeled by the side of the pool, dipped it and counted off to fifteen, then held it up in the light, next to the chart on the kit box, elevated, so Mrs. Richmond could see I was legit. "Oh, it is high," I said. I gave the pool a once-over. No girls swimming, luckily, because the chlorine had jumped to way high since I got here and tested it two hours back—maybe longer.

"Mrs. Richmond, something's wrong. Chlorine's too high for swimmin'. Closed for the rest of the day. Would you mind, ma'am, askin' the girls to leave the pool deck. Grasp is back there. I'm gonna give him a yell to shut it down, and then I gotta open the exterior doors to air this out."

"Oh, of course, Jorgie. I'm grateful you noticed." She turned to the girls and started sharp-clapping and yelled, "Ladies, ladies. High chlorine. We have to get to the lockers, change, and head to the Joes' to dress for dinner. Use the extra time for studies." The girls slowly got up and gathered their things and went to the locker room.

"That's my Jay," Veronica said as she went by. "Always looking out for me." She looked fine walking past.

"Bye, Jorgie," Posenica said, finally giving me all of her attention.

"Thank you, Jorgie," Mrs. Richmond told me. "I'll tell the main office, no more pool today."

I gave her a nod, then went to the mechanical room and yelled down into the well area for Grasp. He came to the bottom of the stair. "Grasp, chlorine is way too high."

"Got it. I'll shut the pump and the chlorinator."

"I'll open the doors and come back."

Out on the pool deck, the girls were all gone. I opened the doors at each end to help get rid of the chlorine odor but figured it would be more than the rest of the day for the level to drop to swim-safe. I went back and met Grasp by the levers.

"I got the pump back on, chlorinator off. I'm pumping to backwash now. That might help, leave it like that for a while, then the autofill will come up and dilute the chlorine."

"Good."

Grasp seemed to have this all under control: knew his stuff.

"Jorgie, the chlorinator was set to sanitize."

"Shock?"

"Yeah. And it wasn't like that when I did my check. That was a while ago."

"Yeah. And Swaine was ticked off and walked away from us all lookin' to get retaliation on the girls."

"Was anyone in the pool?" Grasp asked.

"No. It's all gonna be back to normal by tomorrow, but that Swaine, he might've had us all up the shit creek, paddleless."

Grasp gave me a perplexed look. "I don't think that's the vernacular."

"Trouble."

"I know that. He ain't around. Not like they're going to dust for prints. They'll just snatch the easiest perps to find: me and you."

"I don't like him messin' with Veronica and Posenica, or any of them, whether I get in trouble or not."

"Was it that high, the chemicals?"

"Only red-eyes high. But still, you did the check, if I entered it in the log and we walked away, it could have been bad."

"And we'd be holding the bag." Grasp rubbed his hand across his face. "If I get the boot from this place because of that shit bird, I'm taking him with me. And I'm taking more, because I got another year here after you two are gone."

"It'll be all right," I told him.

I went back up to the pool, grabbed the yellow caution tape from the office locker and taped off the two open doors. I saw a sparrow had gotten in. I went and got a broom and spent a minute waving it around, but he just went up and perched on the bottom chord of a truss. I went back to the office and blasted the classic rock station over the pool speaker system.

Swaine must have heard the music and came walking back in. He came to the office, walked past me to the locker and grabbed an air horn. Out on the pool deck, he blasted the horn in the direction of the bird. It glided down, stopping by the open doorway. Swaine ran at it with his arms outstretched, blasting the horn. The bird flew up and was gone.

Grasp came into the office. "What's up? Loud as anything."

"Chasing a bird off." I turned the PA system off. "Swaine's back. He must have been hangin' around outside."

Swaine was walking back to us.

"Better leave the radio on, Jorgie, until we close the doors."

"Yeah," I agreed and turned the music back on but not at full loudness.

"Did you two see me chase that falcon away?" Swaine yelled, coming into the office. He went to the locker and stowed the air horn.

"You better take an ornithology class, Swaine," I told him. Grasp gave Swaine the cold shoulder.

"I'll be teaching class for you two. Professor Swaine had to bail you out from your bird problem."

"Only reason we got a bird problem is because of you," Grasp said.

"I don't know why you two are lookin' at me like I did something wrong."

"You should fuck off to somewhere else," Grasp said. "Leave me out of your impulse problems."

"That what you think it is?"

"You say what you want. You left me and Jorgie to take the fall."

"Nothing gonna happen."

"You can't shock a pool with people swimmin' in it," I told Swaine. "You know that."

"I'm not saying I did anything. Maybe Veronica would need you to come put some lotion on her irritated skin is all."

"You're the one that's gonna refill the filter media, that I know."

"I always do my share of the work."

"Let's wrap this all up," I said. "Swaine go down and start. I'll come set all the equipment to the correct settings. I'll have to leave the pumps to run overnight. Grasp, can you close the doors?"

Grasp nodded, and we got to it.

Swaine went to the mechanical room. I started entering the pool log info from Grasp's sheet. I knew it was basically all wrong now. It was true at the time taken. I would have to forget all the stuff that happened since then. I couldn't leave an evidence trail, although, it was in my name and I would be filing a false report. Mrs. Richmond was aware of it, and Doc would be too. So I wrote "Chlorine problem fixed" after the last entry of the day.

Grasp came back in, after having closed the near exterior doors. "Hey, Jorgie," he said. "Thanks for getting Swaine off my back when he was talking about mediocre girls and all that shit."

"Nothin'. That's Swaine being Swaine."

"You never think anybody bein' bad, the way they act. Like what? They only havin' their moments and you all right with it?"

"Theory of relativity. Everybody here is relatively okay."

"You mean compared to…"

"You know like we talked before."

"Yeah, I know that. But sometimes people take advantage, even if it's not like it was. Like Swaine today. Brother Dom or Veronica always asking you for stuff."

"I like getting her stuff. You can't compare them."

"No, maybe you're right there," Grasp said but didn't look convinced. "Just keep a suspicious eye out."

Grasp left, and I went to check on Swaine. He had all the levers in the normal spots and was recharging the filter. "Don't mix up the scoop count," I told him. He had the white dust on him and wasn't wearing the respirator or the eye protection like we were supposed to.

"You'll mess up the count. Shut up and let me do it."

"Where's the gear? It's an OSHA violation. You shouldn't breathe that stuff."

"When you ever seen OSHA?" He finished and closed up the system.

I primed and restarted the pump, then checked the gauges. Everything was normal, except I left the chlorinator off and the pump timer set to run overnight.

"Make sure you put in the log we recharged today so we don't do it too soon, again." Swaine rolled the container with the filter media back to its storage location.

"I'll do it on the way out," I said, mad at myself for not doing anything about it before. Now the log would look sloppy, and that drew attention. I could ignore it. But tomorrow the chlorine had to be checked and the auto-chlorinator put back on. Swaine moved his hands up and down, slapping where they passed in the middle to get the dust off. He coughed harshly.

"You two done?" Grasp yelled from behind me at the top of the stairs.

"Yeah," Swaine said and walked past me and up.

"Be right there," I replied and took another look at the gauges. I noticed the pool heater was turned way down to the point it wouldn't kick on. Swaine doing one last jab at me or the girls. I wasn't sure who. I set it back to eighty.

I went to the office and started fixing the log best I could.

"Brother Carey wants me down there next month to help him go through the stuff for their Ñatitas festival. That's his thing." Swaine rubbed his back on the door trim, making a winking, twisted face as he relieved an itch. "They got all the skulls and whatever stored. Gave me the creeps last year, pulling it all out."

"Crazy shit," Grasp said.

"When did you talk to Brother Carey? He's always silently prayin' or communing with the universe or something' when I'm workin' down there."

"They shouldn't fuck with the dead," Swaine said.

"They're honoring the dead, venerating," Grasp said. "The monks that died there. They keep the skulls and do a Day of the Dead type of thing. Lots of religions do it."

"Not Christians," I said, believing Headmistress would lose it if she saw the brothers doing that.

"What do you think Communion is?" Grasp asked.

"No idea," I answered.

"Body of Christ," Swaine said. "But they don't do that here. They said they put the dead brothers' bodies in the ground surrounded by compost and plant a sapling on top of it."

"Circle of life," Grasp says. "Putting you in a concrete vault in the ground is just slowing down what's going to happen anyway. Ashes to ashes and all."

"You two are creeping me," I said.

Swaine chuckled. "Jorgie, when a bear eats a deer and he shits, he feeds the plants, and the deer eats the plants. It's all the same. You're made out of the same thing a bear is."

"I ain't an animal, though. I got the Lord Jesus Christ. Headmistress told me that, and I believe her. No matter what those brothers or Master Kyle says."

"Hell with her," Swaine said, all disrespectful.

"Well, you have to believe somethin'," Grasp said.

"I still don't like them carryin' around those skulls," Swaine said.

"Let's get back." I nodded toward the door. "Lights out."

As we walked out, Grasp said, "I'm not sure those are true skulls. One of them looked like a souvenir from the Pirates of Caribbean ride."

"Where'd you see that?" I asked.

"Foster home. Family took their other kids to the World before I got with them."

"I sure would like to go there, see all that. Ride the monorail."

Swaine had a chuckle at me—again. "Ride the monorail? Jorgie that's not even a ride, it just takes you to your car."

"You've been?" Grasp and I both asked doubtfully.

"Nah. One of the girls told me last year. Seniors go every May, right before graduation."

"That sounds nice," I said.

"Guess you two ain't going, though," Grasp said as we left the building and started walking back to the Butt.

"Fuck that," Swaine said. "Eighteen years old hanging out with Micky the mouse. Shit's for children. That's why they call it: It's a Small World."

"That's just one of the rides," Grasp said.

I spotted Doc driving his golf cart in our direction. I slowed my walk.

"There's big rides like roller coasters and water parks. You don't have to sip tea with princesses."

"Oh," Swaine said, looking surprised. "Lotta stuff there, huh?"

Grasp nodded. My eye started to hurt.

Doc pulled the golf cart up, across our path, his side blocking us. The three of us kept walking, but we all slowed without a cue.

"Well," Doc said. "Keep coming. You know I didn't stop because I was afraid your supper would get cold."

"Yes, sir," I said. We stood in front of him. The other two on either side had stopped behind me so our shoulders wouldn't touch. Swaine might have been Doc's number two, but he didn't mind sheltering behind me in this case.

"Mrs. Richmond gave me a call. Said she had a compliment from the Adjutor's, about you three and the pool. You especially, Jorgie.

She told me she was also going to—how did she put it? 'Impart that sentiment to Headmistress.'"

"Yes, sir," I said. "She told me she would. About the chlorine. I caught a whiff of some high chlorine, and we got it all straightened out. I had asked her to remove the young women from the pool deck. Nobody was in the pool itself—the water, that is—at the time. It may have irritated their eyes or skin."

Doc looked away from me and up at Swaine. "You got something to add to this?"

Swaine shook his head.

"No? Too busy looking at the female form to notice anything?"

Swaine kept quiet. He had the most to lose by anything he spilled.

"I know you weren't, Grasp. Do you have any observations of minutia you want to relay?"

"No, sir. That's the short of it. The rest was just fixing it, and to-morrow it will all be running smooth again."

"Compliment, my ass. Caught your own malfeasance or simple oversight. You want a compliment for that?"

We three shook our heads.

"The chlorinator is broken, I guess?"

"No, sir," I said. "I must have done something wrong."

"You know Jorgie," Grasp said, coming to defend me and keep Swaine out of it. "Jorgie wants to have that pool water perfect for the girls. He kept fidgeting with it an' probably got mixed up and all."

"Fidgeting with it?"

"Yes, sir."

"He's fastidious. Just an honest mistake?"

"Yes, sir," we three said.

"What's that log look like, Jorgie?"

"It's all top-notch now," Swaine said, all relaxed now, feeling like the pressure was off him and on me. He was standing up straight now, towering over the three of us, looking quite self-assured.

"I asked Jorgie about the bread crumb trail. Not you."

"I believe it is proper. Tomorrow, first thing, I'll test it and reset everything, double-check it and all."

"Yeah," Doc said. "No fidgeting this time, I guess."

"No, sir. And I'd be glad to show you the log now, how I made the proper entries."

"I trust you, Jorgie. Besides, gotta eat. The opposite of walking isn't flying, you know. I'm skipping supper tonight at the Butt because of the teachers' meeting at the Joes'."

We stood there, waiting for him to go.

"Well," he said.

I wasn't sure what he was asking, so I kept quiet. Grasp gave a hmm.

"We'll miss you at dinner, sir," Swaine said.

Doc twisted his face up like I believed it might fall off. "Miss me at dinner? You'd be lucky to miss my boot hittin' your ass. Is that the bullshit you are runnin' with these women? Because I could smell that line of crap coming from a mile away. Miss me at dinner."

Swaine had a strained smile like he was hurting himself to look contented. "Yes, sir," he said.

"I was waiting for you three to get on so I could drive you to the Butt."

"Thank you, sir," I said and hopped onto the rear-facing seat with my back to Doc, knowing it wasn't really some offer we could say no to.

Grasp caught my drift and stepped past Swaine and sat next to me. "You're number two, Swaine, you get shotgun."

Swaine took his long steps around to the passenger side of the cart and sat crouched under the roof, straining his neck forward to see ahead. "Thank you for the ride, sir."

"You save it," Doc said. He twisted himself so he could see us all. "I'll say this for the three of you. You kept the ladies out of it. That's what counted. If there had been trouble with them, well, you know who gets to stay and who has to get tossed back into the sewers, don't you?"

We all nodded.

"As for Mrs. Richmond, seems we're in the clear. She don't know about pools or you three. We'll let sleeping dogs lie. No reason to rattle this around anymore." He turned back to front and drove us to the Butt. He dropped us right by the door. "Jorgie, there's a box on the back of the red quad. Take it down to the club after you eat."

I nodded, and he left for the Joes' without another word.

We went to the kit after we washed up. It was rotisserie chickens pieces, mashed and peas. We got our plates fixed up. The chickens gravy was mostly gone, same for the thighs. The others had eaten already, so snooze and lose. At least they did most of the cleanup. Swaine loaded his plate with wings, which there were plenty of because most believed they were dried out on rotisserie nights. Fried chickens nights they were in demand.

We sat at one end of the table, Swaine at the head like he did when Doc wasn't eating with us, even though it was just three of us now. "Hey, what did Doc W mean when he said 'I know you weren't' to Grasp?"

"He knows what's doing, Swaine. Can't try foolin' Doc Washington like Mrs. Richmond."

"I don't think that was it," Swaine said.

Grasp was shaking his head at Swaine. "You keep on moving, but Jorgie's right. Doc got you figured, probably all of us."

"He ain't got me figured. I know I wouldn't have gotten back here with a pile a wings if he knew how many steps ahead I was."

"Swaine, shut up. I had enough out of you."

Swaine laughed at me. Pieces of the chickens meat came out of his mouth and landed on the wings he hadn't eaten yet. Grasp got up and took care of his plate.

Swaine said, "Jorgie, you should be the one shutting up. You're on the hook as much as me, maybe more so. I'm the number two. You can't spill on me; already told Doc W you threw the wrong switch or something. Hey, Grasp, what'd you call him? Fussy?"

Grasp was wrapping up the leftovers. "You were there," he said with his back to us. "Driest chicken yet," he mumbled.

"Hah. Nothing. Your boy Grasp is takin' the fifth."

I felt like Grasp wasn't in my corner, as he was just clanking pans around, but then he came back to the table. "Swaine, you might be number two, but you got two people here who know what really happened."

"Not really," Swaine boasted.

"Enough."

"Yeah. Enough," I agreed.

Swaine got up, dumped his bones and banged his plate on the inside of the garbage can. Then he kicked the metal can a couple of times to be sure he had our attention. "Somethin' to say. Both of you got, huh?" He put his plate in the dishwasher, then went to the freezer, unwrapped an ice cream sandwich and stuck it in his mouth. "Day's coming," he said through his dessert. "You'll see. I got everything mapped out. All these bitches and teachers will be sorry they weren't nicer to me."

"And us?" I asked, trying to impart sarcasm back at his anemic threat. Grasp went back to his chores.

"That's up to you." He left.

"Sick of his crap," Grasp said. "Sometimes he be makin' like he's crazy. He's just crazy to get out of cleanup."

It only took a couple of minutes to finish up. I didn't want to go right to the monastre and deliver the package like Doc said because I figured Brother Dom would want to head to the OBI and would give me the high sign. Then I would have to come back and drive him and everything. Easier to show up later and do it all in one trip.

I went to the office. Swaine was sitting at Doc's desk, on the computer. I didn't want to stay in there with him. Some of the other boys were at a computer station doing their work or watching videos. I grabbed a golfing magazine from a bookshelf and went back to the kitchen. I watched TV and leafed through the magazine during commercials, looking at pictures of the world-class golf courses. Most of them were ads, but ads that I liked. Some were, maybe, a place I would be soon. It made me start to cry, pondering about leaving this place: Headmistress and Veronica. But then, maybe I'd be with Veronica.

12

After ten, I grabbed my coat from my locker and went down to the vehicles. I took the package off the quad that Doc had it secured to and put it on the side-by-side with the long dump-bed. Bonus being it had the covered cab, even if the doors weren't on for the winter yet. It seemed like Doc had a lot of machines parked that didn't get used much. I guess they lasted a long time because we took such good care of them as part of our auto-shop curriculum.

I snapped in the three-point safety belt to keep secure and put my hood up. I hit the garage door's opener remote that was attached to the rearview mirror and headed out. After making sure the door closed fully, I drove slowly with the low beams on toward the back of Upper Joe's. I went to the loading area door that brought you into the building by the kitchen.

I kept still while outside to test how quiet it was: very quiet. The cook staff should have been gone, but I exhibited patience to be sure. I went up and keyed in the passcode Chef Donna had given me when I had been helping her out and went in. The lights were dimmed and the hall empty. I went along the wide hallway quietly and into the kitchen. Everything was straightened out and neat. The stainless was gleaming.

I went to the walk-in refrigerator and started looking around for tomahawk steaks. I didn't see any. There were lots of beef roasts. But no steaks. I was considering taking a few roasts. Maybe Frank could have Manny butcher them. But they wouldn't be tomahawks. I was afraid Frank would berate me over my lack of bovine anatomy, so I moved on.

I saw a box high up and pulled it down. It was heavy. "Ribs, previously frozen." Gotta get Frank something, but these girls might like them ribs. Chef Donna could probably make 'em all different ways: St. Louis Style, Texas Barbeque, Chinese style, smoked. Homemade corn bread too. I opened the box. There were lots of racks individually vacuum-sealed in thick plastic. I pulled one out. It was stamped in purple with an expiration date: expired this past June. Chef Donna must have forgot about these, probably shouldn't have put them up that high. I figured they were bound for the dumpster, and I wouldn't be taking them ribs out of the girl's mouths. I put the whole box outside the walk-in door so I could grab them easy on my way out.

I went into the walk-in freezer. I saw tray after tray of frozen foods marked up—made by Nutrifyed Food Industries. The labels said things like: "Chicken Fingos, Sluppy Jo's, Salisberty Steke in GrayV, Cremey Chicken and Rice, and Potatoes Our Graton." A lot sounded like the stuff we got for our lumps and suppers. No steaks here either. There were sleeves of grass-fed chop meat. I grabbed one to be safe: in case Frank didn't appreciate the ribs. Also I figured they wouldn't miss only one of the sleeves.

I poked my head around the door, eyes darting; coast was clear, as expected. I slipped out and, with the sleeve on top of the rib box, carried it all outside—taking a quick peek around before hustling over to the side-by-side. I covered my commodities with the tarp. I drove slow and quiet (or at least as quiet as possible) to the monastre.

Ride down the decline at night was extra tricky. I took my time, safe as always.

I went to the side door, carrying the box Doc had assigned to me. All was quiet here too. I took a peek inside the janitorial closet, but there wasn't any of Brother Dom's commodities. I walked through the hall looking for someone to ask where the box should go. The brothers were in their rooms, praying with the doors closed. I went upstairs and to the dining hall.

Brother Dom was in there by himself. He had something in his hands in front of him. I would have believed it was a cell telephone except I knew the brothers considered them forbidden. But then I pondered how Brother Dom had his own ways. I stayed in the doorway a moment until he noticed me. He put his device away and then with his head motioned for me to come over. It was quiet time now, like a lot of the monastre time. I put the box down on the table beside him. He looked at it and then at me. He gestured palms up trying to communicate. I shrugged my shoulders.

"I guess I'm gonna have to break the silent code, aye, kiddo?"

"Sorry, Brother Dom," I said low.

"I didn't expect to see you tonight. Special occasion?"

I shook my head.

"So what's in the box?"

I shrugged again.

"Go ahead and talk. You didn't get stuck with a vow, did you?" He laughed.

"No. Doc Washington told me to bring it down, that's all I know."

"He told you to come now?"

"No, after dinner. But I didn't rush, in case I saw you and you were lookin' to have an adventure; then I'd be doin' two trips."

"I don't mind adventuring. Let's take a look." He opened the box quietly. "I got some medications and other bathroom-type stuff." He pulled out a can of shave cream with some French-looking name. "I

know who gets what item. I'll take care of it. Be right back." Brother
Dom got up and walked with the box under his arm toward the hall,
and then as he passed his room, he threw something in there. I followed slowly, lagging. He went downstairs. I looked into his room.
He had a *Rocky* movie poster on the closet door, like the original,
boxer one from before I was born. I was curious to see what was in
the package because Doc had me make a trip here for such a small
box—seemed like shave cream wasn't a rush item. I stepped over to
a gallon-size, red-tinted, zip bag that was on Brother Dom's mat and
opened it: Adderall. I dropped it where it had been. I poked my head
out. No one there.

I went and tiptoe strode down the hall and out to the UTV.
Brother Dom came out in a few minutes wearing his adventuring
clothes. "Did I say meet me outside? I went back up looking."

"I dunno. We going?"

"Yeah," he said, less enthusiastic than usual as he sat next to me.

We had a quiet ride to the OBI. When Brother Dom got out of
the machine, he leaned forward resting his forearms over his head,
on the rollbars. "Why so glum, kiddo?" he asked. "You're not usually
this quiet. And you rode here in the side-by-side. I thought you and
I felt the quads were more fun?"

"Yeah. They are, on the trails. I had a little trouble today. Swaine
fucking around. But Grasp and I, we fixed things up for him. Doc
Washington saw right through. Now I got me a worry. Like maybe
we could get, you know, if word got to Headmistress. She's greatly
defensive of her girls. She might kick us out, or me."

"What happened?" Brother Dom asked as he came to my side and
leaned his backside onto the UTV. He usually ran right into the bar,
so I figured he wanted to hear and he wouldn't snitch.

"Swaine messed up the pool—too much chlorine—while the young
ladies and Mrs. Richmond were in there. Everything's okay. But I do

the pool log and lied straight out. Swaine can rat me anytime. The log's the only thing that's not a he-said, we-said."

"What? You afraid they're gonna kick you out, kiddo? No fucking way they expel you. For that? It's not like you killed someone. Trust me. No fucking way."

"All right."

"I can't say about those other two. I'll bring you a beer round back. Cheer you up a bit." He threw me his jacket and went up the steps quick, waddling a little. He flung the door open, hard, banging it against the front. He yelled, "Norm." Like always.

I drove the UTV around back and parked it further away by the woodland edge. I wanted it hidden more than usual because I had stuff that I didn't tell Brother Dom about. I considered pulling behind the garbage dumpster but believed the rats might try and get at the food. I sat at the employee lounge. Brother Dom came in a minute with my beer. "Cheers, kiddo," he said and went right back in. It wasn't too cold out, so I finished the beer before I went into the kitchen to say hi to Manny.

"Hey, Jorgie." The TV had the news station on. Manny was organizing the spices.

"Slow, huh?"

"Yeah, drinkers tonight. We only did twelve plates, dinnertime."

"I guess bad night for Zoie."

"Bad for everyone. Ski season only thing that's got this place running. Frank talked about closing Monday and Tuesday off-season."

"Bad for you?"

"I only get one day off now, but Frank ain't gonna pay me for six when I only work five, so bad, sure."

Zoie came in. "Hi, sweetie. Nice seein' you."

"She's still not smokin'," Manny said.

"I'm glad of that."

"Sugar, it was hard. Especially you get a slow night like this. Everyone going out for smokes and coming in smellin' like something I want a drag of. But now not too bad. Only the car ride home. How I want to light up after I start the car and kick off these shoes."

"You missed her irritable stage."

"I'm sorry about that, Manny," Zoie said.

"It's okay. You already apologized."

"I would yell at Manny."

"Couple of times only. It was worth it to see you tell Frank off."

"Oh," I said. "Surprised he took it?"

"He can't get a good waitress," Manny said.

"Not like Zoie, he can't," I agreed.

"You two men are sweet for puttin' up with me."

Frank came in. He started making something like the tomahawk chop movement, with his hand straight and whole arm up and down from the shoulder. "Tomahawk chop!" he yelled.

"I don't think you're doin' it right," Manny said.

Zoie laughed. "From the elbow, boss. Bend at the elbow."

"Florida State's thing," Frank said. "Zoie, hustle up to booth three. Their glasses are empty." Zoie returned to the dining area. "Jorgie, outside." At the bottom of the steps he asked, "Any luck with the steaks? Where's the off-roader?"

"I pulled her up a little further back, alongside some trees. I believe I need to be more clandestine. Not just 'cause we didn't tell Brother Dom. Did you?"

"No. I got other business with him. Thanks for the reminder."

"I got ribs and chop meat," I said when I pulled the tarp off the UTV bed.

"How much am I supposed to give you for something I didn't ask for?"

"Well, you got burgers on the menu?"

"You know it."

"Manny can do lots of stuff with ribs."

"Ribs kill your bottom line. They take up a lot of space, most of the weight is bone, especially after they're cooked, which takes a long time. And really, they're just an appetizer. Maybe I can push 'em as bar food."

"Finger food."

"You're optimistic, Jorgie. Help me carry them back. I'll get you a beer, then talk to Manny to see what it's worth."

He grabbed the sleeve of chop meat. I carried the big box of ribs. We put them in the fridge and he said, "Wait outside while I confer with my head chef." Manny had a one-eye-closed, painful look on his face.

"Yeah," I said and went out. I walked past the employee lounge and peered around the dimly lit parking lot. Doc's muscle car was there. "Funny," I said to no one, believing it an odd coincidence: him having dinner here right after I spoke to Brother Dom about him. I went back into the kitchen. Manny was alone. "What'd Frank say, about the food?"

"He said nothing. Soon as you went out, he went to the dining room."

"Guy's got me, and I don't like it."

"I told you these guys don't fuck care about us. He doesn't listen to a thing I say. You shoulda known that."

"Yeah. Frank's Frank. But Brother Dom says he's lookin' out for me." I went by Manny, who was shaking his head at me, and peeked through the door's glass panel. Zoie wasn't too far and had her back to me, making it hard for people to see my head in the window. I spotted Frank going past Doc's booth. They hesitantly waved hi. He then went to a nearer booth with Brother Dom and Terri. He thumbed for Terri to get up from the spot next to Brother Dom and then sat across from him after she left. I put my face full in the window, not caring who saw. Terri was walking this way. I saw Brother Dom push something small across the table to Frank and at the same time held up his phone to him. Frank pocketed the bag with his far hand and took the phone with the other like he was looking at a picture. He pulled something, probably cash, out with the right hand. He switched the phone into the right hand, holding the money against the phone and handed it back. Brother Dom pocketed both.

Frank got up and patted Brother Dom twice on the back of his shoulder as he walked away. He came toward Zoie and Terri, who were having words by now. I quick went to the back door so Frank wouldn't catch on I was spying. The three came in, Frank pushing them a little and the women shouting at each other. Manny joined me by the door.

"Cut the shit in front of the customers."

"She's a fucking cunt," Terri yelled.

I could feel myself getting stubborn, like I shouldn't.

Frank got between them, then noticed me. "I told you to wait outside. Manny, go get a beer for him and you and drink 'em out back."

Manny split into the bar.

"Out," he yelled at me.

I got out but stayed on the steps listening and peeking, just in case Zoie needed backup.

"Tell that bitch to stay away from Dom Dom. My regular."

"Tell him to stay the hell away from me. Fat asshole has his hands on my rump one more time and I'll sue you, Frank."

"You fuckin' love the attention," Terri yelled. "The only way you get any. Cold bitch. You egg him on for tips. My ass works for a livin'."

"I think you're stealing my tips. No way that table of men stiffed me. And I saw you over there trying to get their attention. You swooped in and grabbed the cash after they left. Frank, she's a fuckin' thief."

"Shut the fuck, up! Both of you. And don't you dare talk about suing me."

"Fuck you!" Terri yelled, real close to Zoie's face.

Zoie came out, squeezing past me. "Goddamn it."

"Sorry you're having such a bad night," I said to Zoie, following her over by the bench.

"Son of a bitch Frank. He should have told Terri to fuck off the first night she came in with her slut act. He's getting a cut, I bet. He can't get anyone decent to rent those two rooms upstairs. Fucking cops don't care."

"Not much you can do about human nature. Water finds its own level."

"I don't wanna be in the water with them." Zoie started crying. "Their water is piss."

Manny came over to us. He had walked around from the front door to avoid his boss. We could still hear Terri yelling at Frank and cursing Zoie. Manny handed me my beer, then took a sip of his own.

"Do you want this?" I asked Zoie, offering her the bottle.

"Oh, no," she said and wiped the tears from her face. Then she put her hand onto my cheek for a moment. "That's so sweet of you." She smoothed her apron and tried fixing her hair. She took a paper napkin out from her apron pocket and wiped her face. Then she pulled out her lipstick and checked herself with the phone's camera. "Did I straighten out okay? I still have tables."

"You look real nice," I said even though she was looking a bit worn.

"You're good," Manny added when she turned to him. "Do you want me to walk you back? Through the front door?"

"Yeah, thanks." She cupped her hand to her mouth looking like she would tear up again but didn't. She smoothed her apron one time more—needlessly. "Bad enough night, money-wise, I gotta make the best of it. Thank you," she said, looking at me, "both, for letting me get my composure back."

"Glad to help," I said.

"I'm going to miss you when you graduate." She made me feel nice. I liked helping her. "Good night, Jorgie. I'm going to head home as soon as possible, probably won't see you."

"I'll catch you next time."

They walked away. I went up the steps and listened at the door for a second. It was quiet. I peeked in.

Frank was alone, so I went into the kitchen. "Where's Manny?" he asked right away.

"He's comin'. Terri giving everybody a hard time?"

"Takes two to tango, and two broads are bound to go at it if you give 'em enough time."

"Girls don't fight up at the school."

"Yeah," Frank said. "But those girls ain't got nothing to fight over. Wait 'til they're struggling to earn a buck and they think one's got something they deserve."

"You believe Brother Dom's gotten grabby with Zoie?"

"Shut the fuck up. She flirts with customers. Some get handsy. Dom would bang her if she let him. Nothing else. You would too."

"He's goin' with Terri."

"That's transactional. Wait outside until he's done. Outside."

"I'll do that."

Manny came back in; he must have finished his beer.

Mine was still untouched in my hand. I took a swig. "We got something to finish before I step out."

"What?"

I didn't say anything. I looked at Manny, who had started loading the dishwasher.

"What, you're a fucking kid. What do I have to finish with you? I don't even have to talk to you."

I kept looking at Manny, who had his back to us, ignoring us.

Finally, Frank looked at Manny and then back to me. "All right," he said to me, pulled a twenty out of his pocket and slapped it on my chest. "Don't do me any more favors. Only get what I tell you to get."

I took the money, and then Frank went into the dining room. I sipped some more of my beer, not really enjoying it, just being stubborn standing there. I knew I wasn't supposed to get stubborn like that, led to trouble.

"How about you, Jorgie! You stood up to him. I thought he was going to act all pissed and get you to drop it. He still shorted you."

"Don't matter."

"Oh, it's good you didn't let him completely get away with it."

"You sayin' Frank was acting?" I walked to the dining room door and looked in.

"Yeah, he's manipulative. If there were no customers, he'd let those two punch it out. He feeds on friction." Manny stood next to me looking into the dining room. "I think Frank and Dom went out front to talk before he heads up to meet Terri."

A table of middle-aged men not far from the kitchen got up and started heading out. They stepped over to the bar area, saying good nights to Zoie, who had her back to me. Doc was gone. I went to the table that just emptied and dropped the twenty down near their tip of wet singles that were tucked under an empty glass mug. I continued to the men's room.

When I came back to the kitchen drinking my beer, Manny was watching TV, slowly cleaning the little that was left to do. "Jorgie, you're takin' liberties tonight! You know Frank would go ballistic if he saw you in there walking around with a drink."

"You said it was an act."

"Ain't gonna be an act if he loses his liquor license for having a minor drinking in his booze hole. Oh, Zoie popped her head in here before. She's doing better, heading home. Gotta keep those two apart."

I went outside, around back, and scanned the parking lot. Zoie's car was gone. I went back to the machine and crashed onto the bed, pondering how long Brother Dom would be with his fun. I killed time pretending to shoot the rats moving around the dumpster or trying to discern objects in the darkness of the woods.

Manny came out after a while. "Jorgie, I'm heading home. Frank closed the kitchen to cut an hour off my wages. It's cold. You better wait inside."

"Nah," I told him. "I don't got time to waste on Frank. Besides that, I got to acclimatize."

"Okay." He left without another word.

I heard some yelling and banging around in the kitchen. I went to the door. I could hear Brother Dom, so I went in. He was holding a dishrag with ice balled in it to his head and going through the shelves. He grabbed a bag of no-name chips that Frank would put out on the bar. He ripped the big bag open with one hand while biting it. Chips flew out to the floor. He put the bag on the counter and started eating what slopped out, still keeping the ice to his head.

I got the broom and dustpan. "Leave it, kiddo. Let Frank clean it." Brother Dom sounded intoxicated, more than the usual end-of-night.

"I don't want him to blame Manny. Manny's nice to me here."

"Me, I'm nice to you," he said, chewing and pointing his middle finger to the center of his chest.

"Yeah. You okay? What's that ice for?"

"Fuckin' broads. First that Zoie gives me a hard time, even though I'm the biggest tipper in the joint. Then Terri, that bitch, she ain't happy. Let's me know after the transaction. Starts bitching about the other one, then hits me with the heel of her ankle boot. I tell Frank: he's a dick about it. Says that's between me and Terri. That fuck knows I can't go nowhere else, everything else is too far."

"Want me to have a look at your head?"

"Nah," he said and took a beer bottle out of his back pocket. "Here, open this for me."

I grabbed it, popped the top on the edge of the counter and gave it back.

"Thanks, kiddo. Reliable Jorgie." He got to drinking his beer quick and stuffing the chips in his mouth while I swept.

When he finished the beer, he took a bottle out of his other back pocket, then handed it to me and I opened it.

"Were you talking to Doc Washington in there?"

"Little bit. I talk to everyone. I'm a friendly guy. Sociable by nature. It's my nature, that's it. Can't be helped. The other brothers and Kyle, they wouldn't understand. Those two broads, they can't get it. I'm a butterfly that way. Not enough interaction for me most days."

"Why'd you join up at the monastre?"

"Sorta got locked into something out in the world. I hope it don't happen to you. When you live life at the edges, it's easy to cross the line. It seemed like the offer from Master Kyle was my best offer. Life lesson, kiddo: you get to pick your best offer, but you don't get to choose the offers you get to pick from. Understand?"

I nodded and put the broom back. I started closing up the bag of chips because he had stopped eating.

"I can't remember everything I've said. I'll finish this beer on the way back."

When Brother Dom got outside, he yelled, "Where the hell'd you park?" He threw the kitchen towel and ice down. I kept walking to the machine, and he followed. "You getting suspicious, kiddo?"

"I guess I am," I said at the UTV. "You and Doc Washington? I don't get it. You doing transactions with him?"

Brother Dom got to his side of the machine and got in. "I had to meet with him about some stuff. That's all. In life it's good practices to keep some arrangements separate. That's good human resources. Just know, that provision covers you too. You're not being left to the winds. But that's it. Human resources. Don't talk to him about it. Washington and I got a love-hate relationship. But we're both good with you. Not Terri, she don't like you. Sorry to say, she won't be givin' you your first ride."

He took a long drink, and I pulled away. He dropped the bottle with a clank as we hit the road. He turned back looking at it, and I grabbed his shoulder so he didn't fall out.

"Seat belt," I told him and drove a little slower until he buckled in. He sorta bobbed back and forth for the rest of the ride and mumbled some stuff.

At the monastre, I had to help him out. "I hope this is the beer and not the clock on the skull makin' this difficult."

"Nah. You ain't difficult, kiddo. You're a big help." He turned away from me and pissed, still doing the bob.

When he finished and zipped, I pulled his arm over my shoulder to steady him and grabbed his coat from the cargo bed. "Better help you up to your room." I got him inside. Only the low nighttime lights were on, and it was quiet.

"I can do it, not my first beer," he said. "You shouldn't be in here now."

"I better help you up the stairs."

He gave me plenty of weight on the way up. I got him into his room, and he fell onto his mat. I looked around on my way to hang his coat in the closet, scrutinizing for the bag of Adderall, but I didn't spot it. While facing the closet, I grabbed one of his long cowls and stuffed it in my coveralls, trying to make it as flat as possible to be undetected. I took another and laid it over Brother Dom, who seemed to be out solid. I left, leaving the night-lights on. No one saw me get out.

On the ride back, I stopped at the edge of the field and surveyed the open, beautiful grounds of the school. I was going to miss it for sure. I pondered on whether Brother Dom meant he paid Doc off in stuff to keep him quiet about me taking him for his adventures.

13

My intonation will be broken. I will be positioned in the field of cool grass. The long blades will sway in the dry breeze. It will brush my palms and the bottoms of my feet. I will have serenity, but I will have it interrupted by the sound—harsh sound—of gravel crunching under tires, multiple tires. With physical sight still not restored but hearing acute, I will discern the heavy-duty, six-wheel pickup truck—Patton's truck, an unscheduled visit: never peaceful—descending the path from the world of things. The sound of tires crunching gravel will proceed to the entrance steps and then silence. It will resume slowly, steadily toward me, onto the grass. Before my eyes are restored, I will see the truck—line of sight with the sacred Grouse Pharma Door of Harmony—approaching, closer, nearer, audaciously imminent.

I will raise my hands, the palms ascending above my head, facing the great expanse, giving thanks for the serene moment that was this day I have just pleasured in. I will hear the truck stop, its side doors so close, if they opened fully they could contact me. Palms touching, I will begin my rise. My robes, draped to the ground, will begin fluttering as I ascend from the half lotus. I will not budge my feet. With legs crossed and near straight, I will perceive the truck's passenger doors open, slowly widening, boots touching grass with the slightest gnash.

I will be near to complete vertical and rise inches more. As my feet leave the grass, I will slowly uncross my legs.

"Whoa! Some place. How'd he do that?" an unfamiliar voice will say.

"You detectives should recognize parlor tricks," Patton will answer.

I will open my eyes, spread my arms and allow my feet to resume contact with mother earth, as gently as possible so as not to disturb. I will be set firmly and steadily. "I was expecting you, officers," I will say without knowing why this expectation was within me. "Namaste." I will bow to each of the three.

Patton will stay in the driver's seat. The other two will come and rest their lower backs against the front side panel of the spotless truck.

"That's something," one will say.

"Pretty neat," the other will add. "Great space."

"Only absorbing the time."

"Cops want to ask you somethin'," Patton will scold, half snickering.

"We got this," the taller one will say to Patton (who won't have brought one of his high-school-age lackeys to do all the physical chores he is paid to do). Over across the top of the truck's hood, I will see the barbarian scurrying with a stuffed-full satchel. He will have noticed the police. He will pull his baseball cap down over his face, huff and break into a run, though restrained by his undersized jeans that he insists on wearing beneath his robes.

"Mr. Washington here tells us you are in charge. Is that correct?"

"I am the temporary cornerstone of this domicile of the holy."

"He's the head of the club," Patton will say.

"We will handle the questioning," one will say to Patton and then return his attention to me. "I am Detective Brewer, and this is my partner, Detective Hudson. County police."

"You have been partners for some years. Three."

"Yes," Detective Hudson will say.

"Yeah. Almost four, this coming holiday season. Back to why we came. Quite the place. Remote. We drove to the school in a sedan. Never would have made it down that hill."

"You should enjoy the serenity while visiting. Peaceful. Tranquil."

"Yeah, thanks. Not a bunch of that when I am working. But I do like the woods. You got hunting around this way?"

"Never. We have all the property signed according to state standards to keep hunters off. This is a refuge."

"Yeah, I like the quiet of the woods. Don't mind if I can't get nothing."

"Today as well, I see. About the girl…"

"Yeah. The missing girl."

"She is not from the school," I will say.

"Right. Town girl."

"How did you know about the girl? Not being from the orphanage?" Detective Hudson will ask.

"He knew," Patton will bark. "He knew 'cause I would have been down here and not polite."

"I do not doubt your violence," I will murmur.

"Please, Mr. Washington, we are doing the looking," Detective Brewer will say ambiguously, not alerting me to an investigation.

"Hey, fellas," will be heard from across the field. The barbarian will be coming toward us; his hips move in his unsettling waddle. The knees of his jeans will be dirty from harvesting the medical marijuana from the Key Deer Energy Greenhouse. "Nice to have some visitors down." He will discern easily from past experience that these men are detectives. Patton conspicuously will have his head down staring at the phone in his lap. No acknowledgment between him and the barbarian will be made. The detectives will note this suspicious omission from two people who clearly would be associated.

"Did you have time to properly hang the harvest in the drying room?" I will ask him when he attains our location and before he can say something disruptive.

"Yes, Master Kyle," he will say, unusually formal. "I have the herbs"—the *h* he will pronounce distinctly—"hanging nice." He will distract, as if the medical marijuana we grow were illegal and the detectives came here to investigate it. "Good to see some of the boys in blue."

They will be wearing brown shades of unnatural material mixed with wool—sport coats, elbow patches (similar color), grayed dress shirts (no tie), uncreased khakis and black, thick-soled, above-the-ankle boots—sunglasses dangling from their breast pockets.

"Even if not in blue right now."

"Who are you?" Detective Hudson will ask bluntly, seeing through the barbarian's friendliness.

"This is Brother Domenic. He has been with us seven years."

"We are going to need full names," Detective Hudson will say.

"That's okay," Detective Brewer will correct his partner, briefly holding a hand up to him. "We are just doing some looking around." He will pull a picture from his sports coat's inside pocket.

"Those are our legal names. Many clergy will take a new name when they commit to a religious life. We do that here also. It may seem clunky to the outside world, but as that is exclusively how we refer to each other, it makes everything easier."

"Easier to hide," Detective Hudson will say, inferring his suspicions of the barbarian.

"No, no. I respect the life. My partner and I understand." Detective Brewer's placating manner will be a sign that he is even more suspicious but does not want the barbarian to pick up on it. "Her name is Terri Dover. Hung out at the Old Bavarian Inn."

"Worked," Detective Hudson will interrupt his partner.

"It's just down the road there on the way into town," Detective

Brewer will continue without missing a beat as if inured to such interruptions. "One of their employees quit a little before this, but they checked out. We got flyers around town. County has a standard reward. Few connections for this poor girl. Seemed the down-on-her-luck type since high school. She attended but never graduated from Eastern County High. Pretty girl."

"You ever been to the OBI?" Detective Hudson will ask the barbarian directly.

"What's the OBI Inn?" the barbarian will fumble so dumbly that we all have our suspicions aroused. Even Patton will pick his head up and scowl at the barbarian, who will notice.

"The bar we mentioned, where she worked."

"Hangs out," I will correct Detective Hudson's tense and accusation.

"Yes, hangs out," Detective Brewer will tell his partner. "Excuse him," he will tell the barbarian to put him at ease. "My partner might be jumping the gun. As you can see, she's a young, pretty girl. In this business, you can see some bad things happen to girls like that. Especially if they have no strong bonds to the community, no family glue." He will hand me the picture. I will bow my head and accept reverently, sensing the pain of the dead girl, the pain of the barbarian's hands at her throat as he chokes the living spirit from her. I will shudder, causing my form to rise slightly from the ground.

"Are you all right?" Detective Hudson will ask me.

My physical body will be unable to answer immediately.

The barbarian will say insightfully, "He feels things. Got one going right now."

"He clairvoyant? Got ESP?" Detective Hudson will ask.

"Not like the TV stuff. He feels the future."

"Isn't that what that means?"

"No, no. He just gets feelings."

"You think this is a good feeling or a bad feeling?" Detective Hudson will ask us both.

I will return to them. "I have no knowledge of this girl. I am disheartened that she is missing."

"Will you hang that picture somewhere everyone can see it? That would be a big help."

"Let me see that," the barbarian will say and take the photo from me. "Obviously haven't seen," he will say more to convince me than the detectives.

"I can assure you no one here would be involved. We do not leave the grounds. You can confirm that with Doc Washington. We also do not have representations of the human form of any kind. But for this I will make an exception and display it on our message board in case one of the brothers meets her in the woods or—improbably—on the formal grounds."

"I'll take care of pinning it up, Master Kyle."

"I told them she couldn't come down this road," Patton will say to the barbarian.

"Security," Detective Hudson will say. "Any ability to reach the main road without going through the school?"

"You cannot get a vehicle in or out."

"No way," the barbarian will say.

"But a hearty soul could trek it. The woods are dense, though in winter when nature is barest and if one is assimilated to the cold, you can. Sometimes in winter, from the edge of the field you can make out the sounds of traffic speeding by."

"Phone number's on the back of the picture. Or you could call the barracks. I'll tell Mr. Washington if and when she turns up so you can take the picture down. We didn't get over here the last time we were on campus, when we spoke to Mr. Washington about the minor who took off."

"A runaway," Patton will growl.

"To be thorough: the student hasn't been spotted by anyone, correct?"

"Correct. It is not permitted," I will reassure them. "Unless with Doc Washington's supervision, and then only rarely."

"Practically an adult anyway," Detective Hudson will mutter, already walking to the other side of the truck.

"Still an open investigation until they turn eighteen or return to the system," Detective Brewer will say sympathetically.

"Aloha, and thank you. We will pray for Terri Dover."

"Have a good day," they will say and return to their seats in the truck. Patton will give the barbarian a halfhearted salute and gun the engine. They will drive off, leaving me with the barbarian and the sound of tires straining up the gravel path.

The barbarian will never hang the picture, nor will he destroy it—continuing to emanate guilt. My time will be shattered. Disquiet meditation will be all I can do, because I could not tell the detectives: time is written, the girl will be dead—her body somewhere in the vast wood. The barbarian will continue.

14

Artie pulls into his designated parking spot near the office entrance, right alongside the ones marked handicap.

–This company car is really coming in handy. Good idea you had.

Artie called the Office of General Services and told him the state car required a special, designated parking space. The office-park manager quickly complied.

Artie walks to his desk, almost on time today because he has to leave soon and get upstate. He sits at his desk without saying good morning to any coworkers. He begins eating his bagel with butter and bacon from his new favorite breakfast place. It is a little out of the way for his commute but—without the pressure of having to be punctual—he considers it worthwhile.

–No extra travel expenses either.

After his third bite, his desk phone rings. It is Orange. He continues chewing and glances toward his supervisor's office. He can see Orange in there looking his way with the handset to his ear but the mouthpiece up high. Artie picks up the phone. "Morning, Orange."

"Can I see you in my office?"

–He sounds less friendly than a week ago.

"Be right there," Artie tells him through his breakfast. Artie took a large bite, so he lingers and finishes enjoying his food before wiping his hands, grabbing his coffee and going to meet Orange. He heads right into the office without knocking and sits, slumping, in the lone guest chair.

"Can you close the door?" Orange says impatiently and huffs.

–Could have asked before you sat down.

Artie complies, but this time when he sits, he takes a more formal posture.

"Your work performance has not been in keeping with historical norms."

Artie takes a sip of his coffee.

"Lateness, long lunches. Other employees see this. And the attitude you bring with your idleness is affecting everyone."

"I'll be driving up there again, soon, today. I'll be back late, well after five. I don't get overtime for that. Do they, whoever they are, realize this is a special project? Do they want to trade projects?"

"You know that's not possible. What's today?"

"They are having some announcement. I'll be getting the records."

"Why don't we have these records already?"

"I don't know, Orange. The EdCloud doesn't have the records. OCFS doesn't want to play nice. Legal keeps getting everything sent through them. I sent you what I have. It appears fine. Correct?"

"Yeah. What's there, so far."

"I'll get their records today. Hopefully it will be searchable. They're giving me a thumb drive."

"Bring a laptop, make a copy right away and check if it's at least an effort on their part. And then…" Orange stopped and rubbed his chin.

–Legal.

"Get it to legal before any changes get made by you."

"I'm not going to make changes. You know protocol. What could I even change?"

"I just want to make sure legal has a clean copy."

"Gotcha. I'll have them shut down by Monday."

Orange's jaw starts to twitch slightly left and snap back every couple of seconds.

–Joke.

Artie surprises himself by letting the jest hang in the room, discomfiting his supervisor. "You know I'm kidding, right?"

Orange gets up from behind his desk, goes to the door, opens it and stands there holding the knob for Artie to exit. "Not funny."

Artie stays seated. "Why not?"

–This is not good.

"Maybe you should call your pal the governor and feel her out with your fun."

"Orange, everything is checking out to the point of boredom. I have too much time and not enough to do. Why are you so put off?"

"Can't say."

"I could wrap this up Monday."

"Not until legal says, you can't."

Artie gets up and says, "Well I hope your day gets better."

–You'll be glad to get out of here.

"I'm going to get back to my breakfast and coffee. Then I will head out. Would you like me to check with you when I go?"

"No."

After Artie leaves, Orange picks up his phone. Artie stands at his desk and watches him while he eats.

–Orange is stressed.

Artie wraps up his time at the desk and grabs his items to start out. When he passes Orange's office, he looks in to wave goodbye, but Orange is turned away and on the phone again.

While on the drive up, as the thruway becomes more country and less suburban, Artie hears the distinct ringtone he previously set for the school and sees the number appear on the car's multifunction screen. He presses the accept-call button on the steering wheel and says, "Hiii."

"Hello, Mr. Alston. It's Sandi, from Headmistress' office."

"Hello, Sandi. Everything okay for today? I am on my way, driving now."

"Yes. We are all set for an on-time announcement ceremony. Headmistress is having a busy day, even more so than usual. Would you be able to meet her at the chancellor's lodgings beforehand?"

"I guess?"

"Do you know where that is on the campus?"

"Yes. Jorgie took me by it on the tour. It's near the chapel, correct?"

"That's correct. I'll be at my desk answering the phones, if you need any assistance when you get to campus. But the chapel is easy to spot from the entrance, just head toward it."

"Okay, everything all right?"

"Of course, it's only that she's busy. She wants to get the administrative end completed before the announcement ceremony. She thought that would be best. Save her some time from going back and forth to the main office. She has a fully equipped office in the residence as well."

"That's fine. Thanks for the call. Enjoy your day if I don't see you."

"It's going to be a fantastic day. I'm excited. I'll probably see you at the announcement ceremony. We're not used to such commotion. Goodbye, Mr. Alston." Sandi hangs up before Artie can say bye.

–Meeting at the residence is awkward. You better hope someone else is around. Good thing she is not your type. Why do your thoughts wander like that?

And then Artie is lost in the thought of walking into Headmistress' home, approaching her from behind. Headmistress is sitting at a too-brightly-lit mirror, wearing a baby-pink slip, fixing her hair. Layers of misting hairspray being fired from every angle as she twists with the frantic movement of her arms. She applies red lipstick and talks business with him. "I'm going to take care of everything and I mean everything." She wiggles her ass on the small backless stool, and his eyes dart from her rump flowing over the small, round seat to her made-up face he views reflected in the mirror. He brushes her sticky hair with the back of his hand. He can taste hairspray.

–You better snap to. This is a professional breakdown you're having.

Artie finds a sports-talk AM radio station to take his mind off Headmistress. He sets the car's adaptive cruise control and lane-keeping assist so he can relax. He has mastered the car's features during his work commute. The car is set to travel above the speed limit. Midday traffic is light. He takes a sip of his now warm coffee from the school's travel mug that Headmistress had ordered for him last week. Artie had asked the café to refill it, to save a cup. "Optimum calicem capulus mundi," he reads the italics on the mug.

–You meant to translate that. Mundi is world. Nice mug, better for the environment to reuse and nicer to hold than those paper disposable cups with the plastic lids.

On this trip, with the car more conforming to his wishes, he even speeds on the twisting country roads. As Artie nears the school, he has the lone color-changed tree from his first ride up on his mind. He scans the hillside looking for fall colors. Signs of change are there.

–You are not unlike that lone tree. You stand out at the office and here on campus for your conventionality. Your steady professionalism will see you through this.

The image makes Artie smile. Then the phantasm of Headmistress applying lipstick is back, undermining his self-administered pep talk. He never spots his lone, colorful tree and considers circling back to look again as he has plenty of time and doesn't want to be waiting in Headmistress' office at her residence.

Artie slows as he approaches the driveway. There is a convoy of medium-size, box and flatbed trucks entering the campus ahead of him. He pulls to the shoulder, in line behind them, and puts his hazards on. Cars zoom past.

–Seven trucks. All labeled 'Key Deer Energy Solutions.' There really is something going on today.

Artie moves slowly, following behind the trucks. They all go right when they get to the campus road proper, toward the Butt. He pauses and watches the activity at the Butt. A large, white, open-sided tent has been set up out front. The energy company's colorful logo is stenciled on each plane of the tent top. A low stage with a lectern and folding chairs are covered by the tent. Beyond that, a caterer seems to be setting up some tables and a drink station.

–You hope that isn't a bar. Though you suppose that's fine. Not a flagrant rule to break. It is a private institution.

He proceeds to the chancellor's lodgings. There are two paved parking spots cut into the lawn at the side of the house. A bright pink VW Bug and a golf cart are parked there.

–New golf cart?

Artie squeezes his small car onto the parking pad. He grabs his laptop satchel.

–Should you have brought her something? Didn't expect to be at the residence when you left the office. You are overthinking. This is business.

He notes all the landscaping as he walks to the front of the residence—colorful mums are around the small porch and line the walkway.

–Just done? You can't be sure.

He admires the white woodwork of the rail, the stairs and around the windows.

He climbs to the porch and rings the bell. He admires the half-round, buttery-yellow siding and touches it.

–Not real wood. Fooled you. Maybe all of it?

Headmistress comes on the intercom. "Hello."

"Good afternoon, Headmistress Hunt. It's me, Artie. I hope you were expecting me. Sandi asked me to come here directly. We spoke on—"

"Come in."

–Conventional. Remember: don't let this spin into something else. You're already thinking about it.

Artie grabs the doorknob expecting some kind of buzz to alert him to go in. After a few seconds, he turns the knob and enters. He looks around but does not see her. He looks at the door to see if there is some sort of electronic lock. It appears to just be mechanical and left unlocked. He looks for a security camera; inside none, outside he spots one at each side of the porch but facing outward. He closes the door. "Take your time. I'll wait by the door."

Artie hears the familiar sound of an office chair's wheels rolling. He looks down the white wainscoted hall and sees the tilted head of Headmistress, who has wheeled herself into the doorway at the end of the hall. "Come on to the office, Mr. Alston. Artie."

"Thank you." Artie passes a comfortably modern decorated living room with tall narrow windows. Headmistress wheels herself back into the office. Artie follows. "Nice home."

He enters the office and sits opposite the transparent desk. Headmistress is on the phone, holding up one finger, requesting a minute.

–Obviously this was meant to be the dining room.

Headmistress signs off, hangs up and crosses her legs ladylike and leans back. "Excuse my appearance. I have been too on it to complete my ensemble."

"Oh, but you look so nice."

"Thank you. I'll, of course, put on a jacket for the announcement ceremony. I hope you don't mind."

"No, not at all. Suits. Seems to be a diminishing style in business. Politicians are the new suits." Artie smiles at his attempt to be funny.

"There'll be some politicians at the event. Some suits."

–Sandi didn't tell you in the email how to dress for this.

Headmistress folds her arms under her breasts.

–As expected. Make conversation.

"This room. The dining room originally?"

"Yes. I didn't have dining guests here. So an office made more sense, instead of an unused, upstairs bedroom. Plenty of space for one. Would you like to see the kitchen? Get a drink? You must be thirsty after your drive."

"Yes, a water."

Headmistress stands and bends forward, arranging and turning over some papers.

Artie eyes his new view of her cleavage, pretending to check his phone. "That would be fine."

"Follow me," she says.

Artie follows, while eyeing her swaying hips, into the kitchen. "Very modern interior compared to the outside of the house," he says when they are in the kitchen.

"Yes. Even the retro kitchenette set seems modern. I'm going to have a sweet tea. Not too late for you to change your mind." She goes to the refrigerator and, bending, retrieves a pitcher.

"That'd be nice, thanks. I've actually lost some weight. Funny because I feel like I have been eating more than my usual."

"Seems like a healthy weight for you." She hands him a tumbler of tea.

He tastes it and wishes he had gotten the water because the iced tea is overly sugared to the near point of crunchiness. He sees sugar settled at the bottom of the pitcher.

"I thought it'd be colder by now. I made it today. Steeped it in the sun myself, fresh-squeezed lemon, then put it in the fridge. Ice?"

"No thank you. Fine like this. What's the big announcement?"

"Oh, enjoy the surprise. You don't have to run off, do you?"

"No. The rest of the day is yours. Or the school's, I should say."

"Good."

He follows her back to the office. They sit, and she removes a compact mirror from her desk and touches up her lipstick—turning away and holding the mirror at an angle where Artie can catch the reflection of the lipstick pressing into her plump lips. Artie shifts in his chair. He sees the red mark left on the rim of her glass.

"Now," she says, snapping her large makeup mirror closed and putting it away. She stands and leans across the desk and hands Artie a thumb drive. "All of our required, current filings are on this."

Artie takes it without rising, only shifting forward. She sits. "Great."

"No old records. Paper was maché. You know, shredded for legal reasons."

"I'm not sure that was good advice. There are record-keeping requirements. Legal requirements."

"Yes, we consulted with a law firm. It's all up to legal, the legal requirement, that is. They said there were no issues."

"Would you mind giving me the firm's name and contact information? Save a step if I pass it on to our legal division. They can talk direct."

"I don't think I will. They did this on a pro bono type contract because we are a charity. I don't want to involve them any more than necessary."

"It probably won't be required."

"Right. Your superior, Mr. Benton Orange, called me not too long ago this morning."

–Orange? What's with him?

"Oh. Orange Benton. Orange is his first name."

"Regardless of his name order, he assured me that I can convey to him in all confidence, that is, he said confidentiality would be maintained between us, regarding any issues that arise in this investigation, as you call it."

–Can you believe him? Orange. Confidential. Is she implying Orange told her he would keep her complaints about you confidential? And did she just tell you that? Is she being wily or foolish?

"We call it a focused survey."

"Apples and oranges by any other name. Orange, hmm. Tell me, Artie, is there something to be suspicious of? Why would your superior call me about a survey?" She holds one hand up and does a single air-quotes motion. She swivels back and forth in her office chair. Her skirt retreats up her thigh as she turns. Artie notices. "Is this all really so simple?"

"People are making much of something mundane. Compliance is something we should all support."

"I'm sure there will be no reason to call Mr. Orange. Unless you feel I invited you here, for the announcement, as a red herring." She breaks her lackadaisical swiveling and leans abruptly forward onto her forearms, giving Artie the fully inflated cleavage view.

–She's seen you peek and is exploiting it. Don't say anything.

"The thought never crossed my mind that you would do something to distract me from my mission."

–Stop the sarcasm.

"No, I wouldn't. I like you, Artie." She relaxes and sits back, resuming her gentle swiveling, now with her recrossed leg dangling a designer heel. "You are a true professional. Sometimes I am so protective of these girls, I guess I can believe others don't have the same intention."

"Yes. The students must be placed above the institution."

"Tricky, because there is no optimal. You only get to do the best you can for them. I find myself —now and again—thinking it is difficult to separate what it best for the institution and what is best for the girls. Seems to unify."

"A gestalt."

"I think you get it. We could relax our standards. The girls would still be better off than in so many other situations they have come from, probably all. But we have to fight that urge."

"You seem to be fortunate, budgetary-wise."

"We could do better, always trying to do better for the girls."

–She's unappreciative of all they have at this school.

"Is this lovely house…donated?"

"It is. I am not into material things. It is nice to be able to have this home on campus. Of course it belongs to the institution. When I retire, the new headmistress will live here."

–Or headmaster.

"A new caretaker will, I hope, keep up the fine job you are doing."

–Laying it on a little thick.

"I've always considered myself more of a caregiver than a caretaker."

"I…"

"An inauspicious incumbency. I hope, with the good Lord, to do my best."

"Auspicious."

"Excuse me, Artie?"

"You said inauspicious. You meant, of course, auspicious."

"Of course. Aren't they the same thing?" She stops shaking her foot and swiveling.

–Where did this get off track? She doesn't like you correcting her.

"I guess it's like flammable and inflammable," Headmistress says.

"I knew what you meant." There is some awkward silence. Artie gulps his tea. "I wanted to ask, out of curiosity, not part of the investigation—I mean focused survey—what brought about the change of name from Saint Margaret's Foundling Home?"

"I believe lack of funds. State intrusion had something to do with it also. I wasn't headmistress then. How old do you think I am, Artie?"

"I didn't mean to imply that. I never would have assumed you were here at that time."

"I'm kidding you. Well, the new board went away from the Catholic and state blueprints and traditions. They found enough people willing to donate to this idea. They took down all the saint statues but kept the names."

–That timeline sounds like it doesn't match up.

"We swim against the tide. Some people might say it is an old-fashioned idea, a large home like this for parentless girls. But I feel we are successful."

"Yes. I found some news articles about the change but not much else since then. I had a difficult time just finding who was on your present-day board. Legal found it."

"Many titans of economic power."

"All male. Unless that changed recently."

"I don't have much contact with them."

"They must approve your budget every year?"

"Most of the budgeting process is done by our accounting firm. They also work pro bono. And the board approves the budget every year. That hasn't been an issue. And I hope you won't do anything to change that."

"I don't see how that could be."

"I need to finish a few things. Do you mind waiting in the living room or kitchen? I have to go upstairs. Maybe you would like to head over to the announcement with me. We can take the golf cart."

Artie moves to the kitchen, dumps the rest of his tea into the sink, then rinses and fills his glass with water. He drinks it quickly. After he hears Headmistress go up, he looks in the hall and finds a bathroom. After he urinates, he cannot flush the toilet.

–Ugh.

Artie jiggles the handle. He takes the lid off the tank and sees it is full. He reaches in and pulls the stopper up to release the flow of water.

–You soaked your cuff.

He washes his hands and dries them.

–You should have insisted on meeting at the main office. This was unprofessional. Like some cheap ploy by her to assert dominance.

Back in the kitchen, Artie pats his wet sleeve with paper towels, then gets his laptop running. He loads the thumb drive's data that is in a folder labeled: Artie. He uploads the info to the EdCloud, which takes some time. He shares the files with Orange and legal. Then he starts to go through the data.

–Seems to be in order. Lists of employees, educational staff as well as noneducational, seemingly all proper. Even listings of dates of the students' medical visits without disclosing personal information. Very efficiently done, at first glance anyway.

He checks the students' standardized test scores, and they range from passing easily to impressive. He will have to search some items individually, but it seems like there are no red flags. He emails Orange and legal with the preliminary good news. He spends his time cleaning out his email while he waits.

Artie is all packed up and ready. He strolls quietly into the living room, then heads over to the side of the sofa and caresses the plush velvet, spreading his fingers and allowing the fine fibers to run between them. He picks up an accent pillow and holds it to his cheek. He puts it down, then brushes the pillow and sofa arm back to their previous state of tidiness. Artie walks back to the kitchen, shoulders his messenger bag, and when he hears Headmistress in the upstairs hall, he moves out to the entryway by the bottom step. Headmistress comes down looking completely put together. Artie is looking up at her, her skirt seems shorter from this angle. Her one engaged suit-jacket button is straining below her breasts. She has put on a string of pearls. As she steps, her legs press out against the tight skirt. Her body and her step are at an angle to the stairway, yet she seems sturdy in her tall heels.

–Don't know how, she is so not your type, yet she has you off your game. Look away.

"I hope that wasn't too long for you to wait."

"No," Artie says, looking back up at her heavily made-up face. "I got some work done."

"Good, we will be almost on time. There'll be a photographer there. Had to take that in mind."

"I finished with the thumb drive. You can have it back."

"You are very efficient. Would you put it on my desk?"

"Yes, if you consider that to be safe? Data security wise."

"It's fine."

Artie goes into the office, and she yells after him, "Artie, is my handbag in there? It'll be mostly tan."

Artie sees a large black bag on the floor, the one she had gotten her lipstick from. He puts the drive on the desk and grabs the bag.

"This is the bag that was there," he says when he returns to her.

She is in front of the full-length hall mirror smoothing her jacket and skirt. "No, not that one," she says without turning to face him. "Would you go upstairs and check my bed? I bet I left it there. And that one, could you bring it up and place it on the bed, also?"

"Are you sure that's okay?"

"Of course. You don't just want to watch me on the stairs again, do you?"

–Keep in check. She's getting to you.

"It's only an up and back. I'll wait on the porch."

Artie runs up the stairs. "First room on the right," she yells after him. The sound of the front door opening relaxes him a bit. The bedroom is over-pinked, overstuffed and over-pillowed. The bag is right at the bed corner closest to the door, tan handles straight up. Artie throws the black bag on the bed, grabs the other and is back on the stairs in no time.

"See, I knew you'd be a bunch quicker than me," Headmistress says and begins down the porch stairs before Artie can reach her and hand her the bag. At the bottom she turns back to Artie, who is on the porch looking down at her. She puts on her sunglasses and says, "Artie, would you close the door?"

Artie is starting to breathe heavily, not sure if it is because of the stairs or Headmistress. "Shall I lock it?"

"No, just close it. I don't lock it."

"You have the security system at home? I didn't notice anything."

"No. Some cameras, but we have staff that comes in at various times, so I leave it unlocked."

–Odd.

Artie pulls the door closed, then meets her at the pink golf cart. She is standing by the passenger side. Artie approaches from the front and asks, "Did you want me to drive?" Then he walks over to her side and holds out the purse for her to take.

Instead, she grabs his hand and holds it while she slides her rump up and onto the seat. After she is settled, she takes the bag and holds it on her lap with both hands, handles up.

"You've played golf before, haven't you?"

"Been a long time."

She doesn't respond, so he puts his satchel in his car and then gets into the driver's seat.

–The sun really warmed things up.

"No seat belt for me. Please drive with care."

"Certainly."

He finds reverse and attempts to ease the golf cart back out of the tight spot between car and grass, but it lurches and he hits the brake. After the short stop, he shakes his head and looks at Headmistress.

She is unruffled. "You might be more comfortable going forward. Don't worry about the lawn."

"Good idea." Artie turns the wheel and makes a tight semicircle across the grass. He allows the cart to roll to a stop after spotting a landscape feature beyond the chancellor's lodging that he hadn't noticed before. "Is that a labyrinth?"

"Yes. That is the labyrinth. Donated a few years back. You see the retaining wall, there, beautiful stone. We needed that because of the slope. The contractor had the foundlings right with him learning masonry skills. It's not used much. Reverend Mathis will stroll it if he arrives early for service and has invited me to join him for contemplation. Fishy origins, labyrinths, if you ask me. But hard to look a gift horse in the mouth, and the boys learned a lot from it."

"Very nice feature." Artie lightly presses the gas pedal down and is soon on the pavement rolling along comfortably.

–This is fine.

"They'll wait for us, no rush. I'm not really dressed for a golf cart ride."

"I'll ease up. I noticed you have president as your official title in the filings. Is there a reason you don't use that professionally? Here on campus?"

"It's the job and tradition, that's all. Don't rain on the parade, Artie. We can talk business some other time."

"I was just making friendly, education-professional to education-professional talk. I didn't consider it to be business."

At the tent, everyone looks ready. Headmistress directs Artie around the tent and up near the front. The female students are milling around under the tent, some sitting. The boys are in new-looking, pressed coveralls standing in the back, beyond the tent, in the sun. There are some suits milling about near the front of the lectern.

–Mostly men.

When they stop, the crowd has their attention on them.

Headmistress asks, "Will you assist me gentlemanlike, Artie?"

Artie gets out, and as he walks around the cart, he spots and nods a hello to Doc Washington. It is returned without a smile. Headmistress hands Artie her bag when he gets around to her and then holds his other hand while she slides out. "There'll be some light refreshment after. By the Butt. Couldn't do much about the location."

"I'll see you then," Artie says.

Headmistress walks away and goes to the suits. She seems familiar with them all. She looks back at Artie and swings an index finger his way with her bag in the crux of her bent elbow. The suits all look.

–What's she telling them?

Artie walks over to Doc Washington and asks him, "Is it okay to leave the cart here?"

"It's Headmistress' cart. She can leave it where she likes."

"Everything looks great. You have done a superlative job."

Doc Washington only nods back. Artie walks away and finds an empty chair, at the end of a row, under the tent, and checks his email again.

–No response from Orange or legal.

Artie turns away from the lectern and sees, back by a far corner of the tent, a group of students.

–There's that nice young man, Jorgie, with some of his classmates. Is that Veronica he's with?

15

I'm conversin' with my girl Posenica, and of course for the big announcement—the one that Headmistress told us we were havin' with
dignitaries comin' on campus and all, including some of whom run
companies that have endowed scholarships at universities—we are
lookin' our finest: the finest we can in our school uniforms. And sure
as be all, my boy Jay, he wants to come right over to me.

"Hi, Veronica," he say.

"Just because Posenica and I are standin' here by the tent tryin' to
get some sun and warm up our bare legs because we didn't want to
ruin our look with coats doesn't mean we wanted you to come over."

"Hi, Posenica. I know. Only sayin' hi."

"Hi, Jorgie. You boys all got new coveralls, and dark blue too, for
this?" Unusually, she sound all complimentary to her ex-fostermate.

"Yeah. They came this morning. They're stiff."

"They look starched and pressed."

"Headmistress must want us lookin' good."

"Did you see that state dude you were makin' friends with ridin' over, drivin' Headmistress from the candy cane palace in the world's slowest golf cart. He must be tense."

"I saw. Not my friend 'cause I was bein' friendly. My job. I am a professional."

"You are, Jay. I know why Headmistress picked you for that."

Jay smiles like I knew he would.

"More attention coming our way, Veronica," Posenica say.

I turn and look. "Jay, here comes your BFFs, Splain and Gasp, sportin' their starched onesies." I say it so they hear me as they approach.

"Hey, Posenica," Splain say with a big dumb smile, lookin' only at her. Gasp is beside him lookin' up all skeptical.

"Gasp, hello," I say. He nods back and says hi to Posenica and me. "Splain, I'm surprised they let your oxygen-depleted face around today."

He ignores.

"Hi, Grasp. Hi, Swaine," Posenica say. "I see you have your new uniforms. Looks nice."

"Thank you," Gasp say. "You two look nice also."

"We know it."

Splain moves close to Posenica, almost against her. "Do you want to feel my stiff onesie?"

"Splain, you are goin' off rails actin' like that around all this." I motion with my hand (French manicure done by yours truly to a tee) at all the outsiders gathered under the tent.

"No one asked you. They ain't payin' attention to us, and I'm payin' all my attention on my girl Posenica, not you. Stop bein' so proprietary."

"Slow it down, Swaine," Gasp say. Jorgie has a one-eye-closed and hurtin' look on his face that Splain notices and steps back.

"What's going on, children?" Miss Irma is callin' across the way and speed walkin' toward us. She's wearin'—like always—her Saint Margaret's softball uniform, like she's managing an MLB team. Her elbows jut out, and her hips rock with each step: she always walks like that. She says it keeps her young, and maybe it does. She super skinny and a bit hunched. Looks eighty but people say she'll hit triple digits soon.

"Hi, Miss Irma." I wave all friendly and actively. Posenica does too.

The three boys shuffle back and give us some space now that some authority has caught their attention. "Ma'am," they all say, like they've been practicin'.

"That's why we don't have dances anymore," she say to us all when she gets near. "The young fellows dancing too close to the ladies."

"They were only showing us their new uniforms."

"You fellers do look sharper than usual today. You girls also."

"Your uniform is major league," I say to get her happy and moving on.

"Better not be any bullying."

"No, ma'am," the boys say together.

"We wouldn't bully these three," I say, and Posenica laughs.

"Don't worry. I wouldn't let no one get bullied around," Splain tells her, lookin' down from like nearly twice her height.

"You look more like the bullying type, with that smirk on your face, Mr. Smarty Britches."

Splain looks like he's knowin' he got trouble comin' his way, the way he got his head hung down now. Doc or Headmistress catches this act with Miss Irma, and then troubles will all surround him.

But my boy Jay, he bails him out. "Ma'am, if I may, with all due respect."

"Go on, Jorgie."

"I believe there ain't no bullying here because before, ain't none of us had no confidence to stand up to bullyin'. Now we know. This school did that for us. Nor have we got regards to pick on another. People like you help us see that."

"Yeah, Miss Irma," Posenica say. "There isn't even a cool crowd in this place. We're all the same. No reason to be jealous or wanting to join a clique, and no one has to act like the nerd protector. We all in it together."

"You certainly are well-spoken young ladies," Miss Irma say. "I will miss you two after the summer. And I am hoping we will get the softball team going in spring. I loved watching you hit that ball in Physical Education, Posenica. And you too, Veronica. You have a good arm. I tried to order the uniforms, but Headmistress said there weren't enough girls. I would have loved to have put a team on the field. A pitcher would have been our weak link."

"Yes, Miss Irma," Posenica and I say.

"I'll see you students in gym class. Say no to drugs." She speed walks away, around the tent, wavin' at other girls as she goes.

"Thanks for coming up with that one, Jorgie," Gasp say, tryin' to get all tight with my Jay.

"Just tellin' the truth," Jay say, and then we—all the rest—quiet for a moment, wonderin' on why he said that.

Gasp finally say, "Swaine, you twice now got the trouble finger turned on me and Jorgie. What's up with that? You two short timers, I got another year."

Posenica laughs at him.

"What?"

Splain say, "Step back down the mountain, Grasp. Your mountain of bullshit. I'll do as I please. You'll all see what's going to go down. You're used to bein' down."

"Splain, you are an apex moron. Shut your mouth." I go hands on hips. "You might be Doc's number two in the greenkeepers, but you nothin' but number two out here with us."

Splain and Gasp both be lookin' mad as hell at each other. Jay got like one eye goin' from full squint to slammed shut. Then Jay's face goes all straight and calm, and he say, "I believe these two just unhappy rib night got canceled yesterday evening, and we had chickens again, not even fried: rotisserie or somethin'."

"That was bullshit," Gasp say.

"Goddamn chicken and string bean casserole," Splain say, pumpin' his fist straight down. "Again. And again."

"I sure would like to get some barbecue ribs sometimes," Posenica say.

"Cornbread too," Gasp say.

"I do too," I agree. "We never have no comfort food like that. Not even pizza."

"I liked the rotisserie chickens," Jay say.

"Chicken," Posenica corrects.

"There were a whole bunch of them."

"I would like some fried chicken too sometime," I say. "Sit in sweatpants and eat a leg in front of the TV, instead of dressin' and 'which fork I need?' But, Jay, it's just chicken, not plural." The other three laugh. "It's a tray of chicken, not chickens."

"So that old joke, why did the chicken cross the road? That's actually about a whole brood of birds?"

"No."

Jay got the rest of us laughin' at an old, corny joke.

"You can raise chickens. You can eat chicken legs. But it's just a bucket of chicken."

Jay smiles. I start thinkin': he's bein' too smart; he playin' dumb to defuse the situation.

"I'm sure you're right, Veronica, you being so smart about everything."

"Only a misunderstandin', Jay."

"You're a misunderstanding, Jorgie," Splain say, not appreciating how light the atmosphere got. Jay still smilin' though.

I see Brother Dum and the head robe walkin' toward the side of the tent, taking a wide loop. I wave and yell, "Hi, Mister Kyle." They pause, face us square and do that head bow with prayer-hands-emoji thing that Headmistress can't stand. Posenica waves with me, the boys just stare. The two robes continue their walk. "Jay, why that brother gotta wear those crazy tight jeans under his robe? Why is he the only one wears jeans at all?"

"I don't know. Don't talk that much. I'm just workin' when I'm down there."

"So tight, makes him walk funny. And that shabby baseball cap."

"Wish I could sport around in some jeans," Posenica say. "We'd be lookin' taut, Veronica."

"All the way," I say and then smooth my skirt down across my ass. "Do you know them dudes' real names?" I ask the boys.

"Nah," Jay say. "I believe Brother Dom's old name was Norm. I heard somethin'."

"You think they got any spinach on them?"

"No," Gasp say. "Headmistress and Doc would go bat, ape, shit if they had weed up here."

"Probably all their green energy drawing them mother-earth types for this announcement ceremony," Posenica say.

"How'd you know?" Splain ask. "I heard it was a big secret. Headmistress didn't want anyone to know 'til she said it. Brother Carey told me."

Gasp turns his face up to Splain again like he does when Splain confuse everything. "When you talkin' to that brother?"

"He's helpin' me with my plannin'. He's got good advice."

"Like what?" Gasp ask. Jay unusually steppin' back from this conversation.

"Like keep a textbook in a pillowcase by my bed so I can clobber you when you come at me. Brother Carey told me I have to watch others: suspies. It's the bitter angels of our nature, as he called it."

Gasp shake his head and I do too, but I can't be bothered to correct Splain.

"Sandi told me," Posenica say, all of us ready to move on from Splain's fatuity. "These bigwigs around, lovin' green energy, getting photo ops with Headmistress. This school run on big donors from the business world."

"State pays for this," Splain say.

"It don't cost nothin'. They got us doin' work, and they got an endowment," Gasp say.

"Endowments are money," I tell him. "It's got to come from somewhere."

"Dividends," Gasp say.

"If they don't need more money, why do they do this thing today? And why they got empty rooms?"

Posenica looks at me like she wants to shut me down. Probably thinks I shouldn't talk in front of these three. Then she say, "They got those rooms. Money got those rooms. The money decides who gets them. Something pops up. Looks bad for their image: they send the kid over, nobody knows. And the kids are happy, so they don't say nothing."

Jay has his head hung down, not making eye contact, kickin' the dirt a little with his new boots. I know this got somethin' to do with their two pasts together. He knows somethin' about Posenica, maybe how she got here.

"And who told you this?" I ask her.

"Sandi."

"When you get tight with her?"

"She's nice to me. Everybody's nice to you. We don't all get to be the valedictorian."

Posenica got me feelin' bad for her, except we all got our past. I see Sandi comin' our way with some executive type. His suit is all Savile Row, dollar-to-sterling lookin'. He has thin, wire-frame glasses and short hair.

"Hello, everyone," Sandi say as she approaches. "Excuse us, boys." She waves them back from us. "Veronica, Posenica, this is Mr. Nerit Jacksen."

"Hello, Mr. Jacksen," I say and extend my hand like Headmistress taught. "It's a pleasure to make your acquaintance."

"Nice to meet you," Posenica say and shakes his hand.

"Nice to meet you both. Two top students, I hear."

"Thank you, sir," I say, but not Posenica because she knows he's mostly talkin' about me.

"Mr. Jacksen is running this whole show today; you know, outside of Headmistress," Sandi continues her introduction.

"Beautiful school," Mr. Jacksen say.

"He also is steering the Key Deer Energy scholarship this year," Sandi say.

"For a lot of years, I hope," he say, smilin'. The boys are behind him, shufflin' about uncomfortably. "It's great to meet students who have excelled after a difficult beginning."

"Good to have you here, Mr. Jacksen."

"Oh, call me Nerit."

"Welcome to our campus, Nerit," Posenica and I say, knowin' Sandi wouldn't go for the familiarity but couldn't say anything in front of Nerit.

Another man in a suit, lackey-looking type, comes over. "Sir, Headmistress Hunt wants to have a quick run-through and then get started."

"Very good. First get a couple of pictures with me and these two girls. I mean students."

"Yes, sir."

Sandi steps back behind the lackey, who takes out his phone. Nerit moves between Posenica and me, and he say, "Veronica, we are near the same height, I see."

"I have a small heel on today." I kick a leg up and back to show him. He takes a long look down my legs. I glance over at Jay, and he's not too happy. Splain elbows Gasp to get him to look. "Headmistress says we should always look our best."

"Sir," the lackey say. "And girls, students, could you look this way."

"Shoulders, girls, shoulders," Sandi say, trying to get us in a formal posture, like we don't know how to pose for snaps. The three of us stand there stiff and straight, hands clasped in front. The lackey motions for us to get closer together, and we do, with Posenica and me getting our shoulders in front of Nerit.

"I got a couple," the lackey say.

Sandi steps forward with her hand out like she gonna guide Nerit back to the other suits when he say, "Let's get a couple of friendlier pictures. Then he puts his arms around our shoulders and squeezes us in. Lackey's a bit put off but quickly takes a snap. Sandi is frowning and shakin' her head a bit. But Posenica and I just smilin' and posin'. We pop our forward knee in at an angle and go full shoulders back. Posenica even pulls her skirt up a little with the hand she had on her waist.

"Girls, you'll have to find your seats," Sandi say, wantin' to end this immodest photo op by tryin' to handle us and give a pass to Nerit. She holds her arm out, directing. Nerit and the lackey follow.

"That guy gonna give you a scholarship?" Jay ask me and Posenica when the boys move back over.

"We hope," Posenica say.

"He's a little old," Gasp say.

"Posenica, he didn't pull you too hard, did he?" Splain ask.

"No, Splain," I say. "You know we got to play the game for them money-meting types. They want photos for their PR when they be handin' out scholarships."

"Handin' out his hands on girls," Splain say.

I see State Dude comin' our way next. Posenica and I are used to all this attention, but the boys don't look happy. "Hello, Jorgie," he say. "Hello, everyone."

"Hi," I say.

"'Nuff of this," Gasp say and walk away, givin' State Dude no respect. Splain and Posenica drift off too while State Dude talkin'.

"It's good to see you again, Veronica. That's correct?" He dips his head a little when he ask.

"Yes. I see you are back so soon. How's your investigation coming?" I ask.

"Fine. I guess. I see your fellow students have left us. Sorry."

"That's okay."

"The school is passing with flying colors. Headmistress gave me some records today. I gave them a quick look, and it all seems to be in order. I feel like this is the home stretch."

"Are we exemplary students?" I ask.

Jay's head is just goin' back and forth as State Dude and I talk.

"Yes, thus far. I must congratulate you on your performance. You have a heavy load of AP courses, I noticed."

"Are you paying special attention to my records?"

"I did a quick look. I would wager Headmistress wanted me to see her top-ranked student's remarkable effort and organized the files in that manner."

"She's the valer victorian." Jay finally talks. "That exec that was over here, he's gonna award her a scholarship."

"We'll see about that," I say, and then to State Dude, "Jay's going to be my PR rep."

"Yes," State Dude agrees. "Have you ever considered something in the STEM field, or medicine, instead of fashion? You seem to have the mind for it."

"Fashion takes a lot of intelligence. People need clothes. Good clothes."

"Yes, I'm sure you'll excel in whatever you do."

"You know, not everybody has clothes," Jay say.

"Yes," State Dude say but then expands. "There are so many under-privileged, in this country and throughout the world. But look who I'm telling."

"Are you implying we are underprivileged?" I ask him teasingly because it seems too easy.

"Well, I mean. Yes. I didn't mean to be insulting." He steps back, all nervous.

"Take a lot more to insult us," Jay say respectfully, but I didn't know if State Dude took it that way.

"I hope I didn't put my foot in my mouth. It is a school for orphans. I could assume you had difficult starts."

"We did," I say, tryin' to let him off the hook. "Jay doesn't talk too much about it. Do you?"

"You are under no obligation to tell me about your past," State Dude say.

"It's okay," Jay say.

"I admire both of your efforts. Do you mind if I ask about your parents, Jorgie?"

"I guess, sure. I ain't got time for detail, but Headmistress wants us to be good hosts."

"I won't share. What happened to your parents?"

"They were murdered," Jay say, cold. I ain't never heard him say that. Did Posenica know it?

"Sorry to hear," State Dude say, all humble. "Sorry to bring up such a painful memory."

"It's okay. They were terrible people."

"A difficult background, indeed," State Dude say.

"Indeed," I say, hopin' I didn't sound sarcastic to him. "Jay's got it together now."

"He does," State Dude say. "Was there no other family to take you in after the episode?"

"None that would have me."

"It must have been greatly difficult," State Dude say, all sincere, maybe his eyes welling up a bit, almost creepy. "I bet Headmistress is very proud of you having gone through all that."

"I believe she is, and I want to try my best to make her proud. I don't know where I would be without her and this orphanary."

"That's right," I say. "All of us."

"Well, it was nice speaking to you two," State Dude say. "I'm going to find my seat. It looks as if they are almost ready. Thanks for allowing me to see that difficult, inspiring part of you, Jorgie. Good luck to you both. If you ever need a letter of recommendation, I would be proud to give it."

We say bye. He walks away.

"Jay, you never told me that, about your bios."

"Oh, maybe I shouldn't have conveyed it."

"No. I won't tell people. You had State Dude all emoting. You weren't makin' it up, were you? To get him off us?"

"Nah," Jay say, all casual but believable. "I couldn't lie to the State and get the orphanary into trouble."

"We don't have to talk about it no more."

"I like talkin' to you, Veronica. I really hope after graduation, we won't lose contact."

"Contact, huh," I say, wonderin' if Jay gonna go quiet when this is over. He seem all puppy dog, but you can't tell. Maybe Posenica suspicious for a reason. "Well, before you even get close to gettin' contact to me, you gotta get pay checks. I'm goin' to college and then high-fashion world. You gotta be in the same league to hang with me."

"I know that, Veronica. I'm gonna work hard, you'll see, as long as you're not too far away to notice."

"Well, I'll be in NYC."

"Hey, do you believe that, what Posenica said before, when she was talkin' to Coach Irma, us bein' all the same? You know, at the orphanary?"

"I do."

"Sometimes it don't seem it."

"We all got warm beds and hot food and get to live here, learn a career for success. Doesn't matter how we got put, they treat us all the same."

"Some things," he say.

"You're not gonna go all woe-is-me, are you? Because State Dude brought up your past?"

He's looking down, kickin' the dirt again.

"I need you to get some confidence, Jay."

He looks up at the sun and squints his eyes real hard.

The lackey is at the lectern, on mic, doin' a sound check and asking everyone to take their seats. I see Doc comin' around the tent.

"Hep, boys. Line up in the back like you were told."

"Headmistress is always tellin' me that too. Be the best Jorgie you can be."

"Right, we both got her and the other teachers. I like to say you got to be the Jay you can be, my Jay."

"Really? Thanks."

"Hep, hep," Doc is boomin' again.

"You better sit, Veronica."

I touch his shoulder and say, "I'll see you after, Jay."

He smiles.

16

Artie returns to his chair. The seats are mostly full now, with faculty and guests in the first two rows and the girls—looking all put together in their pressed uniforms—filling in the rest. The boys stand in the back, resembling parade rest, with long-handled gardening tools. Headmistress is center, first row. Doc Washington stands well behind the lectern, in the background, between the Butt and the trucks from Key Deer Energy. A suited, neat young man uses the microphone to introduce himself and welcome everyone to this beautiful day and after saying, "Let's get started," introduces Headmistress.

Headmistress walks to the lectern and says thank you to the polite applause that seems rehearsed. "I actually will not be starting," she says, eyeballing the man who introduced her and that has now taken his place standing to the side. "We will start with our Lord. Please welcome the Reverend Mathis."

–Awkward.

Headmistress returns to her seat. Artie watches as she smooths her skirt-back while sitting. Reverend Mathis, in all black attire (other than his Roman collar), approaches the lectern. A thin woman comes and takes the seat next to Artie. She has short hair and a designer pantsuit.

–More your type.

Reverend Mathis begins by thanking Nerit Jacksen of Key Deer Energy and Headmistress and his coreligionists. He looks to the side, past the tent, at Master Kyle and the other monk from the monastery. They bow to accept the thanks.

–You thought they stayed down there.

As the reverend delivers his invocation, Artie's mind drifts to the news of Jorgie's parents.

–You shouldn't have been asking those questions. You act like it could have been mundane, like drugs or abandonment. But murder, it must be hard to live with that. He must appreciate all this security.

Artie takes out his phone with the intention of searching sites to see if the murderer or murderers were ever caught. The woman next to him notices and gives him a stern look. He pretends to be checking to make sure his ringer is silent.

–Shouldn't be looking into that boy's past. Just because he is friendly and nice. You have to maintain professionalism.

After putting his phone away, Artie smiles at his seatmate, but she has already switched her attention to the reverend. He spots Sandi at the far end of the row. She is leaning forward and waving to him. He smiles and waves back.

The oration is concluded with an amen, and the crowd returns it. "I would also like to add," Reverend Mathis says. "What a pleasure it is to be working with Headmistress. She is undaunting in her devotion to these girls. She is really making a terrific educational home for them. She is protective and a fantastic role model to these future women leaders of America. God bless you, Headmistress Hunt."

The reverend sits to a slightly louder and longer round of applause.

–He knows what his audience likes.

Headmistress returns to the lectern. Artie's eyes dart back and forth between her and the woman sitting next to him, comparing body types. Headmistress calls for all to stand and face the flagpole at the Saints' building and pledge. After the Pledge of Allegiance, Headmistress adds another amen, and the audience under the tent sits.

"Thank you all for coming today, for this generous day the Lord has made. Soon I will be asking Mr. Nerit Jacksen to join me at the lectern for the announcement. But first I would like to introduce and thank some guests that have joined us today on our beautiful campus. A special thank you to all the faculty for doing such a wonderful job with the girls. And a special blessing and thank you to the Reverend Mathis for his beautiful invocation. We are truly blessed." Reverend Mathis stands, faces the crowd and waves.

"We also have with us State Senator Ursula Lastings."

The woman beside Artie stands and waves politely to the audience.

"She's been a big supporter of our mission. And also, Mayor Keane, the mayor of the great little town down the road, Laffton."

He stands and sits quickly.

"And my new friend, Mr. Artie Alston, representing the New York State Education Department."

Artie stands timidly and waves to the least applause. He notices Jorgie and the other boys in the back standing and not clapping.

–She didn't.

Artie sits and eyes the state senator next to him.

–Did she get lured into this also? Is Headmistress that devious as to purposely drag you up to her school to make it look like the Education Department was giving some kind of approval to this event? To this school? In front of a state senator no less. You have no authorization for that. In fact the opposite; you're scrutinizing them.

"I believe we all have challenges. Some of us have our biggest challenges ahead of us. I hope and pray every day that these girls have their biggest challenges behind them."

–No notes?

"They have all gone through so much, but they are persevering. These girls have arrived here, some with only the clothes on their backs. No personal items. No favorite toy or stuffed animal. No brush for their knotty hair. No makeup. Plain, unwashed faces. But with the human spirit that our Lord has instilled in all of us. That is to say, they had the most important part. The part that keeps us separated from the beasts of the field and the forest."

–Intellect.

"God, our savior."

"Amen," Reverend Mathis says.

"The spirit within these girls is so powerful that with our guidance, they can't help but succeed. Despite having so little, we endeavor to carry on our task of saving these beautiful girls and supporting them in all the aspects of becoming fine, beautiful, gorgeous women."

The students stand and clap. Artie joins the rest but unenthusiastically.

"Now," Headmistress continues as the audience sits again, "as we march together into the great future that awaits us, we take another step toward being environmentally friendly. We've had some campaigns. Coach Irma's 'Turn Off the Lights' campaign and Mrs. Richmond's recycling campaign. We have been composting and feeding our own plantings for three years now. And today another leap forward for our world. Please welcome the representative from Key Deer Energy, our partners on the planet, Mr. Nerit Jacksen."

Nerit walks up to the lectern to a smattering of applause. He stands next to Headmistress, who has stepped to the side. Artie pulls out his phone and searches Key Deer Energy.

"Thank you all. We at Key Deer Energy believe clean energy is our future, and we plan to put our money where our mouths are. Today, as part of our cleanest energy postu...position. I'm sorry."

Artie looks up from his phone.

–He seems flustered by her. Why is she standing so close to him?

Nerit turns his head and smiles at Headmistress. She nods back.

"I saw Headmistress do this impeccably, without notes. I thought I could do the same." The man who started it off walks across the front to Nerit's chair and picks up a sheet of paper and attempts to hand it to him, but Nerit waves him off. "Our planet deserves our cleanest energy. That's why we are partnering with this remarkable facility to show how well clean energy can be done. Now I would first like to thank Headmistress for allowing us to have this partnership with the campus. I assure you we are not just here for the day; this is a commitment. Thank you also, Reverend Mathis, for your blessing, and thanks to the people's representatives for coming, Senator Lastings and Mayor Keane. Also, I would like to thank Master Kyle for his prayers."

Headmistress rolls her eyes plainly. Master Kyle and Brother Dom bow. Artie strains his neck to watch the two monks.

"And for partnering with us. Thank all the brothers at the Universal Communion of the Mountain. And now the main event. Key Deer Energy is proud to donate and support new, green-energy, fully electric vehicles."

The energy company employees pull down ramps from the backs of the trucks parked between the Butt and the tent. With the clang of the metal ramps, out roll eight various off-road vehicles. Four pull up along each side of the tent. The drivers all have full-face-covering helmets. "Key Deer Energy" is on their shirts and on the sides of the vehicles.

–They're unexpectedly quiet. Seems anticlimactic.

"These are for the school's use. We also have an all-electric pickup truck on the way and a golf cart. And we didn't forget about you, Master Kyle. We have a UTV coming that is specially outfitted for your needs arriving early tomorrow. You can tell how quiet they are just by listening." Artie notices Doc Washington chuckling and shaking his head. "And starting next week we will be installing solar panels, right there on the roof of this building behind me, enough to charge these and the pickup, and with the battery storage, we will even run most of the building. Plenty of charging stations. Then our workers will move on to install solar panels on all the buildings, with battery storage. You will be a very green campus indeed. And, Master Kyle, we didn't forget you, solar panels on your building also. Key Deer Energy is the supporter of the communion's greenhouse."

Artie goes back to his phone, checking news stories about the company.

—A lot of hydrofracking, and not too far from campus.

"Let's all check out these gleaming, all-terrain, all-electric, Key Deer Energy vehicles," Nerit wraps up.

Headmistress pops over to the microphone and says, "Enjoy the vehicles and some light refreshments. That concludes the announcement ceremony. God bless." She turns off the microphone and walks with Nerit (holding his left bicep with both hands) to the closest side-by-side.

Nerit's assistant rushes back to the microphone, turns it on and announces, "That was Nerit Jacksen, vice president. The Key Deer Energy, Northeast, Head of Operations. Thank you." No one is paying attention to him. He turns the microphone back off.

Nerit holds Headmistress' hand while she slides into a well-cushioned seat. He goes to the other side and gets behind the wheel. Pictures are being taken, and Nerit is encouraging the girls to get in the vehicle and the pictures. The monks are declining to have their picture taken.

Artie is reading press articles about the energy company when Ursula Lastings, standing over him, says, "I would think someone from the State Department of Education could avoid social media long enough to get through a speech or two. I thought they deserved our full attention."

"I was reading about all the hydrofracking that Key Deer wants to do around here," Artie says. "They are already over the Pennsylvania border going full steam ahead."

"Today is green energy day," she says and walks away.

Artie continues searching.

–You wonder if the slinky senator will pull a power play and report you to Orange. Maybe she is single. Much more your type than Headmistress.

Artie picks up his head once in a while to see who is about but keeps reading. He adds the county name to the query and sees State Senator Lastings mentioned in an article. She is in the minority of supporting hydrofracking jobs in New York's economically unempowered areas. She mentions tax credits.

–No surprise there. Guess she won't be making any formal complaint.

Artie walks to the refreshments. There are chips, pretzels, crudités, and a cheese and cracker platter.

–They all look like they were in the sun too long.

Artie samples some of each and goes to the drink station.

–No alcohol. Makes sense.

He orders a seltzer. He drinks it quickly and gets another. He starts to wander away from the crowd, toward the Butt. An energy company employee drives a quad past him and stops it by Doc Washington, who had been standing alone. Artie walks over. The employee busies herself by the trucks.

"I was wondering if these were even more fun to ride than the side-by-sides that Jorgie gave me a ride on. You know, the last time I visited."

"They can be fun to drive the trails. We use them for work mostly. I'll have to request a utility trailer for a couple. I know the boys like to take some liberties when out of sight with the quads. I don't mind. Need to wear a helmet with these. They gotta get a little adventure or they get fidgety. Young men want to get out on their own. Some don't have the patience."

"What's your opinion of these new ones? I didn't even know they came in electric motors."

"I think they're dog crap. Can't beat a gasoline engine. Hard to believe these get the same horses. Batteries degrade over time. We're going to have to get them serviced somewhere off campus. We don't have the equipment or training to work on these high-voltage batteries."

"I guess…sometimes progress…maybe the Key Deer people will have a certified mechanic come and train everyone."

"Maybe. I don't know if Headmistress will want an outsider teaching these boys."

"Maybe they could train you up at their shop."

"I'm needed here."

"Maybe in the summer."

"This isn't a camp. The boys don't have a home to go to in the summer. I'm needed here then as well."

–You got your foot in your mouth again. He seems to twist things to make your words look thoughtless.

Artie swirls the ice at the bottom of his cup. "There do seem to be some hurdles with all advancements, but it's a tremendous gift for the environment. And you're getting a new truck."

Jorgie and Veronica come walking over. Jorgie breaks the uncomfortable silence between Doc Washington and Artie. "I would like to show Veronica the quad, with your permission, sir."

"Okay, Jorgie. There are some new helmets in the cab of this box truck behind me."

Jorgie walks around to the front of the truck.

Veronica says, "Mr. Alston, did you uncover the coven?"

Artie smiles and looks to Doc Washington, who has turned away to read the laminated instruction packet that is cable-tied to the quad.

"You know those robes come up and train us all to be witches."

"Do they come to campus and interact with students?" Artie asks seriously.

"No. I'm just kidding. We never see the robes. I was surprised to see them today. I guess that expensive suit guy made sure they showed their happy faces to get their donation."

"That could be. Difficult to run a charity."

"Religious buskers," Doc Washington huffs, not looking up. Jorgie returns with two helmets and helps Veronica get one on over her long hair.

—Really notice her height with Jorgie reaching up with the helmet.

"I hope no one takes a snap of me looking silly with this pasta bowl on my head."

"You look good," Jorgie says.

Artie walks around to Doc Washington's side, leaving the children on the other end of the quad. "You have suspicions as to the sincerity of the uh, Universal Communion of the Mountain, if that's what it's called?"

Doc Washington frowns. "I never heard them called that before. Who knows what they told that guy? These energy people are simply paying indulgences. And the monks are taking the money to help other crooks exiled to save some other corporation's good name—if they ever had a good name. Key Deer people trying to settle their conscience."

—Too cynical.

"How do I look sitting on this go-kart?" Veronica asks, straddling the quad, leaning forward, gripping the handlebars, the face shield of her helmet up. Jorgie is beside her, holding his helmet.

"You look like you know what you're doing," Artie says.

"Mr. Alston, are you talking about the extra rooms we were discussing before?"

"He wasn't there for that," Jorgie says. Doc Washington is giving Jorgie a stare.

"No. What extra rooms?"

"Rumor. School keeps extra rooms in case some girl a corporate type wants to get out of sight, out of mind; they get her right in."

"Sounds unlikely."

"Headmistress coming this way," Veronica says.

Artie turns and watches Headmistress step gingerly in her heels across the grass to their position.

"Hello, all," she says when she finally arrives. "I think the day is a success."

Artie nods, and the other three say, "Yes, Headmistress."

"I see Veronica has her helmet on, that's good. But maybe young ladies should only be on the side-by-sides. More appropriate. You are wearing a skirt, Veronica."

"Yes, Headmistress," Veronica says. "I was just trying it out. Jorgie was showing me. He knows all about these."

"Okay for today. Don't let him sit behind you. Go for a little ride. Slowly. Jorgie, you run along with her and keep watch."

"Yes, ma'am," Jorgie says, and Veronica is already moving away, headed around the back of the Butt toward the trees.

"I don't know why we have two-seater, double-motorcycle things. If two people need to ride they should sit next to each other, properly. Like what the side-by-sides are for."

"He seems like a gentleman," Artie says. "The right man to keep an eye on her."

"Hm," Doc Washington blurts.

"I'm sure they'll be fine," Headmistress says. "I hope you enjoyed the day a little, Artie."

"A fine day."

"What were you talking to Veronica about?"

"Oh, the quads, and earlier when I first came with you to the tent, I had asked her about switching to a STEM field in college. I noticed how prominently you placed her academic records in the files."

"Sandi must have done that."

"Well, either way she is an academically gifted student. We need women, young women like her, to go into the sciences."

"She'll find her own way. Maybe you didn't need to speak to her about it. We have an excellent guidance department here."

"It wasn't a knock against the school. Not everyone has her aptitude."

"I believe the good Lord gave all of us the tools to be our best."

"Hear, hear, Headmistress," Doc Washington adds.

"Anywho. Come walk around back with me, Artie."

Artie and Headmistress leave Doc Washington and walk around the Butt. Her stride becomes more natural when they get to the paved path. "I just want to check on Veronica. Plenty of time for running around with boys in college. We could have picked a prettier background than the Butt for this. Something more naturey. But Nerit wanted this spot because they are emphasizing the solar panels, and they are going up on this roof to charge all these things."

When they clear the building they can see, on the inclined field, Jorgie still holding his helmet, yelling instructions and cautions to Veronica, who is riding circles around him. "I guess they're fine," Headmistress says.

"Jorgie appears quite adept with the quads."

"Ah, Jorgie. I hope he's not too crushed when he has to go. He is smitten with her. Jorgie is like a boy running with his face up to the sky: he has to look down past his nose to see where he is going."

"An optimist?"

"Maybe," she says.

Artie looks downhill as they turn back and notices two boys using pitchforks on spaced-apart, steaming piles. "Is that the composting area?"

"Yes," Headmistress says as they leave the path headed back to the front.

"Turning the piles, I see. Is that part of some farm training?"

"Oh, I don't know. You'll have to ask Doc Washington about that one. All I know is it stinks when they flip it."

Doc Washington is gone. Artie crinkles his nose at the odor as they continue their walk past the Butt and stop by the tent where the Key Deer employees have begun removing the chairs and lectern. All the quads and side-by-sides are gone.

"I see it's wrapped up and people are moving on. I have to catch up with Nerit at the Joes'. I will stay on top of Sandi and make sure she touches base with you to confirm you have everything."

"Oh, is that it?" Artie asks, noticing people heading up the campus's slope.

–Thought you were getting another sumptuous dinner. Ready for some food.

"That's it. We have to say goodbye here. I am afraid I am a little tardy for all I was doing. I got sidetracked."

Artie follows her to her golf cart.

She gets behind the wheel and puts on a pair of leather gloves that were tucked in by the seat back. "Goodbye, Artie," Headmistress says and holds out her hand for an awkward shake.

"Oh, yes, I'll be in touch."

She drives off. He watches, wishing he had been invited to the Joes' for dinner—invited by Headmistress personally. He looks around and notices he is alone save for the Key Deer workers who are loading the trucks and disassembling the tent. He remembers his car is at the chancellor's lodgings. He looks for Jorgie to ask for a ride but sees him driving away on the quad with Veronica seated behind him.

–Oh, well, good for Jorgie.

The sun is behind the trees, and the temperature is dropping. The landscape lighting is coming on in stages. Artie wanders past the open garage doors of the Butt. No one is inside.

–Guess you'll have to walk.

Artie gets to walking, his hands jammed into his pockets against the cold.

–You wish Sandi told you to wear a blazer now.

Artie arrives at his car and starts it up. He feels the vents, but no heat. He listens and determines he is on battery power only.

–How long for this thing to warm up? Gotta keep a sweatshirt handy or something.

Artie pulls his phone out and opens the map app and looks for a place to eat. The OBI is the closest by a lot. He checks the reviews. All five stars, which makes him suspicious because he assumes it is the place he saw from the outside when he left for home on his first visit. He reads a review: "The place where locals come."

–Is that supposed to imply home cooking? Check the outside and make up your mind.

Artie sets the app and is quickly in the OBI parking lot. There is a neon sign for an IPA Artie enjoys in the window of the small porch. There are a few cars in the parking lot.

–Not many people for a Friday evening. Got to be better than the thruway rest stop though? Maybe?

Artie goes in and waits by the door to be seated. He notices a few people at the bar and that a few dining tables and booths are occupied. The lighting is dim with a hint of reddishness from some neon alcohol ads.

An older man behind the bar yells, "You can sit anywhere you like if you're here for grub, or you're welcome to the bar. Only do apps at the bar."

Artie says thank you, waves and sits in a booth. There are laminated menus and some paper specials menus by the wall, stuffed between the ketchup and three different kinds of hot sauce. A man in a stained white apron comes and asks Artie what he wants.

–The cook also?

"A craft IPA, the one on the window sign I saw: Annadale Brewers IPA."

–One or two beers should be fine. State car, though.

"I don't think we have those anymore."

"It's in your front window, the neon sign."

"I could ask Carton?"

"Please."

"Carton," the waiter yells without even turning away from Artie. "We got those Annadale IPAs?"

"No, Manny. Only the Adams IPA."

"Okay. I'll have one of those."

"Adams," Manny yells, and then asks Artie, "Do you know what you want to eat?"

"I didn't really look yet. I am hungry though, Manny."

"The ribs are on the specials menu tonight. People get them all the time. Slow-cooked baby backs in homemade, honey barbecue sauce. I put them in the oven at nine a.m. myself."

"I see it seems you are doing double duty."

"Yeah, waitress left very suddenly. Boss has a college kid starting some days next week."

"Well, good of you to pick up the slack. If you recommend the ribs, I will have them."

"Uh, okay. Do you want fries? You could get baked if you don't want the fries. Or the homemade baked beans."

"Is there a vegetable?"

"Tonight, there's just fries or baked. Baked potato: I don't think people say that's a vegetable. It's the slow season. No one orders a veggie, and then they get thrown out. So we stopped making them except Saturday and Sundays."

"Fries."

"Okay," Manny says and walks away to the kitchen, past a table of customers waving to get his attention. Carton brings Artie his beer.

–No glass? Not worth asking. Seems like this place is having a tough time. No waitress. Good man that Manny.

Artie kills time looking at his email but is distracted by thoughts of Headmistress' ass sliding onto the golf cart seat, of her putting on her leather driving gloves. He wonders if Headmistress could have been devious enough to make it appear that he showed up today with the imprimatur of the New York State Education Department. Or—as he now likes to believe—she guessed Artie was a greenie and wanted to impress him.

–Maybe she noticed your hybrid car?

Artie spots a thin, pretty girl at the bar glancing at him.

–Much too young for you. More your type than Headmistress, though.

He keeps glancing at the girl. She keeps noticing and smiling as he convinces himself that Headmistress has no future with him when the focused survey is complete or more likely ended, complete or not.

Carton brings him another beer when he still has a few ounces left of the first.

Artie thanks him and says, "This will be my last one. I have a good drive ahead of me."

"Okay," Carton says and walks away.

Manny comes back with the ribs and clanks the plate down in front of Artie.

"That was quick."

"Had them cooking all day," Manny says. "They should be tender as can be, fall right off the bone. Just had to get the fries done. I was supposed to tell you fries were a dollar extra."

"Okay. It looks good. Thank you."

Manny walks away—again not aware of the tables trying to get his attention. Artie eats and keeps glancing at the young girl at the bar. When Artie is almost done, he hears the entry door slam open behind him.

"Norm," someone yells.

Artie turns his head to see the back of the yeller as he walks, tilting slightly side-to-side, toward the bar. Artie does not recognize him.

–Buffoon.

Artie finishes the last rib but leaves a majority of the greasy, now cold fries on his plate.

–Delicious ribs. Haven't had good barbecue like that in a long time.

He nurses his beer, checking his phone and looking at the thin girl at the bar, who has the buffoon occasionally yelling something at her. She returns glances to Artie with a crooked, yellow-teeth-showing smile. She gets up and walks back to the kitchen. Artie tries to catch the face of the all-in-black buffoon in the bar mirror, but the liquor bottles block his view of the reflection.

–Maybe you should buy her a drink.

17

After Brother Dom slammed the door open and yelled, "Norm," I drove the quad around back. I parked it and took my helmet off, pondering if the new electric ones were better. It seemed quick off the start. Only got to drive it a little on campus (nice giving Veronica a ride to the dining hall) before Doc got all worried like they were fragile and stashed all the keys in his desk somewhere. He had said, "None of you better mess up them DC ones," and something about the quick chargers not being installed yet, and so we had to run extension cords out to them. He wasn't happy about where he was going to keep them and didn't want to make room in the Butt by selling off the older gas ones or parking his car outside. He had me and Grasp strap tarps over the quads because they didn't have enclosed cabs. Doc said always have some clean tarps around, a hundred uses for them. Weather wasn't expecting rain, but new stuff required caution.

Swaine was hanging around Grasp and me, pretending to supervise our tarp-securing like he was some expert.

Doc had given me some extension cords and stuff to bring down to the monastre. I had put warm clothes on because I knew Brother Dom would want to get to adventuring.

I grabbed the bag of shrimp off the back and started for the door. I heard people messing around inside the kitchen. I went up to the screen door and looked to the right, over by the open pantry door. It was Terri fellating Frank like Swaine says whores do. Frank, leaning back against the open pantry door, glanced at me and waved me off while trying to keep his pants from falling all the way to the floor.

I went back down the steps and sat on them, waiting. In a minute Frank walked out, still buckling his belt. "Just a quickie work break. What have you brought for me?"

"Brother Dom got shrimp. I'm the driver."

Terri came out too. Her jacket was open, and she was smoking.

"Well, you should get something. I'll send a beer back to the kitchen."

"Thank you."

"Your old, and I mean old, bitch waitress friend split," Terri said and took another long drag. "Left Frank high and dry without a server."

"All right, Terri, cut the kid some slack. You act like you're jealous he liked her better."

"Bullshit. But I am better than all those skirt-shortening sluts up at that school you go to."

"Hey, Jorgie, how about, to show our appreciation, I pay for Terri to give you a speed suction."

"Nah. I'm okay."

"He'd rather bang that old bitch Zoie. But no more of her for you, never see her around again." Terri walked up the steps and inside.

"Is that true, about Zoie?"

"Yeah. She left. Don't worry, I'll get another waitress." Frank reached into his pocket and pulled out a ten. "There you go. The ribs are selling better than I thought."

I took the money, then followed him in. I put the shrimp on the counter. Manny walked in from the dining room and said hi. He looked tired. "Long day?" I asked.

"I been here since eleven, the usual, but I'm doing double duty as a waiter." Frank and Manny looked at the shrimp, then Manny put them in the freezer, and Frank went to the dining room.

I took my seat by the door and asked Manny, "What happened with Zoie? Is she okay?"

"Yeah, she was. You saw her fighting with Terri. Then she said she couldn't take her, and she couldn't take another winter of obnoxious skiers grabbing her ass. I think she wanted someplace warmer."

"Did she say anything about me? She say goodbye?"

"She told me what I told you. Frank wasn't too nice to her on the way out, gave her a hard time about getting the wages he owed her."

"Yeah?"

"Yeah, but he paid her."

"Nothin' about me?"

"No."

"Terri fightin' with her again?"

"Like usual. Nothing stands out."

Frank came back in and gave me a beer. "What's with the face?"

"Nothin'," I told him. He left.

"Was I making a face?" I asked Manny.

"Yeah, a little. You okay?"

"I know I shouldn't get stubborn, but I feel like Terri drove Zoie away."

"People don't always get along."

I went to the dining room door and looked in. Terri was standing by a booth talking with Mister State. She was bending and putting her hand on the table, her shirt riding up above the waist of her jeans. She rolled her ass a bit, making sure he got a look at it. Brother Dom was at the bar. He did a shot of something brown, then threw a couple of bitten chicken wing bones at Carton's chest. Carton just laughed, and everybody at the bar, including Brother Dom, laughed along with him. I went back to my seat.

"Looks like same fun as always for them, even without Zoie," I told Manny.

"That reminds me I gotta check some tables," he said and left me there.

I killed time walking some of the woods in back. I had noticed Mister State left not long after I saw him chatting up Terri. I wasn't sure how he could spend his day with a quality lady like Headmistress and then engage with the likes of Terri. But what did he know? He wasn't from around here.

Brother Dom wrapped up his night in style, as he put it, and I drove him back. When we got off the quad, he said, "Frank told me he gave you a ten. That true?"

"Yeah."

"Had to make sure he was straight with me."

"I wanted to ask you about this place, the monastre, last time, but I didn't…"

"What's up, kiddo?"

"Are there a lot of gay monks?"

"I know I got hammered last time, but what were we talking about?"

"Nothin'."

"I don't know if there are gay guys around. I never ask. We ain't allowed to ask about what happened before they came here. They take their vows, give up earthly pleasures. That means vagina."

"Oh. Huh."

"But I never heard of no gay guy givin' up dick. But I don't really know, kiddo. Does it matter?"

"No. People is people. Brothers is brothers. Pondered on it: bunch of only men livin' in isolation."

"Human spirit," Brother Dom said. "Can't figure it out. Everyone's an oddball somewhere."

"You hear anything about Zoie leavin', saying goodbye to me or anything?"

"Yeah, yeah, kiddo. Carton, he told me, sure. She had to go. She wanted him to relay to me, goodbye, take care of yourself, to me, for me to watch out for you." I didn't believe him. "You okay? Were you close with her?"

"Terri and her were fightin'."

"You should sleep on it, kiddo. Don't look so down."

"Good night, Brother Dom." I got back on the quad but skipped the helmet.

"Get some rest, kiddo."

18

Doc was driving me and Swaine to the Home Center USA store to get some stuff for general repairs. Doc was real organized and kept all supplies and spare parts on hand to make sure the orphanary was always running smooth. I was in the pickup's crew cab—the seats were a little tight. Swaine was the number two, so he got to ride up front in the big, comfortable captain's chair that's got heating and ventilation. I sat behind Doc because Swaine had the seat all the way back. I figured I'll never get that seat because I'll graduate without ever being the number two. Swaine was too tall for the crew cab part of the truck anyways. If I were the number two, I'd probably still let him sit in the front.

We pulled into a parking lot. This was the nice part of going to the HCU. Doc always had to stop and get him a pastrami on rye at this diner that was on the way. Swaine and I always got cheeseburgers and fries. They were good. The burgers at the Butt were good, but they sat in the warming trays for a time and cooked all the way through. So they got a little rubbery and a bunch would lose their cheese. These diner cheeseburgers had grill marks that you could taste. And the fries had a crunch you didn't get from the warming trays.

Doc always ordered them from his phone before we left, and they were ready by the time we got there. Doc inched his seat forward for me, and I got out. I always fetched the food. Doc liked to eat on the road, said it shortened his time away from his wards. I stopped at his window. He took a fifty out, gave it to me and said, "Tip three bucks."

"Like usual," I said politely.

He took his school credit card out of his wallet, put it in his shirt pocket and then put the wallet in the center console.

At the bottom of the steps to the door there was a middle-aged, heavy guy in a mobility scooter yelling for someone to bring him his food. "Hey, you," he said to me.

"Yes, sir."

"When you get in, tell 'em Tommy's here waiting for his food. I know they can hear me. I already paid for it."

"Okay. They ain't got no ramp for you?"

"I'm gonna sue."

I went to the counter, by the register. "Doc Washington's order," I said to the uniformed waitress.

"Okay, honey," she said, went to the pass-through window and spoke to someone on the other side.

I heard the guy outside yelling, "I want my food."

She came back with our bag and was ringing me up when I said, "That guy Tommy, yellin', he told me to say he's waitin' for his order, that he paid for it."

"I can hear him, honey. He's just a pain in the ass. He calls from the parking lot and expects us to run out with his food. He don't even tip us."

She gave me the change. I left the three singles like always. "I'll be happy to bring it out if it's ready. If that would help you." I looked around: the diner wasn't too busy. It was a little early for a lumps crowd.

"Well, I could check with the kitchen, but he ain't gonna tip you neither."

"I could wait a minute."

She returned with the bag and handed it to me, saying, "If he complains something is missing or messed up, just keep going. He'd have you back and forth all day."

"Bye," I said and went out.

I gave the guy his bag. He grabbed it roughly, and I started back for the pickup. "Hold on. Let me check it. They're always messing with me and my order."

"I gotta go," I told him without looking back, pondering how that whole situation evolved. At the truck I handed the bag to Swaine because he was in charge of passing out the food. He handed Doc half a sandwich—half at a time because he had the wheel. I walked around, gave back the change and got in.

Doc told me (through his sandwich) as he drove away, "You can't solve everyone's problems."

I looked back at the scooter guy. He was unhappily holding up his food sack with one hand and pointing a finger at it with the other.

Swaine handed me my container and bag of fries. Can't have no ketchup because of the condition of the car, but Doc had lots of that special mustard he says only this diner has. It was dripping off his mustache; it seemed like he ordered it with extra.

"Thank you for the burger," I said.

"You're welcome," Swaine said.

"Not you."

Swaine laughed. Doc just kept eating and driving. I knew he didn't want us to interrupt his pastrami sandwich. I dug in.

At the HCU, we parked away from all the other cars. Doc didn't want any door dings on his pickup. Swaine and I were still eating. Doc had smashed his sandwich down already and stuffed the wrapper and his dirty napkin into the diner bag even though Swaine was still eating his fries out of it. "Make sure it all gets in the trash," he said. He went to give Swaine the keys. "Lock it up."

Swaine held up his burger to show he was still eating and nodded back at me. Doc gave me the keys. I took them. I was still at my lumps too but couldn't be that ungrateful.

"Catch up to me by the building supply checkout. I got a few things to grab, then I'll be over there and hopefully my order is ready."

"Okay," Swaine said. "Mind if Jorgie and I check out some power tools?"

"Go right ahead. Try and learn something." Doc walked away.

After we finished and cleaned up, we went in and walked past all the registers, as Swaine always wanted to see if there were any new, hot checkout girls. "I like your apron and work-boot elegance," he would usually tell them. We turned down the tool aisle.

I picked up a titanium hammer that was priced over $200. "Check this," I said to Swaine, but he kept on, right out of the tool section. "Where you goin'?"

"I got some materiels to procure." He glanced at his phone. "Got time."

I followed him, bouncing the hammer's head on my palm to check how balanced it was. I had to step quick to keep up with his long strides. "What materiel you buyin'?"

"Plumbing supply aisle."

When we got there, he looked around the aisle and picked up three one-pound propane tanks.

"You gonna start learnin' to sweat pipe?"

"I told you, I got plans, Jorgie. I'm gonna drop these in the pickup before we meet up Doc W." He started walking. "And by the way, I know where his gun safe is now."

"You better end what scheme you believe you're gonna run."

"You just keep your mouth shut. Follow me out back, this way. And tell your girl Veronica she can shut her mouth around me too."

We started for the outside area that was the garden center, past electrical. We went through the auto-slide, glass doors, leaving the interior of the store proper. The garden area was surrounded by a high hurricane fence with a sheer, green mesh hanging on it. Half of the area was covered with a metal roof that sloped from the building to the far fence. By where we first entered was the gardening supplies, and past that was the outdoor plants. We turned and moved toward the hardscape section that had the tall shelves with different loose rocks and other aggregate, pavers, water features and retaining-wall blocks. It was dim back there because of the cover and the shelves.

"I found this fence opening previous time. Not bound properly to the post. It's unwatched, near all these plants and peat moss bags and behind the hardscaping stuff. I think the workers use it to take breaks or smoke pot out in the woods. Lots of butts in the dirt back that way."

"What, you're gonna run out, around through the woods to the truck?"

"Shut up, Jorgie."

We got around at the back of the garden center, and I saw the fence opening he was talking about. Beyond it, the woods were thick, almost growing through the fence.

"You're not even gonna pay for that stuff?"

"Shut up or you'll get yours before everyone else even."

"Can't go with you on this. Can't endure you anymore. I'm out."

When I got back to the pickup, Doc was waiting for me. "Where's the other one?" he said. He had pushed his trolley full of construction material over to the truck by himself and was waiting for us to load it. I had walked to the meetup spot at checkout, but he had been gone. I unlocked the truck.

"He's comin'. We split up. I told him he was takin' too long." I set to loading the truck.

"Text him," he told me, handing me his flip phone. "No reason he should let you load all this."

I sent a short text while Doc opened the tailgate. I started loading, and Doc pitched in.

"Didn't we have a tarp in there? Has he replied?"

I shook my head.

He scanned the parking lot. "Give him a call."

I called from Doc's phone. I heard a ringing as I followed Doc to the cab. I heard and saw Swaine's phone by his seat, in the cup holder.

"What's he playin' at? If he is straggling to get out of work, he'll be turning the compost piles for a month."

"Should I leave a message?" I asked as a mood lightener, but I could tell from Doc's face he didn't take it that way. Not sure if the look was the you're-an-idiot look or an angry look.

When we were loaded up, Doc took both phones and the keys. We drove to the loading area. He parked where he wasn't supposed to, and we went inside. He asked the manager he dealt with, "You seen that tall kid I come in with?"

The woman told him no. He explained to her he had to leave the truck there while we walked around looking for Swaine. He gave her his number and asked for her to look out for Swaine, explaining we should have met right there. Doc always had a plan. I walked along the first row of aisles and he the middle. We made eye contact down the aisles as we crossed. Then we went through the garden center. I couldn't say anything about it. Then we came back along the last row and checked the men's room.

Before we got back in the truck, Doc asked the manager lady to hold his number and watch for Swaine. She said she had it on the account, and she already told security. Doc told her that wasn't necessary and we would drive around. Inside the truck—I sat in back again—Doc took his wallet out of the center console, went to put his school credit card away and said, "Crap."

Doc looked around a bit, then at me. He didn't look like he wanted me to say anything. "We're going to have to call Headmistress about this if we don't see him. He took my money. I had cash, about three, three fifty in here." He waved the wallet up and down like he was trying to guess how much lighter it was now. "Do you have any ideas?"

"No, sir. You believe he's a runaway? That he's taken off?"

We drove around the parking lot. Then he checked in with the manager again, but he had me wait in the truck. "I have to come back with at least one of you," he'd said. He appeared back outside, by the truck, talking on the phone, probably Headmistress. He was all calm.

"Nothing to say?" Doc asked while we were driving back to the orphanary.

"Swaine's been actin' a little off. I was looking at this two-hundred-dollar titanium hammer, and he just was gone. He didn't even stop in the tool aisle."

"Two-hundred-dollar hammer? That's what you were looking at instead of sticking together?"

"He had to stick together too."

"I know, Jorgie. Was he talking to anyone outside the school, old friends and family?"

"No. Not that I know or would know. We been a little at odds."

Doc drove quietly, and when we got on campus I said, "Remember the pool thing?"

"Yeah."

"I got to go there and show you somethin'." We went to the Adjutor's, and I took him to the spare-parts closet. He took off his big ring of keys and opened up the dead bolt. Soon as we opened the door, we got an odor of gasoline. There was a gallon-size gas can there.

Doc picked up the can. "Not nearly full." He handed it to me. "Take it out and leave it next to the truck, by the driver's-side door, so we don't forget."

I did as he said and came right back.

I opened the box of ball bearings to show him. "There was even more last time, a lot more. Only about a quarter left."

Doc moved the box with his foot, checking the weight. He grunted, looked around and then picked up a mostly empty box of nails. Then he went to where there was a muriatic acid jug. He tapped it with his toe—the hollow thump made it seem like it was all gone. We usually didn't have much on hand for only-indoor-pool season, but there had been some.

"That would usually be stored with the other pool chemicals down by the filters. And funny about the gasoline can," I said. "He had told me he was goin' to the plumbing section to look for propane canisters."

"I thought he just walked away."

"That was before I picked up the hammer."

Doc spent a bit of time looking around the big closet. He found the blackberry, dumped it out in the slop sink and then threw the bottle away. "Hard to say what this is all about," he said as he came back to the closet. He closed the door, locked the deadbolt and then pushed the key head sideways with his palm and snapped the key. "I'll call the locksmith later." We headed for the truck. "I don't think you should over-worry, Jorgie. Swaine, he wasn't that serious of a person."

He opened the tailgate, and I loaded the gas can. "Do you want me to take that filter media out of the truck bed and stow it, while we're here?"

"No. Dallied enough. We got to get to Headmistress' office." While we drove over, he said, "Between you and me, all this: the ball bearings and the combustibles and the brandy. But I'm going to tell Headmistress about the stolen money. Not sure if she'll think that means he ran away or wanted to go on a tear."

I nodded. "Swaine said he knew where your gun safe was."

Doc nodded, contemplated. I wasn't sure it was best to tell him, but Swaine was cooked now, nothing I could do.

"Don't you know where my gun safe is, Jorgie?"

"Yes, sir. Seen you bring them out."

"He must've too. Did he say he knew the combo?"

I shook my head.

"I saw they were all accounted for last night."

I waited in Sandi's room while Doc and Headmistress spoke in the office. Couldn't make out too much.

One time Headmistress raised her voice a bit and said, "Washington, why are you so calm?"

Doc came out looking as collected as ever. "She doesn't need to talk to you, Jorgie. I explained it all. Unless you left something out. Better say it now."

"No, sir."

Sandi's phone rang. She stood after listening to the first few seconds of the call. She started pointing and waving to the office door like she wanted us to get Headmistress. When she hung up, she yelled, "Headmistress, the police, detectives are on campus." She quick tottered to the door in her high heels. "They are talking to a student."

"Go take my cart out to meet them and get them to come right back. Bring the student with you."

"Right away," Sandi said and headed out.

Doc and I went to follow, but Headmistress was in the doorway. "You two wait here. We'll all talk to them. Sandi will be fine. Don't need men to do every little thing."

"Okay," Doc said.

"How long ago was it when you called the police from the hardware store?"

"Right after I hung up with you. Less than two hours."

"They were quick."

19

I am walkin' out from the Cousin's, headin' toward the front of the Saints', when a black sedan comes rollin' up the hill from the main road. They see me and pull right up to me. Slick Number One is passenger side and starts to slow roll his window down when they get close. I hold my bookbag and train case in front of me with my arms crossed, cradling them.

"Hello," Slick One say.

"Hi."

Slick Two gets out from behind the wheel, sportin' a white, short-sleeve dress shirt and too-short tie. As he come around the car to me, he does a big display of flippin' around his blue suit jacket to his back as he slips his arms in and then tugs his lapels forward tight to his neck with a shrug. He buttons all his buttons (sartorial error) and slips his shoulders back, all like he's, 'I'm dressed so fine.' Both of their suit jackets look like they have no handwork whatsoever: lapels bubbled, lapel rolls pressed flat like trouser creases, plastic buttons, sleeve holes big enough for a hippo, crumpled shoulder lines. Slick One's shoulder line on one side looks like he has a big, old-fashioned shoulder pad but the other side don't. Slick Two's jacket pockets look like they're full of nickels, and the flaps are frayed.

"Are you a student?" Slick One ask.

"Yes."

Slick Two leans an elbow onto the hood and ask, "What's your name? Are you a senior?"

"Maybe she doesn't want to tell her name to two strangers," Slick One say.

"I don't mind tellin' you cops. It's Veronica."

"How'd you know we were cops, Veronica?" Slick Two ask and puts his Bans on.

"You look like you're auditioning to be a cop. And those suits look like you bought them in the discount section of the super store next to the box mac 'n' cheese."

Slick One laugh and holds out a pic: a five-by-seven of a young Splain. "You know this boy?"

"What'd he do?"

"He's a senior here. He ran away, we think."

"Splain ain't smart enough to get lost, never mind run away. Where did you get that picture of him from like four, five years ago?"

"He was in the system."

"What did he do, knock over a gumball machine?"

"Has he been telling you anything?" Slick One ask, puttin' the picture away.

Slick Two is leanin' into me a little too much. I give him a sideways glance and lean away so he knows I noticed.

"Mentioned wanting to get out of school? Unhappy? Speaking with friends or relatives from outside the school?"

"No. He don't like me much and likewise. You should ask the other boys. Gasp maybe." I gave them Gasp, hopin' they'd leave my Jay be.

"I can't believe he didn't like you," Slick Two say, but I don't even look his way.

"Veronica! Veronica!" we all hear and look across the lawn to the Saints' and see Sandi tryin' to high-heel-run down the stairs, holdin' the rail with both hands, torso twisted. "Veronica!" She gets Headmistress' golf cart and starts drivin' straight toward us. She has both hands together, high center on the steering wheel, tuggin' it back and forth, yellin', "Veronica!" She's speeding on grass, and we all three see the hump she's about to hit.

"Oooh," Slick Two say as she gets a bounce off her seat goin' over the hump.

"Don't talk to those men," she say as she pulls next to us and gets out.

"They are cops," I say.

"The adults will handle this. You police officers shouldn't interrogate a student without getting permission from the office first."

"Interrogation? We were called about the runaway," Slick One say. "I'm Detective Brewer, and this is Detective Hudson, from the county PD. Mr. Washington called."

"How did you know we were cops?" Slick Two ask.

"The security company called as soon as you got on campus."

"How would they know? Unmarked car."

"License plate."

"This is an undercover vehicle. If you run these tags, it comes up as an auto financing corporation."

"Well, they did. Veronica, you get in the cart."

"Okay, but don't drive so fast." I sit and lean over to make sure I hear.

"We want to work with you on this and get the young man back," Slick One say. He takes out his phone. "Excuse me, I have to take this. What's up, boss?" he say into the phone. "Yeah…We are here, talking to a student right now, along with someone from the school…Yes, both female…Right…We'll get to the office…Right away." He puts his phone away. "The Lieu," he say to Slick Two. "Says go right to the office, not to interview anyone without school permission."

"How'd he know?"

Slick One doesn't answer his partner but tells Sandi and me, "We'll follow you to the office."

"Gentleman," Sandi say and gets in with me.

As we drive away, I give the Slicks a finger-wiggling wave. They think they got trouble handlin' Sandi, wait till they meet Headmistress. I watch them over the back of the cart as Sandi drives, slower this time, across the grass back to the Saints'. They confer for a bit, then Slick Two gets back in the car, and they lazily drive toward the front of the building, looping around along the campus road.

The Slicks really take their time, eyeballin' up the whole campus. Sandi and I get inside before their car even parks. Headmistress is there, out of her office, waitin'. Doc is also standin'. And my Jay.

"Are they coming?" Headmistress ask Sandi.

I give Jay a wave and a smile. He smiles back, like we both know not to talk.

"Yes."

"You run Splain off for me?" I ask Jay.

"No, Veronica. You know I didn't. Ditched us at the HCU."

"Veronica," Headmistress say. "Let's wait for the detectives. I'll hear from you after."

When the Slicks come in, Headmistress stops them, cold, from talkin' and asks for their IDs. They meekly comply. "Detectives," she say when they have put their bifold wallets with badges and ID cards away, and everyone has been introduced. "We require permission before anyone interviews minors under my authority at our displaced childhood assembly."

"We were just getting a feel for things, preliminaries. Not a formal interview. We wanted to know if Veronica had intel that would be helpful."

"Did you tell them anything helpful?"

"No, Headmistress. Probably not. I didn't even know Splain was mislaid. He is easily flummoxed."

"We have guests, Veronica. Swaine is one of the school's. We all appreciate him even if he isn't in high-level classes like you."

"They have an old pic of Splain."

"Yes," Slick One say. He pulls the pic out and shows Headmistress.

"When and where is this from?" Headmistress ask.

"Juvenile records. We ran him. Let me tell you what we know so far, and then you can fill us in on things that can help us find him."

"I thought the children's records were sealed?" Sandi ask.

"We have access. It's sealed to the public. Usually only accessed for a criminal investigation. But a missing minor is serious, and we can check if there were—how to put it—previous cohorts who might have resurfaced who may want to interact with Swaine, or vice versa. There wasn't a crime, was there?"

"No," Headmistress say.

"Someone, one of the foundling boys, stole some food," Sandi say. Headmistress gives her a glare. Sandi wilts and say, "Not a big thing. We didn't call the police."

The Slicks look at each other, confused. "We'll let that issue go; more of an internal problem."

"Definitely," Headmistress say.

"So," Slick One continue, "we have our information technology people checking things. I know you have the phone. Any chance he had another one?"

"No," Doc grunts.

"Well, this woman, the IT forensic officer, she'll make the usual rounds, social media. We already spoke with a manager at the Home Center store. We'll have a picture over to her. We are familiar with the layout of that area. We drove through on the way and gave it a look-see."

"I'm there every other week," Slick Two adds. "I know the place like the back of my hand."

"Yes," Slick One continues. "If you have an updated picture, that'd be great. This one has already gone out for the BOLO, the Be On the Lookout. But we can get an up-to-date one out, and he's tall, correct?" Doc nods. "An exact height and build will help."

"Sandi," Headmistress say, "get these men that file picture and the height from the last medical."

"Six and a half feet, two hundred pounds," Doc say. "I'm sure of it."

Sandi goes to her desk.

Slick Two follows her, sayin', "A digital picture would be best. If you could drop it to my phone, then I can get it to the field right away."

Sandi gets to the desk and leans over her chair that's pushed in. She's bendin' past ninety degrees because of the high heels. Slick Two checks her BOLO as he walks behind her, then leans in beside her and tight to her, pretendin' to be ever so interested with what's on-screen.

As my eyes come back from those two, I notice Jay lookin' upset. "You okay, Jay?"

"Yeah, I got a little stubborn with Swaine. He wanted to do his thing. I know I should have stuck with him."

"Probably planning to ditch this place all along. Wait till I tell Posenica."

"If any students know some information about him contacting anyone, drug or alcohol use, and the connections to those substances, that could help us. If there was a PC he had. I know it was a flip phone that he left, but there may still be some traces there. If we could get those to our IT forensics person, with passwords, when you have them."

Headmistress sighs. "We have a security department, SecureThrust. They have been notified. I spoke with the president. Nothing stood out. The school owns the phone he had. We were able to immediately get the records. He hasn't been off campus without supervision or contacted anyone. Most of these kids came from tough backgrounds, and they leave them behind when they come. It's the only way, the only choice."

"I'm sure," Slick One say. "Very difficult. We'll do our best. As far as his age, he turns eighteen in January. Then—and hopefully he'll be back here to celebrate that day—he becomes a missing person, no longer a missing minor. Which is very different, because he can legally refuse to return as an adult."

"I am aware," Headmistress say. "That's something we deal with once in a while. We persuade them to stay through graduation. Legally there's some recourse for that, but it's never gone that far."

"Do you think Swaine was aware of his right to leave in a few months?"

"Splain wasn't aware of too much."

"That's enough, Veronica. We all cared for Swaine."

"You should ask those monks down the hill," I say. "They were just up here walking around for that energy announcement."

Slick Two and Sandi are havin' a quiet chitchat lookin' at his phone. Doc is scrunchin' his lips together behind his moustache.

"We had an event on campus. A company made a donation, and we had a welcoming event with light refreshments. There were some politicians, our minister and a representative from the State Education Department, as well as two of the men—monks as some call them—at the school. They are religious types, and I say types because I don't know what it is they do, but it doesn't involve our Lord Jesus."

"That colony are sketch."

"They have a monastery down the hill," Doc say. "It's school property. They lease it. You can only come and go through campus. But they don't come and go. They're cloistered. Energy folk insisted they make an appearance. They didn't interact with Swaine, did they?"

"No, sir," Jay say.

"He ran from off-campus. The club had nothing to do with it."

"The club?" Slick One ask.

"That's my name for the place, 'cause not much of anything goes on down there."

Sandi and Slick Two—who is all smiles—suddenly rejoin us. He say, "I got the updated picture out to the field. They're going to hit all the nearby bus stops and the main stations. He probably hitched his way out of the area. A lot of day laborers come and go over there. It's a makeshift employment hub for them. We'll get there early tomorrow and canvas them. We got the Port Authority PD in the city looking out for incoming." He looks right at Sandi. "Common for teens to head to the city."

"Oh, the big city, sure," she say.

"You two go anywhere else this afternoon?" Slick One asks Doc and Jay.

"No, Detective," Jay say.

"We stopped at the diner on the way. Swaine stayed in the truck with me. Jorgie here got the food. We ate on the way."

"Diner normal routine, Jorgie?"

"Just diner stuff. They got good burgers in there."

"Yeah," Slick One say. "And of course, if you hear from him, you know. He might be out for the night and maybe come back tomorrow."

"We will, Detective," Headmistress say. "And we'll pray."

"Any reason he might not have been happy with the school?"

"No," Doc say.

"He lucky to be here," I say. "He probably make a play for attention."

"How about you, Jorgie? You feel that way?"

"I wouldn't know. Some people like bad attention, maybe he's one."

"And the student Gasp, he was close to Swaine? Veronica mentioned his name."

"It's Grasp. I'll speak to him," Doc say. "Let you know."

"Did he have a girlfriend? At the school? Anywhere?"

"No," Headmistress say before anyone could answer. I know I shouldn't bring up his hittin' on Posenica. Can't drag her into it for no reason.

"We'll be outside, make some calls for a few minutes," Slick One say. "If anyone is reminded of anything, let us know."

"Bye," Slick Two say, mostly to Sandi. "You have my cell."

When they are gone, Headmistress calls me to the office. I stand in front of the desk. She fixes her face real quick, then say, "Veronica, were those two men sliming on you?"

"No, Headmistress."

"Just because they are the police—detectives—doesn't change the fact that they are adult men. And you can come to me if they were. I'll make sure it doesn't happen again."

"I'm fine, Headmistress," I say. She should be askin' Sandi these questions, but Sandi was lookin' receptive as hell.

"You're a fine young lady," she say. "Don't let this kerfuffle get to you. Swaine's got himself in a difficult spot. He lost hope. You shouldn't."

"Can't lose hope if you are hopeless."

"You should go back to your room, have a lie-down after all this. I'll have Ms. Stanley bring you some tea and a snack."

"Like we're British."

She smiles but doesn't say anything, so I start out. She yells past my back as I go through the doorway. "Sandi, have Jorgie drive Veronica back to the Joes'. She's dealt with a lot. He can use my golf cart. And return it."

We're all in the room and can hear her.

"I sure will," Jay say.

Sandi gives him the key. Doc goes into the Headmistress' office.

"Bye, Sandi," I say, and then low to only her, "Is he going to call you?" Then I wink like I assume someone her age would do. She smile all coy and goes back behind her desk. I walk out with Jorgie. He carries my bookbag and train case, going ahead of me to put them onto the backseat of the golf cart.

The Slicks are at the bottom of the stairs on the far side of their car talkin' louder than needed. "Thank you, Jorgie," I say to get their attention so they can watch me walk down the stairs. They nod at me and Jorgie, then go back to talkin'.

"Please, sir, can I have some more?" I hear Slick Two say.

The other snorts and say, "What'd the kid want? Seconds? Extra fries?"

I keep walkin'.

"Big kid, was probably just hungry," one of them say.

"Detectives," Doc say, usin' his outdoor holler as he pushes through the too-slow-for-him door. He quick steps down to the Slicks. "I know you have my cell. I am the one to call if you have any concerns."

"Our point of contact? Is that it?" Slick One say.

Jay walks me around Headmistress' golf cart and then pretends to fuss with my bags, taking his time strappin' them in with the seat belt so he can eavesdrop.

"I knew Swaine best, all the young men. I run the boys' dorm."

"How long has Swaine been here?" Slick Two ask.

"Three years, give or take."

"That's how long we've been partners. Brewer made detective long before me, though."

"Oh, nice. If you need anything, call me. Anytime. I'll be searching, doing my best to find him. He's a good one. Hard worker. He's very capable. Or if you have to come back to campus, need some office space, or a meal, you let me know."

"That's nice of you," Slick Two say.

"And how long have you been with the school, Mr. Washington?" Slick One ask.

"Fifteen years or so."

"From where?"

"Private sector. Support for private schools, some public."

"Security?"

"Lots of contract items these large facilities require."

"We're all lashed," Jay say. He hops in next to me.

"We appreciate the assist," Slick Two say as Jay and me drive off.

"You hear those two tecs, Jay?" I ask when we get far enough away from those three.

"Oh, I guess. Talkin' 'bout that movie with the singing orphans."

"You know Splain was stealin' food?"

"We got all-you-can-eat, every night. He wouldn't have no reason to steal food."

"Well, he wasn't as happy as you here," I say as we pull up to the entrance of the dorm.

"Maybe."

"You observe that one tec currying favor with Sandi? Believe it."

"No. But she's nice."

"You have to pay attention, Jay. People got motives. And not all of them are nice."

Jorgie gets out to unstrap and hand me my stuff. I go and wait on the first step.

"Maybe. Most people, though, are true."

"Anything else? You want to tell me somethin' about this you didn't want them all to hear?"

"No. I mean, you know Swaine."

I fold my arms while he holds out my bags. He knows I'll wait him out.

"I believe, if they, Sandi, meant he was stealin' bulk food, like boxes of it, not extra fries. The detectives didn't take her comment seriously. He wasn't stealin' food, though."

He's quiet for a bit, then I decide to let him off the hook. "All right." I take my bookbag and train case. "I got to tell Posenica while I have my tea. I'll let you know if she say anythin'."

"She won't know," he say.

"The other day he proclaim he missed fightin'." I turn and head inside.

"He didn't really have that much fight in him."

20

My intonation will be broken. The mop cadet will come noisily into the Key Deer Energy Greenhouse. I will hear him moving things about, metallic scraping. I will sense he is missing something.

"Hey, kiddo," the barbarian will bellow.

"Hi, Brother Dom. I was told to rake out the greenhouse. Is it okay to do now?"

"Sure, kiddo. Sure."

"I'm not gonna bother Master Kyle, am I?"

"No. He's trancing. Won't even hear us."

"Why does he have no cowl on? Just those boxer briefs and them ashes all over his body? And his kukri across his lap?"

"He's doing atonement for some future misdeed. He's got a good sweat going."

"What'd he do?"

"He felt it in his future. Some omissive transgression."

The mop cadet will go back to raking, clumsily banging his tool against the plant beds.

"We're getting an apiary. Those big cheese energy dudes are gonna have it sent to us, and we'll be making our own honey in spring."

"Bees make the honey."

"Aw, kiddo. You got a lot to learn. People ain't bears. Can't just pull out a honeycomb and eat it. There's a lot of know-how. I gotta get all caught up."

"Nice those executives donate all the stuff to the monastre. Sometimes, I don't believe like this is a real vow of poverty, what with gettin' people donating everything. Good food, heat, this medical marijuana. Brother Carey lies around all day. You have people cleanin' and cookin' for you. Other people work on their feet all day and have less than this. Like Zoie. They don't understand where they're gonna get the money from for their next bill. I don't see none of that down here."

"You miss Zoie? Don't ya, kiddo?"

"She was real nice to me."

"Well, people give voluntarily. We don't make 'em. Half the world took a vow of poverty and they don't even know it. We give things up to be monks. Just because we got food and heat—this is America, most people do. We change. I always thought I would want to die before I became somebody else. It's not like you get to step into the phone booth and come out as Superman. But it's not so bad. You'll see. Change is a constant. I'm not the man I was when I was your age, and you won't be the same when you've got my years."

"You sure are wise, Brother Dom. What's a phone booth?"

"Exactly. You have to adjust, but don't lie to yourself. Remember: an unbearable lie and an unbareable lie are antonyms."

"You know, Brother Dom, Mister State told me: 'It's hard to forget the world when the world won't forget you.'"

"Don't I know it. You think he's really working for the education bureaucracy? He's not law enforcement?"

"I believe he's true."

"From what you told me he's said, it sounds like he's looking for someone. When things seem hunky-dory is when you got to start thinking we're not in canvas anymore."

"Well, I didn't tell him anything. He might have misunderestimated me. But I played along. And like I said, I believe he is true."

"Okay, kiddo. I gotta run. I'll see you later. We got some gift boxes sent to us, pricey ones from some Manhattan chocolatier. Most monks won't touch 'em. Come up to the eats hall; have a few or bring Veronica a box of chocolate, if you want."

"Thanks, Brother Dom."

The barbarian will exit the Key Deer Energy Greenhouse, allowing the door to slam behind him. The mop cadet will resume raking vigorously.

I will struggle to maintain my serenity as the mop cadet bangs around. Maybe I will observe him humming. He will be by the entrance door, possibly finished, and then I can return to my inner peace.

"Master Kyle," I will hear him call in a whisper. "Master Kyle."

I will place my kukri to the side and rise. After I stand, I will open my eyes—they are clouded by the ashes of atonement, forcing me to blink vigorously to clear them. "Why whisper when you want my attention? We are alone here. What is the urgency?"

"I just know how important all this green earth stuff is, and I wasn't sure if this organic debris from the medical marijuana should go in the regular compost piles or be thrown away."

"What did you do with it the other times?"

"We were throwin' it away with everything else. But Doc Washington has us doing more composting now. 'Came straight from the top,' as he put it. So we got to put organics in the bed of the side-by-side and drive it up to the compost piles. I didn't know if the vegetation from the cannabis plants went in with it. Didn't want the girls smellin' the cannabis and all."

He will have me fully returned to the world and wishing I could take aspirin. "I believe you will find it no different from the rest of the organics, and you should mix them all together. It won't bother the girls. No more than the other compost."

"Well, thank you, Master Kyle. I hope I didn't disturb you too much." He will go back to raking.

"I perceive you have other questions."

"I do. I have a lot of questions. If you don't mind."

"You have this moment."

"I was ponderin' about how you feel the future."

"Time is not a straight line. Once you understand… Please stop raking."

He will stop, face me with the rake to his side at arm's length (tines down and bending severely, thick wood handle grasped with a gloved hand near the top) and lean into it.

"Lesson in concentration: focus your attention on the immediacy. Live in the now with your mind. We are not as good at multitasking as commonly perceived."

"Yes, Master Kyle."

"Namaste," I will say and bow.

He will return the bow, still holding the rake parallel and at arm's length to his body.

"Time: Picture a cheetah, who, as nature made him, wants to hunt. He chooses a gazelle in his area. If he sprints to where the gazelle is grazing, his prey will be gone when he gets there—having run off well before the cheetah arrives. If he predicts where the gazelle will run and races to that spot, the gazelle will sit and continue to graze, thinking he is not the target of the predator. The cheetah will find the empty spot he ran to is still empty."

"Are you sayin' if you predict the future, it can't come true?"

"Cheetahs exist, so there must be some way they know their prey's future path. But it is not obvious. It is some part in us and some part learned. It is not fatalism, and yet it is."

"I get that. Needs to be fatal for the cheetah to eat."

I will consider correcting him, but he will continue.

"What about Brother Carey? He really go supine one day and not get back up? He really findin' synchronicity with the universe?"

"He believes he has. He believes he has transited the ethereal and returned. What your Headmistress would call the afterlife."

"What'd he say it was like."

"Kindergarten."

"I didn't go to kindergarten."

"There was pleasant supervision—"

"Our creator?"

"It is his vision. They performed pleasant tasks. Finger painting and stapling are some he mentioned. His journey is his alone, as with all sentient beings. It doesn't allow for all. It is his. I would say he has been successful."

"So that, it's not everyone's heaven?"

"Only his. His beauty, his creator. Nothing lasts forever. Even gods crumble: the Roman, the Greek, the Egyptian. They have all retreated. Remember when we discussed time. Brother Carey questioned whether he had proven the universe doesn't even exist. He called it a simple renormalization, like a slip to another dimension. He worried that as he slipped, he might cause a break in the path and that the entirety of the universe would disappear with him."

"Good thing that didn't happen."

"His journey is beautiful to him, but there is no beauty in perfection."

"Veronica is perfectly beautiful."

"And she is if you believe that. The nature of the cheetah exists, so it must be true. And yet perfection is just a human construct."

"I guess a lot of contemplation is occurrin' here." The mop cadet will pause, and I let him as I sense he will want to confess something to me. He will place his rake in front of his body, slap a palm on top and rest his chin on the back of his hand. He will scratch his nose and then continue his questioning while oscillating his head slightly—correlating with the tines rolling along their curve as they contact and leave the ground. "Do you believe all your prayin' helps people's souls? Brother Dom does."

"We do."

"Uhmm."

"We do not believe in confession. Remember time. We can't say it is unbending, in the same way the cheetah can't pursue in a straight line. If it isn't straight, we cannot know what is next. We have to accept it to understand it. We who commit to this way of life leave our past lives; we do not revisit them. Not looking to your past makes the path forward seem aligned. It is very different from other religious movements like the Catholics or the twelve steps."

"Just bury it?"

"You cannot bury it. You burden it but not on others. But what is one's past? A blip in the universe? Or a constant? That is what must be established. Fated and faithful can mean the same path with predetermination."

"I was gonna ask. I know Brother Dom, he said he would ask you about me signin' up, joining after graduation. I wanted to know what you believed. If I learned some more, could I?"

"The school provides the workmen for the monastery. We do not take them on."

"I meant as a brother, like Brother Dom."

"It is unlikely, but it could be your future. We would not directly accept postulants from that school. We are brethren of learned men, magi. We all have at least secondary degrees. Master's in business, accounting, finance, computer engineering and also corporate lawyers. We have all lived in the outside world first. All have had other, financially lucrative careers. If we hadn't had possessions, how could we be enlightened by foregoing them? Plus, there is the hurdle of the endowment. All come with some backing. Many companies—Key

Deer, Dragon AI, SecureThrust, Grouse Pharma, Bangoro—made donations so these men could enter. This endowment is necessary, and even the school benefits. It is a symbiotic relationship. And being wise in the world already allows one to then see it through the veil of maya, and in this manner the truth of the universe can be revealed."

"Oh." The mop cadet will be disappointed.

"You will find your place. It is not here. Not now. It is the individual that is special. Individuals end. Everything else just changes: atoms reforming."

"Our spirits?"

"I see you understand, our bodies and spirits are one, and then they are not."

"I'm not quite sure I understand."

"You need to continue, to learn and educate yourself."

"I gotta ask Brother Dom about this."

I will consider what the barbarian has told the mop cadet and will caution him. "Brother Dom is too tough for his own good. And I mean the good, as in good versus evil, not personal welfare. He has his own improvements to make. He is faking confidence."

"Are you sayin' something Brother Dom is doin' that's not right?"

"No. Only everyone has their own difficulties. I want you to accept that. It doesn't mean something is not right or not good. It simply is."

"Do you know the bad hide among the good? That's where the term a wolf in sheep's clothing comes from."

"I know the adage. And yet the wolf exists. The wolf is not good nor bad, only hungry."

"I can't argue with that. You sure are wise, Master Kyle. I gotta ponder on all this. Okay if I get back to my chores?"

"Yes. I appreciate your focus. I hope you keep that top of mind in your activities. Even small tasks can be improved with a focused mind. Also, more worldly matters: I wanted to let you know that misunderestimated is not a word. It is just underestimated."

"I don't remember sayin' that."

"When you were speaking a moment ago with Brother Dom. He misquoted the Oz movie."

"I don't know what movie he was quotin' from, if he was."

"Perhaps, at the time, my conscious was more with the god Kū than I realized." I will think the mop cadet stubborn with that previously unseen, odd, twitchy-eye look on his face.

The mop cadet will give me the little jerky bow, and after I return peace, he will resume his raking. I will watch and notice his care and the silence as he avoids clumsily striking things with the rake. Soon he will be at the door, pulling all the material out. Then he will slowly close the door and leave me alone but not at ease.

21

Artie is driving onto campus. He carefully turns his car toward the break in the trees that he had approached so very slowly because of the darkness.

–Very dark.

He turns his brights on as he leaves the road.

–A student is missing. Swaine, missing for three days. Police detectives involved. And this Headmistress doesn't call you immediately? In the middle of a focused survey? Callous. She has no idea what pressure was already created for you personally. Now? She has her secretary call late in the day and casually mention it. Like no big deal: police on campus, searching for a ward of the school. And of the State. You demanded an immediate meeting. Sandi wouldn't put you on the phone with her, so you insisted. Had to. She isn't taking your required oversight seriously. "She'll meet with me today." You were right to say that.

Artie drives out from the narrow, tree-dense entry road and into the pleasantly lit landscape of the campus. He pulls up to the main building and turns off the car. He gets out and puts on his jacket. There are lights on inside, on the first floor.

–The Saints'. She better not have thought you were going to her office in the chancellor's lodgings. Well, you are not going there. She'll have to get over here and act professional.

Artie takes out his phone as he climbs the steps.

–Should you call and let them know you arrived? To let you in?

He puts his phone away expecting the doors to be locked, but they open, as do the secondary doors. He walks down the echoing hall. The hallway behind him is dim. He turns into the main office.

Sandi is sitting at her desk. "Hi, Artie," she says cheerily.

–She looks fresh: all made-up and dressed up. Guessed she would look a little tired or glum for having to be here this late.

"Good evening, Sandi. Sorry you also had to be in the office at this hour."

–Stop apologizing.

"Oh, I don't mind. If Headmistress wants extra work, I'm fine with it. 'It's for the girls,' she would say, but she doesn't have to."

"Should I go in?" Artie says, heading for Headmistress' office.

"Better if you waited outside with me; she doesn't like people in her office when she isn't there."

–Power play?

"Have you told her I've arrived for our meeting?"

"Oh, she knows about the powwow. She'll be along."

Artie sits in the wood-and-leather two-seat bench opposite Sandi and takes out his phone, checking emails. Orange wanted to be alerted right away of any pertinent information he could pry out of the school. He browses through the usual irrelevant emails, deleting as he goes. Orange emailed him after five, stating what he had already verbalized at the office.

–Probably did it while on his way home.

"Did you have a nice ride up?" Sandi asks with her hands folded on her desk, staring straight at Artie.

–Apparently no other work for her.

"It was long."

–Don't play nice, even though Sandi has nothing to do with this visit, she'll be relaying all to Headmistress.

"Oh, I don't like the long drives in the dark. I think I might need special glasses for night driving. Do you find long, night drives to be tedious?"

"I did today. And probably will again going back."

"I hope you got something to eat on the way up."

"I didn't. Actually, I—"

"We had the most delicious meal tonight at the Saint Isidore's Dining Hall."

–She doesn't care. She just wants to pass the time talking. Or butter you up as per Headmistress.

"Have you ever had a tomahawk steak?" Her eyes light up, and she sits back, pulling her arms up and out. "It was so big! And delicious. The thing had this big, long bone on it. That's where it gets the name from: tomahawk. Well, the thing was bigger than the plates. We could hardly keep from hitting other people's services with the ends. Ms. Richmond—she's such a character—she picks this thing up by the bone." Sandi mimes and laughs, covering her mouth. Artie is smiling with her. "She goes…" Another gasp slows her storytelling. "Yabba dabba doo!" Sandi laughs open-mouthed and even lightly slaps her desk. Artie chuckles along, feeling hungrier. "The girls wouldn't get that one. Way before their time. You know, except the vitamins."

"And the cereal."

"Oh, I forgot the cereal. We were all cracking up, even Headmistress. She never brought up decorousness once. That's how funny Ms. Richmond was."

"It sounds like a nice evening. Hope I didn't cut it short."

"No. We didn't rush. Couldn't. Too much food and so yummy. Creamed spinach and these huge baked potatoes. A fixins bar for the potatoes. With cheddar, bacon bits, sour cream, chives, fried or raw chopped onion, butter, olive oil, Parmesan. We're going to have to get some bigger plates donated."

"A real New-York-steakhouse meal. Sounds delicious."

"Oh, it so was."

The room is silent for a bit before Sandi asks, "Would you like some tea or coffee?"

"No. Do you estimate she'll be long?"

"Not easy being the boss. A lot on her plate. Just like at dinner tonight." Sandi chuckles, but Artie only nods along, feeling left out of the joke. He hears Headmistress' heels clacking down the hallway, getting closer.

"Hello, Sandi. Good evening, Artie. How is the investigation?"

"Grinding along," Artie says, standing and starting toward the office.

"Thanks for meeting with me and agreeing to make the trip this late." Headmistress turns from Artie, walking away, and starts talking low to Sandi about updates on the situation.

–Thanking you? For the meeting you demanded. She can't consider you that pliable? Could she?

As Artie waits in the doorway, he looks in the office and sees no chair has been placed near the desk. He moves one to a position close to the desk but off to one side, slightly turned so he can also face the doorway as his host enters.

–Forgot how heavy these were.

"He didn't want tea or anything," he hears Sandi say as Headmistress enters and goes to her desk.

"Is there an update for the State?" Artie asks, trying to skip pleasantries.

"About Swaine?"

—She knows why you came. Don't answer.

"No. The PD are looking, a Detective Brewer and Detective Hudson—handsome men. They have included the State Police as well now. Doc Washington has gone to the hardware store a few times, retracing the route and expanding to places he thought Swaine may go in the vicinity. He referred to them as…shitholes."

—The one-handed air quotes again.

"The security company has done a thorough investigation of the cellular telephone and all the PCs he accessed on the campus. Each foundling boy has his own sign-on code. Although, I believe, they did a more expansive search due to the likelihood he was trying to cover his tracks. But they thought he would not have enough technological capability to do that."

"Yes. Have the students been recanvassed for any contact since he left or other pertinent information?"

"Relevant ones, yes." She sits forward, resting her elbows on the desk, rerunning the cleavage show she put on for Artie's other visits. He notices how done up she is.

—You would have guessed she'd be a little more business casual (at least) at this hour. And last minute. Though she had the entire time you were driving to get herself ready. Part of her strategy for handling you?

"What about child services for the county?"

"Notified. They were not involved in his case previously, as Mr. Swaine was not from this county. Also, they have no children under their care that would know the boy."

"New York State Office of Children and Family Services? Did they have anything?"

"Nothing they wouldn't have shared with your office. I spoke with Orange, your superior, about a half hour ago. He had no information. And I assured him there was no purposeful delay in notifying State

ED." Headmistress pushes her chair away from her desk, leans back and crosses her legs. Artie looks and notices the tension turn slightly sexual.

"Orange has repeatedly assured me that this is my focused survey. If I decided this was urgent, then he will back me up."

"There's no reason for backup. The boy is going to be eighteen in a couple of months. He feels…How did Doc Washington put it? Like he has come into his manhood. Now, that's the family law, and we, at this institution, do not agree with that. We want all of the children to complete their studies."

"Difficult for a boy, even a near eighteen-year-old, physically capable one, to make it, and by make it, I mean survive out of harm's way, without some adult assistance. He could easily fall in with criminality, whether that was his initial intention or not."

"Agreed. Doc Washington felt there was some ego involved. Like he had to prove himself."

"Yes. I believe there to be some truth in that statement. Has there been an internal review of faculty and policy?"

"We've had formal interviews with all staff and contracted employees."

"Have you considered a girlfriend's involvement. Maybe he was taken with one of the young women and was trying to prove something and set up a future rendezvous?"

"We interviewed the young women who had some small interaction with Swaine, and the school will keep that quiet."

"Do you think that's best?"

"Yes, I do. And I am the one who decides these things. That's the way it will stay. And if there was something that could help find Swaine, we would have taken immediate action on it." Headmistress stands, flattens her skirt, walks to a cabinet and opens it, revealing a small, built-in refrigerator. She pulls out a plastic water bottle and walks back to the side of the desk. Artie admires her shape in each direction—strutting away from and coming toward him. She stands by Artie's side, peering down at him. She places the bottle on the desk, keeping her hand on it, leaning onto it slightly.

Artie is looking up, past her bosom, to her perfectly made-up, now smiling face. "Could I have one of those?" he asks.

"I thought Sandi offered you a refresher. I'll have to scold her inhospitality."

"She did. I'm feeling like a cold water now."

Headmistress uncaps the bottle and slides it slightly closer to Artie, then walks back to the refrigerator as Artie watches again.

To recover, he says, "I don't see how this incident and the school's response to it bodes well for the focused survey."

–You sound awkward.

"Oh really," Headmistress says and returns to her chair and leans onto her desk. "And where will this comeuppance come from, Artie?"

"That's not what I meant. Comeuppance. This could drag out the report's timeline."

"Tired of seeing me, Artie?"

"No. Not that. I actually enjoy our professional meetings." He takes a long drink.

–Try and take a breath. She's leading you down a dead end.

"I have found your school welcoming and enjoyable. But I have a task assigned to me, and as I am sure you, as a fellow education professional, would want me to do, I will execute it properly."

"Execute? Artie?"

–Why is she saying your name so many times?

Artie stands and steps over to the front of her desk. "The State expects full cooperation. The open filings require immediate notification if there are major changes."

She doesn't move. From his spot standing in front of her, he has another view of her face and down her cleavage.

–Pretty lipstick. Is she going to respond?

"I have a long drive; I better say good night." Artie turns to go.

"Bradley. Your legal eagle guy. He called today, probably while you were on the road, asking if we had a spot for a boy now that Swaine has run off."

Artie turns back. "Really?"

"I told him we expect Swaine to return."

"Well, I agree with you. That's best. I don't know what purpose he would have to do that."

"People know people. And so on. He probably heard about all our great programs from you."

"Well, I have certainly only been pleased by the school. But he did not speak to me directly about it. He would have gotten it from my status reports or my verbal assurances to my superior. I mean boss, Orange Benton."

Headmistress swivels her butt in her chair and then sits back, placing her forearms onto the chair armrests. "Those two do seem to talk quite a bit, from what I can glean."

"Well, good night."

"Good night, Artie. I'll have Sandi email you the detectives' contact information. Don't forget your water."

Artie takes his water as he leaves, saying a quick goodbye to Sandi, who stays quiet but waves enthusiastically. He finishes his water before he gets to his car.

—Forgot to use the bathroom, and you need to eat. Feeling weak. Guess you'll have to stop at that OBI. Hopefully they'll have fixed their staffing issue. I wonder if that skinny girl will be there—take your mind off Headmistress?

Artie drives away with his face flush and his mind drifting to his last view of Headmistress' full red lips set above her breasts.

Artie goes into the OBI and sits at the same booth as last time. He notices the skinny girl is at the bar but not the loudmouth. Same bartender. Not many people are eating, only one other occupied table.

There are a dozen or so chatty people lining the bar. Artie orders the garlic shrimp over rice (the special tonight) and an IPA from a young woman who doesn't introduce herself.

Terri surprises Artie by sitting suddenly, opposite him. "If you're gonna become a regular at this dive, ya gotta start saying hi."

"Oh, hello."

"We're country friendly around here. I can tell you're not a local. Didn't get your name last time?"

"I'm not local. I'm Artie, from Long Island."

"Terri. Artie, you are a long drive from home, and it ain't ski season. What's your angle?"

The waitress brings Artie his beer. He notices the two women ignore each other.

–What happened between these two?

"I'm with the State Education Department."

"Shutting down that school?" She smiles.

"No. Not at all. I can't speak to specifics. Really, it's boring—administrative details. Government requirements and all. What do you do, Terri?"

"Besides being the head diva of this place—Laffton, not this shithole—I am between careers. On unemployment."

"Well, good luck to you finding something. Maybe when ski season gets back."

"Yeah, I'm sure I'll be plenty busy then."

The waitress brings Artie's food.

"I guess you don't want a stranger staring at you while you eat."

"Have you eaten?"

"Not hungry tonight."

–She might be thinner than the ex.

"I'm gonna head back to the bar. Look for me when you're done. You know, so we can say good night."

"Okay, I have that long drive, so I won't hang out."

"Wanna buy me a drink?"

–Forward.

"Well, I…I did enjoy your company, short company. Very well."

–Maybe you could get her number, take your mind of Headmistress.

"I'll tell Carton to put it on your tab," she says and goes back to the bar.

Artie returns to his food.

–Tight jeans. Do all females find you gullible? She and her country friendly. Left quickly after you agreed to buy. What? Was that her maneuver for free drinks? That Manny is a good cook, enjoying this. She is a younger version of the ex. Same small-boobs body. This Terri may be thinner, but such bad teeth. Guess it's difficult to be unemployed and get a dentist up this way.

Artie cleans his plate and starts another beer but deicides not to finish it.

–It will only make you sleepy for the ride back. Can't have that.

He gets the bill, then leaves the money on the table. He takes a peek at the bar area and sees Terri engaged with her friends—mostly male and all older than her. He goes to his car and starts it up. While plugging his destination into his phone, he is roused by a knock at the passenger-side window.

It's Terri. He puts the window down. She leans on the door, bent at the waist, face almost inside, bare elbows on top of the window opening. "You didn't say good night."

"You were having fun. I have the long drive. Aren't you cold? No jacket?"

"I'm good. I didn't even get to thank you for buying me the drink."

"No problem, none at all." Artie leans into the gap between the front seat backs and looks past her full hair, along her curved back to the top of her ass as it sways from the switching of her weight from right leg to left.

–You should give her your phone number.

"Maybe you should stay."

"I don't feel I could stay any later."

Terri pulls her head away from the window opening and turns it left, looking beyond the car at something in the distance behind them. "Are you going to come back soon?" She stands facing the rear of the OBI.

"Sometime. I could maybe reach out to you then." Artie adjusts his rearview mirror, trying to determine what she is looking at. But it's just the empty, dark space along the side of the pub.

"Wait for me. I'll be right back." Terri half jogs—swinging her bent arms awkwardly—toward the end of the building. Artie turns and looks over his shoulder to see her get to the back and turn the corner. He takes out his phone and finishes putting in the address but then checks the time and route to his ex. He occasionally glances at the rearview mirror and then turns his head to check the front door.

–How long does she expect you to wait?

Artie switches the route to home, does a quick check of email in case Orange wanted an urgent update.

–Maybe you should drive around there, make sure she's all right. Bet she knows everyone here; she's fine.

Artie hits start on his map app and heads home. He compares Terri and his ex, but his mind wanders to Headmistress and the late night in her office and her red lips. He pulls to a stop while in Laffton and calls his ex.

–Voicemail. She's ignoring your call.

"Dear, I am on my way home, going past your place. Again. Hoping you were free. Let me know. I'm driving, so call."

Artie hangs up. He fantasizes about stopping by his ex's apartment, but instead of the ex, Headmistress is there waiting on the dilapidated couch. He continues driving home—uninterrupted.

22

I went out on a quad, past the line of the new electric machines still sitting under tarps charging. The company was supposed to come this week and start on the power cells and fast charge hookups, but they were delayed. I drove slow along the woodland edge, crossing the driveway that leads to the main road. Then I went back uphill toward the monastre turnoff. I slowed and looked back across the campus fields to the Butt. I believed I could make out Doc standing in his window watching me. I wasn't as quiet as I had guessed.

I made my way down the decline, running through my mind if I should have used the other ways to get down here that made it less likely to get spotted. There were some trails in the woods, branching off campus proper—I have driven them before—that would lace way around, dipping in and out of the forest. That way was: go out back away from the Butt, then uphill, looping around the Adjutor's, Cousin's and the Joes'. There was a good-size deer path—that's what Swaine had said it was—that you could circle around from behind the Adjutor's and be out of sight before coming out of the woods, for only maybe twenty yards, and to the monastre's decline. I had checked them all out before, knew the trails well.

I didn't believe that was the best thing to do every time. Going later in the night would have been best, I believed, but Brother Dom set the schedule. I was going along. He got the adventuring; I got a break from the campus. I didn't mind driving him; it was the waiting around. And now Zoie wasn't even there. Driving down was nice and all, but waiting around wasn't, and you couldn't pick the time to head back or even get an estimate from Brother Dom. I liked Manny fine, but with Zoie gone now, he would be the only one there that would be friendly enough to me.

I parked and took my helmet off, then ducked inside and checked the closet. I saw Brother Dom had left some commodities there in a plastic storage bin. I popped it open and touched the wrapping: it was cold. I gently unfolded the butcher paper and saw two long colonnades of ribs jutting out of nice hunks of beef. I closed it all back up, then hefted the bin: heavy, twenty-five pounds at least. Got to be the tomahawk steaks Frank wanted. He must've asked Brother Dom to get them. That's probably what it looks like before they're sliced into individual steaks.

I poked my head in and looked down the hall: quiet. I carried the bin outside and went about bungee-cording it down to the back of the quad. I made extra sure it was secure because of the weight. The quad didn't have much room.

Brother Dom came out. "Hey, kiddo. Right on time, like always."

"Doc Washington saw me."

"No worries. I worked something out with him. I got these steaks Frank wanted. He better appreciate it."

"Master Kyle told me it might be too difficult to get a spot at the monastre."

"Yeah, he spoke to me about it. You can do a lot better than this place. You won't need a fallback. Shoot for the stars. Besides, you don't need the aggravation. You're young. And you ain't gonna see your girl Veronica hangin' around these monks. You're going to sweep her off her feet, reconnect and have a family."

"I don't know."

"Kiddo, you got a long, amazing life going forward. It's a big world. It's not all like what you went through before you got here. Let's ride."

After we pulled away, I asked, "Do you know what I went through?"

"No. No, I mean, I understand you lost your parents. But we at the monastery, we don't discuss the past. Everyone's got one. I don't tell you mine. You don't tell me yours. That's how Master Kyle wants it."

"I guess it's for the best."

"But your future is bright, good head on your shoulders. Loyal, good-natured. A worker. That's what success is made out of every time. Some people say it's the ass-kissers that get ahead. They might start out fast, but then they get bunched up in a company—too many lips, not enough ass cheek to kiss. Yes-men can't be at the top. They got no one to kowtow to, and they implode. You, you're your own man. You juggle a lot at the school and for me. I got confidence in you." We were quiet for the rest of the ride.

"I wish I had it," I said after we stopped in front of the OBI.

Brother Dom got off, struggling to swing his leg over because of the bin on the back and his tight pants. "The confidence? Self-assurance?"

I nodded.

"It will come when you get out in the world and see some of the losers that are getting by. Hard to believe."

I was surprised a brother would talk like that.

"You ever hear from your friend? The kid that took off?"

I shook my head.

"Think he'll come back?"

"Can't say. I guess they believe he will. Doc Washington hasn't made me, or anyone, his number two yet. That would look good on my resume."

"Don't worry about all that stuff now. I'll bring you out a beer." Brother Dom went up the steps and yelled, "Norm," as he banged the door open and walked in.

I drove around back, unstrapped the bin and carried it in. "Hi, Manny," I said.

"Jorgie," Manny said. He was watching a game show.

"Slow?"

He shrugged, not even looking at me.

"I got a bin for Frank from Brother Dom. Wanna see?"

He shrugged again.

"Have you heard from Zoie? How she is doin'? If she got settled somewhere?"

"I…" He turned to me. "No. Haven't heard a thing. And now Terri disappeared, just gone one night. Didn't take anything, not even her jacket. It was hanging on a barstool at the end of the night. No one knew where she went."

"Frank look upstairs?"

"Yeah. No sign. All her stuff there. I told Frank to call the police. He's afraid." He went back to the TV.

I put the bin on the counter and started unpacking the meat. "Should we put this in the walk-in?"

He shrugged.

"You mad at me?"

"Weird stuff goin' on, Jorgie. Best to unsituate yourself."

Frank came in and handed me a beer. "Don't open it until you're outside." He set to unwrapping the butcher paper. "Oh, beauties. Too good for anyone here. I might sell these back to my meat distributor or freeze them for ski season. Manny, look at these. We gotta find a recipe."

"Nice piece of meat," Manny said after barely looking.

"Slice them up. Make sure each steak has its own bone."

"Gonna be a big steak."

"We'll sell it as a steak for two. Triple the price that way. Maybe bring it out to the table and carve it into manageable slices in front of the customer."

"Who's gonna do that? The new waitress? Me?"

"All right, just butcher it up for now."

Frank left. Manny set to work. I went outside to the employee lounge to have my beer.

The night dragged. Nobody came out to talk to me like Zoie always would. I missed the way she touched my cheek that night, could still feel it, like it was warm there compared to the other side. I didn't have, now or before, anything that lingered the way that warmth did. Finally, Brother Dom came out. Not having Terri in there saved me some wait time.

He yelled, "Ride, muchachos!"

After we were on and had started her up, I asked, "Did you get any update about Zoie?"

"Nah, kiddo. Manny said something about someplace in Florida and a construction company job. Her cousin is down there. Nothing media worthy."

"Oh. I guess you were hearin' about Terri leaving and you wanted her around tonight?"

"No. Fucking bitch wasn't worth the trouble. Nobody gives a shit. Took off with some john with a shit-ton of drugs. That's everybody's guess."

"Too bad she ran Zoie off first."

"Neither one liked me much. What do I care?"

I drove Brother Dom back and then went up the hill and straight across the fields to the Butt, feeling all stubborn and pondering on if I would be able to sleep. But I did. I fell asleep right quick.

23

Artie is at his desk slowly going through emails. He is killing time, so he reads each one before deleting. He is bored. The long lunches, the late arrivals and early departures still don't make the day pass quickly. The focused survey is at a standstill. He has nothing but good things to report. He could finalize, but legal and the higher-ups won't allow him to close it and won't give him any other assignments.

Orange comes to Artie's desk. "We should talk in my office."

"Good," Artie says, popping up enthusiastically.

–Hope this is the start of the end for this unvaried hassle.

Orange waits for Artie to sit, then closes the door to his office before taking his seat. "Artie, there are going to be some changes."

"I'm for that. This is becoming a mind-numbing grind."

"Well, some people would be happy to not be busy."

"I'll trade."

"You and I know that's not an option. And not my call."

"Yes. I know, it's not personal. It's personnel."

Orange smirks. "This, what I brought you in to talk to you about today, is separate from your present duties."

"Oh, okay."

"I'm getting promoted. I'm moving to the NYC offices. I'll be heading up compliance and certifications for the lower part of the state. They were initially looking to move me to an Albany position. But you know how I dislike the snow." He grimaces at Artie—his eyes squinty.

–Expecting a laugh?

"This other position happened to open up, and they grabbed me. I haven't told anyone in the office yet. I won't go for a bit. As far as this position, I thought, because of your seniority you may have some expectation of getting the office. You know, promoted to my supervisory role."

–You have to feel the *but* coming. No doubt.

"However."

–Close enough.

"I didn't consider you to be enough of a people person to get the most out of it. Also, could be some animosity from the troops. They might consider it favoritism. Or that, because of your required extracurricular diversity training, you couldn't be fair to all employees."

"That was required to be expunged from my file by now."

"But everyone's aware of it, aren't they? Also, and I feel, as you probably will, that the higher-ups would see a recent drop in your productivity."

"What?"

"Your fault or not. They couldn't overlook it. Not at this time."

"That's ridiculous. They give me nothing to do and hold it against me."

–You don't even want his job, but this is detestable.

"I see your point. The whole office has productivity difficulties because of this particular school's issues. When you get back to your familiar assignments, things will return to normal."

–Guess they didn't hold the unit's productivity drop against you, Orange.

"The school doesn't seem to have any issues. It's like scrutiny for scrutiny's sake. Turn up the heat to see if they boil over, and then you can blame them for the mess."

"That may be, but as far as this office, that is the situation."

"I don't want your job. Maybe someday. I want my job. What I used to do. I liked it. It wasn't exciting, but I now have nothing to do. I have to sit at my desk and look busy. And I expect some coworkers know and resent me for it."

"I'm glad you're not disappointed. Keep this between us. Word is they are looking to promote from a different location. That way, no one in this office can think they were slighted."

"Or they'll all feel slighted."

"Except you."

–Not nice.

"Will I be able to discuss my situation with the new boss?"

"I wouldn't, until legal gives the go-ahead."

Artie's phone rings, and he glances at it. "It's the police from upstate. All right if I take it? It's probably about the missing student."

Orange leans forward. "Put me on speaker. I'd like to hear."

Artie answers.

"Hello, Mr. Alston. I'm Detective Brewer, and on speaker with me is Detective Hudson. You had called us a couple of weeks back, about the school near Laffton. About the student."

"Hello. My boss here at the State Education Department, Orange Benton, is on speaker with me. If that's okay."

There's a pause before Brewer says, "Yes, if you are. Is he aware of your car usage, the car with the official New York State tags?"

"Yes, certainly. For the focused survey I'm doing on the school and orphanage. That's why you're calling, isn't it? The missing boy? Swaine?"

"Well, we are the detectives assigned to that case, yes."

"Hey, Orange," Hudson says.

"Yes, Detective."

"Anyone ever call you O?"

"Not professionally."

"I meant friends. Like, 'Hey, O, it's good to see you.'"

"I was saying," Brewer interjects.

"Maybe high school," Orange responds anyway.

"I worked with this guy one time, he thought these other cops, he thought Bobby Neal was related to Tim O'Neill. Thought O was his middle initial. Or like a nickname: Tim-Oh!"

"We gotta…" Brewer says. "Let's get back to why we called. We don't have any new information on the missing student, Swaine. We are still actively pursuing that case. Do you have anything about that to tell us?"

"No," Artie says. "I was actually glad to see your call, hoping you had something good to report on that front."

"Is there anything else you want to tell us? About you going to the school?"

"What's a focused survey?" Hudson says over his partner.

"It's like an investigation. The school fell behind in administrative filings only. Nothing to do with the boy running off. The school and orphanage appear to be fine, and the survey will hopefully…" Artie looks at Orange. "End soon."

"Mr. Alston—"

"Please call me Artie."

"Artie, were you up by the school about two weeks ago?"

"Yes, that was the last time I was there. I went up after I had demanded a meeting with the school's principal, the headmistress, after they informed us—and not right away—that Swaine was missing, had run away. I had reached out to you the next morning. I was sure that was why you were calling today."

"So you were up there, driving the state vehicle?"

"Yes."

"At night?"

"I returned at night, due to the meeting time. I felt it couldn't wait, so I drove up that day, soon as I heard."

"Did you go anywhere else?"

"I stopped to eat on the way home."

"Where'd you eat?" Brewer asks.

"The closest place. The Old Bavarian Inn."

"The OBI," Hudson says enthusiastically.

"Have you been to that pub before?"

"Yes. One other time. There aren't many places to eat around the school."

"You're on a cell phone?"

"Yes, a work phone."

"I'm going to text you two pictures of a woman. Let me know when you get it."

Artie holds the phone back and answers the text when it comes in. He enlarges the mugshot of Terri and another photo of her that he can tell was taken at the OBI.

–Her.

"Do you know that woman?" Brewer continues.

"I saw her at the pub. That last night."

"She's missing. No one even called us to report it for a while. We think that night was the last night anyone ever saw her."

–She ran to the back of the pub. Into the darkness. Can't say that in front of Orange.

"I did interact with her, Detectives. She sat at my booth while I was eating. Said she was country friendly. She asked me to buy her a drink, and I did. Then she got up to get it at the bar. I left, thought maybe she scammed me. I was embarrassed."

"You stopped in town, in Laffton?"

"Yes. I pulled over to call my ex-wife. She didn't pick up, and I drove home."

"We grabbed your license plate from a security camera in town. That's how we came to you. Traced the plates to the NYSED. And they told us it was assigned to you."

"It is."

"We'd like to talk. Will you be back at the school soon?"

—You better go and discuss this away from Orange.

"I can drop everything and come up today. Be there in the afternoon. Have you checked into those men who live off that path, down the hill from the school campus? They call it a monastery. It's a religious group."

"We know about them. We are going to have to get over there. Only as a matter of procedure, of course. Apparently the school takes care of their grounds and plant ops. They have people up and down."

—Hope you didn't get Jorgie caught up in this, because of his going there.

"Probably head over there today. Will you be able to meet at the orphanage? Or maybe we meet at the OBI, to see if that rings any bells?"

"The school. If you want."

"Text me, and we'll pick one, meet up. Try to remember if she had a fight or other interesting interaction with anyone either time you were there."

"I remember she was very thin."

"Drug addict," Hudson says.

"We'll see you later," Brewer says and hangs up.

—When it rains, it pours.

Orange is making big eyes at Artie. "You got something to do now."

"This has nothing to do with the school."

"You brought up those men."

"If they're involved, they will have to dissolve their relationship."

"Better get going," Orange says. He gets up and opens the office door for Artie.

Artie buys a sandwich and two bottles of water to have later in the car so he won't have to stop on the trip back.

When Artie enters the campus, he stops the car, closes his eyes, lays his head back and exhales open-mouthed at the car's ceiling. The detective had texted him saying they would wait for him at the orphanage.

–Just tell the truth. Nothing was inappropriate.

He looks to what he assumes must be the detectives' car over near the Butt, in front of Doc Washington's pickup truck. He heads that way. He sees Headmistress and Doc Washington. His stomach hurts. He had only eaten half his sandwich.

–Too much raw onion in that chicken salad.

Before he gets out of the car, he takes a gulp of water. His stomach is gurgling loudly.

He walks to the side of the Butt where the four people are waiting for him. Headmistress is sitting in her golf cart. Driving gloves on. Skirt bunched above her knees. Light, tight sweater despite the fall chill. Detectives in brown sport coats. Doc Washington dressed for labor, hands behind his back.

–Like he's handcuffed.

"Hello, Artie," Doc Washington says. "These are the detectives that wanted to speak with you. Detective Brewer and Hudson."

–Unusually friendly to you? Or gloating?

"Hello. Hello, Detectives. Good afternoon, Headmistress."

"Hudson," the closest detective says and shakes Artie's hand.

"Brewer," the other says and shakes. "Thanks for making the drive."

–Headmistress is suspicious? Why no greeting?

"Part of the job. Under different circumstances, I would say it's nice to get out of the office."

"Yeah. Know what you mean," Hudson says.

"Anything you want to tell us, Artie?" Headmistress says.

"I hope you and the rest of the school aren't too put off by all this."

"You seem rather cool about it." She twists away from Artie, facing the woods.

"I doubt this has anything to do with the school."

"But here we are," Headmistress says. Doc Washington huffs and rocks on his heels.

—You can't allow her this moment, not so easily.

"Any news on Swaine, Detectives? Any possible connection with the girl, umm?"

"Terri," Brewer says. "Nothing really. We are looking all around. Terri had no connection to the school or the monastery. Can't see how she could know Swaine."

"Do you suspect foul play?" Artie asks.

"Drugs and prostitution," Hudson says plainly.

"Allegedly," Brewer corrects. "Regarding Terri, she's a name that has come up before. She was arrested for suspicion of prostitution when a former landlord had her tossed out. He dropped the charges after he got rid of her. Must have been happy to be done with it, I guess."

"People get prescription drugs and sell them all the time, all around the county," Hudson says. "They go to multiple clinics. There isn't any real top of an organization. Everyone involved is low-level, and drug addicts don't get time, only treatment."

"It's just this sort of organically developed wave of drugs. Glad to hear it hasn't reached these children."

"Blessed by the Lord," Headmistress says. "These girls have had enough hardship. And I will tell you officers, honestly, some of them had drug issues before enrolling. No addicts, we don't have the re-sources to deal with that. And thank you for fighting this scourge and keeping it away from my girls."

"You're welcome," Hudson says, beaming.

"Artie, can I speak with you alone?" Brewer asks.

"Of course." The two step away from the group.

–You're not really out of earshot.

"Did you think about your interactions with Terri?"

"Yes. It was short. Like I said, I bought her a drink and regretted it. I didn't know she was having a difficult time."

"You didn't suspect she was a prostitute?"

"No."

"Young, pretty women approach you often?"

"I am a trusting person, I suppose."

"Did Terri mention any names? Any plans for later that night?"

–Should you tell them about her leaving the side of your car and going behind the pub? Someone may have seen you.

"The bartender's name, Carton, about buying the drink. She asked if I'd be coming back sometime."

Brewer thinks for a moment. "Did she offer you drugs or other services? Try to sell you?"

"No."

"Exchange phone numbers?"

"No."

–Are you a suspect?

"Professionally, do you feel anyone at this school could be involved?"

"No, Detective. I have only the highest regard for how this place is run."

"But you're investigating it."

"As I explained on the phone, this is a focused survey. It was initiated for administrative reasons. No complaints were filed, and certainly no criminal activity was ever suspected. It has been mostly routine, except that the facility is overseen by both the Education Department and Family Services. Maybe because of that, some paperwork fell through the cracks."

"Well, I know all about how that can happen with paperwork. Not always an accident, though. Is it?"

"They have complied with all the requests from the State. Nothing fishy."

"Okay, well, thanks for coming up." Brewer hands Artie his card. "Call if you remember anything. Oh, and the guys down the hill. You meet any of them?"

"My first day here. I was given a tour by Headmistress. She didn't want to go down there and was busy. It's school property. I thought I should see what was going on. One of the students, Jorgie—very nice young man—drove me down there. I met the leader. Kyle."

"Master Kyle. We met him today."

"Yes, that was how he was introduced."

"What's your impression of them?"

"Sincere. I had a quick look around. I was assured they didn't interact with the students and stayed in their own area: isolated. I did see two of them at the eco-friendly announcement a couple of weeks ago."

"What did they say?"

"Nothing. They kept to themselves. We didn't interact at all."

"Thanks." Brewer turns and rejoins the others. Artie follows. "We are going to get back. Thanks for your help today, Mr. Washington, Headmistress Hunt."

Doc Washington nods.

Headmistress says, "Thank you for your service. I'm praying for you, as well as Swaine, and now I'm going to add that poor woman to the list of people that need our Lord."

The detectives nod, get in their sedan and drive away.

"That was a long trip, just for that," Headmistress says. "Odd they wanted to grill you away from Doc Washington and me."

"I wasn't being grilled. I was allaying their fears about the school."

"Not allaying about yourself?"

Doc Washington again huffs and rocks on his heels.

–Suspicious of you?

"That wasn't necessary. I was glad to come up. It seemed important."

"I heard your investigation is winding down, ever...so...slowly."

"Slowly indeed. I wouldn't worry about this missing woman changing that. No relationship at all."

"Only if you make it."

"There's nothing there," Doc Washington says. "Detectives are just being thorough. I hope it doesn't distract them from finding Swaine."

"Such a shame," Headmistress says.

"Indeed," Doc Washington agrees.

"Very sad," Artie says. "Getting colder. Can't see how he could survive on the streets."

"He's a wily young man," Doc Washington says.

"Really?" Headmistress says.

−Glad someone else is getting some hot water.

"Yes, Headmistress. Boy's learned a lot. He could get a job in an auto shop. Landscaping. Apprentice a plumber. Even a restaurant. Good with his hands. Runs things through."

"You almost sound proud. It's like you're pedestaling him."

"He was a good boy."

−Is.

"I've got my girls to see to. To make sure they don't wind up like that Torri."

−Terri.

"I'll get back to it also."

"I will keep in touch," Artie says. "Please, again, I would like to hear any news about Swaine as soon as you two do. Anything."

"Of course," Headmistress says. "Have a smooth ride back to your office."

"At this hour, I will probably go straight home."

"Behave yourself on the way," Headmistress says and drives away.

−What?

"Did she mean something by that?" Artie asks Doc Washington.

"She's suspicious. You know how she is about those girls. Protective.

She likes you, though. Imagine if she didn't? When the investigation is over and the police are done, you'll see."

–Could he mean that?

"I don't see how I rated her last comment," Artie says as Doc Washington turns and walks away toward the open garage doors of the Butt.

–No goodbye?

"Doc Washington. Could I use the bathroom before I go?"

"This way," he says, not turning back or stopping. He points Artie to a narrow wood door along the side of the garage bay. Artie goes in.

–Old-fashioned water closet.

The room is small and only has a seatless toilet bowl with a pipe running down to it from the ceiling and a hanging, pull-chain light bulb.

–Smells, no ventilation or sink. Not even a mirror.

When Artie is done, he exits the room and finds a slop sink along a wall. There is only a cold-water tap. He washes his hands with pumiced, grease-cleaner soap. He grabs some rags from a box above the sink and dries his hands. He looks around for Doc Washington, even checking the office, but doesn't see him. Artie looks around the shop: no one is there. He heads outside.

–Would have been nice to talk with Jorgie, see how he's handling his friend's disappearance.

Coach Irma speed walks across Artie's path and past him. "Coach Irma" is sewn in an arc across her back above the number fourteen; St Margaret's is below. "Better get to class, young man. Extra push-ups today for being Larry Lateness." She doesn't look back.

Artie walks back to his car. He considers stopping by Headmistress' office to chat over tea.

–It's a bad time.

He leaves a voicemail for his ex and drives home.

24

Artie has been off the thruway for more than twenty minutes. The few flakes he noticed at the toll booth have become sleety, and increased in speed, they crackle when they strike his windshield.

—There are many fewer cars on the road, even less than usual. You should have checked the weather forecast for Laffton, NY, not just for by the office. It was unseasonably cold when you left work, but this is more severe.

Before Artie left the office, and despite the fact that the office was being decorated for Thanksgiving by some of his coworkers, Orange had been in a surly mood. Weeks later, he was still rooted in the same office, at the same desk, at the same pay level. He had called Artie's phone. "Can I see you in my office?" It had sounded to Artie like a little bad news was coming his way.

"It's over," was mostly what Orange had said. Then they went over bureaucratic things like his assignments being returned. The school was done with. Legal agreed all was in order. Paperwork completed long ago was now satisfactory. They didn't talk about outside interference or Orange's lack of movement. Artie had to return the car at the end of the week and had no specific work to do until Monday, so he had decided to get in a last trip upstate, tell Headmistress in person. His last chance to make the ride in the state-paid-for vehicle.

–She'll feel like you're giving her great news. A big burden will be lifted from her. And after the professional supervisory role is lifted, you can speak to her as a colleague: ask her for coffee, discuss education trends. Dinner? Maybe she would consider meeting you in Manhattan for a date.

The snow picks up. The roads are wet but not icy. Snow accumulates in the trees and is beginning to form a slushy layer on the roadway.

–Front-wheel-drive cars do very well in snow. Besides, this area knows how to handle winter conditions. It's not a problem. Could even stay over if you had to—if things go very well.

Artie smiles. He slows on the curves and admires the beauty of the ever-whitening trees at each side of the road. He fiddles with the wipers and defroster.

–Not far now. Big decision, why rehash it? Such messy litter in the background. Let it go; it's over. Maybe the relationship with Headmistress will be better. Maybe she would like to hear about all the funding the monastery is getting from ethically compromised corporations. But they are passing it on to the orphanage; she has to know.

Artie had passed time at work investigating, first, Key Deer Energy's ties to the school and monastery, and then some other corporate sponsors whose names he had heard. And the background of the monks. They were all former corporate execs who fell out of favor, made stocks tumble or caused investigations to be started by different, mostly federal, oversight agencies. Then a legal name change and they become a monk—following a large donation, with lots of pass-through fees that wind up as rent and other monies paid to the school, to the orphanage. The board of the orphanage was mostly people tied in with the same corporations. Corporations with histories of making large political donations.

–Master Kyle? He's Edward Dill. You have to move on. Not the Education Department's bailiwick. If you tell Headmistress, then she may tell some other agency—you know what contempt she has for those monks. Do you? Is the school providing cover for this? Which one is primary? No way to tell.

Artie sees the sign for the school is pelted white. He turns up the driveway and notices the snow is beginning to accumulate. When he exits the path onto campus proper, he sees they have an inch or two of fluffy snow covering the landscape. He sees a boy on a quad, wearing a helmet and heavy clothes, emerging from the Butt building's garage. There is a plow attached to the front of his machine, and he has begun to clear the school's roads and pathways.

–Jorgie? Swaine? You can't tell with that big helmet he has on. Wouldn't be surprised if Swaine returned and the school never notified you. He wouldn't fare well on his own in this climate. Tough winters up here, not just the fact that it's farther north. It's altitude. No one else is outside. I wonder if they do snow days?

Artie pulls in front of the Saints' building and puts his jacket on. He considers wearing his hat but fixes his hair instead. He heads inside.

–Car is going to be freezing when you get back in it.

"Hello, Sandi," he says, trying to sound cheery.

–Was that forced? Still need to sound professional.

"Good afternoon, Artie. What brings you visiting in this terrible weather?"

"I had good news that I wanted to give you, you all, Headmistress, in person."

"We all like to get good news," Sandi says, getting up. She walks to Headmistress' office and knocks on the jamb. "Knock, knock. Artie is here for you, with good news." She turns back to Artie, stretching out her hand, inviting him into the office. "The intercom is broken."

Artie goes past her, squeezing sideways through the doorway so as not to make contact with her body. "Hello there." He grabs a chair and lugs it to the front of her desk.

"Hello, Artie. Nice to see you. Haven't visited in a while. Rough day to travel."

"Yes, well, not on the way up, it wasn't. But I suppose I will have to take it slow on the way back. The road crews in this area must be used to and well prepared for these occurrences. Winter comes every year, as I say."

–You do?

"I'd hate to get stuck and have to spend the night."

"Where would you do that?" Headmistress asks.

"Anyway, the good news."

"Everyone likes to give good news in person. Bad news, not so much."

"True. You haven't heard? Have you?"

"No. I didn't talk with any state personnel recently. It has been some time."

"Yes. The focused survey did bog down. I was waiting for legal to clear it. I wasn't sure if they would notify you directly."

"No," Headmistress says plainly, slowly shaking her head and smiling.

"The focused survey has concluded, and the school has gone back to full accreditation and good standing all around."

"That is good for you," Headmistress says, leaning forward onto her forearms that she has crossed on her desk. "You won't have to make the trip anymore."

"Oh, I didn't mind. Maybe I would like a position where I get out more often. In the field, as we say."

"I knew we would be here one day. Comparing us to other schools that have students with more mainstream backgrounds would be unfair to our girls."

"That's the thing. You have so many fine students enrolled, it is hard to believe they are orphans, I mean displaced children. Your test scores are more than competitive. There seems to be only a disparity with the boys, perhaps relating to their career track in which they are placed."

"I don't want to hear you talk down these boys."

"I wasn't…"

–How does she twist you into these tight spots?

"Well, now that the survey has concluded, the school will receive written notice. Probably on Monday. I hope it wasn't too much of an inconvenience?"

–Nothing?

"Do you ever go out for coffee?" Artie asks. "Is there a good coffeehouse? Not too far a drive?"

"Sandi," Headmistress calls out, and Sandi appears in the doorway. "What's the name of the coffeehouse with the delicious cinnamon pecan ring? In Creeks Ridge?"

"I think that's it. Creeks Ridge Bakery and Café. Big with the skiers."

"Thank you," Artie says to Sandi, who lingers in the doorway.

–Is she going to stay there?

"Delicious cake," Headmistress repeats, and Sandi disappears.

"Would you like to meet for coffee sometime?"

–You left that one hanging out there.

"We could confer on all matters educational, personal, this beautiful area."

"Artie. We have a professional relationship."

"The focused survey is complete."

"It sounds like you are asking me on a date. Is that professional?"

"I…at this moment…we have completed that relationship. And I would like to get to know you better. Date? Oh, I suppose."

"I don't think I want to date a pencil pusher who only cares about the orderliness of his paperwork. I have the best interest of these girls to look out for, not paperwork. I don't see how I could."

–Shot down. You were impulsive.

"I understand. I never thought you were my type but felt, and I wish you understood this about me, I also only have the best interests of the students in mind. I thought that was something we had in common, and we had a professional bond there, as well as a cordial one."

"Well, we won't be bonding, as you call it," Headmistress says, stands and walks toward the door.

Artie eyes her rear and asks, "Any word on Swaine? I was hoping he would have returned. We haven't heard a thing at my office. I am still quite concerned."

Headmistress gets to the doorway, leans against the jamb with her hands crossed, lifting her breasts, and crosses her high heels. "No sign of Swaine. We have a new foundling boy now. Some emergency that Mr. Bradley alerted us to."

"Oh really?"

"Yes. Police seem to have lost interest. Doc Washington still drives around looking for him, at night after the boys go to bed. He even asked some drug-dealing-looking types. It sounded awful. Swaine's still in my prayers. Sandi, what was that rumor you were telling me about the woman in town the police went to the monks about?"

Sandi comes back to the doorway. "Oh, Townie Terri. That's what I heard someone say. Apparently the police found a body, female body. They are waiting to make a definitive ID before announcing it, but there are rumors around. Someone told me. Sounds just ugly."

"At least her parents will have closure. I will pray for them as well."

"If it is her," Artie says, remaining in his seat, twisting to face the women.

–That sounded awkward.

"Oh," Sandi says. "It's not like there's a serial killer around." And she slips off.

"I only meant, they haven't IDed her re—"

"Who else could it be?"

"Yes. That would be a huge coincidence, if it weren't."

"Coincidence? Is that how you would describe it?"

–You're floundering.

"I did want to ask about something else, if you have a moment."

"All right," she says, remaining in the doorway, arms and legs crossed.

–Was hoping she would rejoin.

"I, as I stated previously, recognize that you are doing a superb job with the students. There was an old note that was expunged, concerning your Regents' standardized test scores."

"Old news."

"Yes. Was there something particular you would like to share that allowed you to make those improvements."

"The students change, Artie. That's all. If I remember, we had some boys who dragged down our averages. They didn't take serious things seriously. You know our motto: a sua intentione relaxaretur. Latin for proud woman. We take it seriously."

–Isn't *femina* Latin for woman?

"Well, I am happy for your success."

–Still won't budge from her goodbye position in the door.

"I was interested in mentoring Jorgie. He has good test scores. I discern he could do better than his current track."

"This again? Doc Washington is the boy's mentor. We don't need another."

"It would be voluntarily, on my own time. I am qualified and have the background check per state regulations."

"No."

–Strike three. Time to go—gave it your best shot.

Artie gets up slowly. "Should I put this chair back?"

Headmistress comes to Artie, lifts the chair and returns it to its place by the wall.

"I'll be on my way." Artie walks out.

"It's bad out there," Sandi says to Artie as he passes her desk. "Take it slow. Nice seeing you."

"It was nice seeing you. Take care." Artie zips his jacket as he steps outside. Snow pelts him, and cold slices through his pants. The sky has turned dark. The wind is picking up.

–Visibility really diminished. Drive slowly until the thruway. You'll be fine once you get south and down from the mountains.

Artie gets in the car and starts it.

–Cold. No snow brush.

Artie exits the car and uses his forearm to quickly clear the front and rear windows. He pulls out his phone after getting back in, calls his ex and leaves her a voicemail about wanting to stop by. He notices an incoming voicemail from an unknown number that could be work. He sets his guidance on the phone and starts out. He sees the school's roads are in good shape as three quads with their headlights on are now working to plow and salt the roads and paths.

–What will become of Jorgie when he graduates? Maybe you pick up a coffee for the ride?

Artie stops before entering the road and searches his map app for the coffeehouse, but it is out of his way.

–If the weather wasn't this bad, you could go. Check out the lay of the land in case something worked out with her? You never know.

Artie resets his guidance to home, then hits play on his voicemail. The car fishtails as it enters the road. The guidance is taking him away from town.

–Roads not so good. This app sends you a different way every time. But I'm glad not to be going by the pub, that poor girl.

He realizes he can't hear the voicemail and fiddles with it to restart the message with the volume up. Artie turns his wipers and defroster to high because of the worsening conditions. He leans over the steering wheel, unable to see the center line of the road. The speedometer is out of his view.

"Mr. Alston, this is Yancy from Albany. We recently received—well, this morning actually—your name for our position search. This would be a promotion to a supervisor's role in the Manhattan office. I was told you did a great job in your previous assignment. We would love to interview you. It would have to be in person, sorry about that. Previous searches haven't turned up a qualified candidate. I think it would be a good fit for you."

–What? Can't be.

The car slides some more.

–Orange's job? Could you do that to him? Would be just deserts. Nice to get a change of offices. Tougher commute. Would need a company car. Have to listen again.

Artie adjusts the phone to replay. He smiles. The car gets sluggish in the deepening snow. He sees a rise followed by a decline as the road curves left. He gives the car gas.

–Hope you can make it up this hill.

25

Artie is woken by Brother Dom. "How are you doing, Crash?"

Artie groans and looks around.

–Where are you?

When he turns his head, he gets a sharp pain that feels like his skull is being pressed from the inside out. His ears are ringing. "What? Where?"

"You had a car accident, Art. You were driving in the snow, went off the road, down a steep hill and hit a tree dead-on. You'd a been dead-on if you didn't have the airbags."

"I remember. I was...It was hard to see. I was going over the hill. I turned the wheel for a curve, and the car just went the other way."

"Do you remember me and the kiddo bringing you inside?"

"No." Artie moves his hand slowly up to his head and touches the large bandages.

"I changed that for you last night. You didn't wake up during the procedure. I was worried. Worried that the gash wasn't your problem. You seem concussed."

"Yeah. Thank you. I could have frozen to death without you."

"A can of corn. Made me feel young. Basic first aid stuff I learned in the army, a long time ago."

"Who's kiddo?"

"Jorgie. He got stuck down here also. Snow was crazy for this time of year."

"It was bad."

"He went up on the quad to get someone to call you an ambulance. It really warmed up already. Snow is melting. Main roads should all be cleared so we can get you to the hospital."

"My car?"

"Totaled. Worse shape than you. Are you warm enough? You didn't bleed through the bandage again. I'll leave it for the pros." Brother Dom holds Artie's head still with one hand and checks the placement and security of the bandage with the other. He looks at Artie's eyes. "Any other pains anywhere?"

Artie pulls his knees up one at a time. "Ugh. Nothing like my head, but knees hurt, my back."

"You're havin' a rough time of it, Art. You know what the monks say: it's tough to forget that harsh world when the world don't wanna forget you."

"Yes?"

Jorgie comes into the Dragon AI Prayer Room. Two monks are with him, who say, "Namaste," as they enter. One is carrying a stretcher. Brother Dom carefully slides Artie's glasses on, slipping the temples under the bandages.

–Better.

"Thank you, Jorgie."

"It was all Brother Dom. Shoulda seen him go through that snowstorm."

"Thank you all."

The two new monks do not speak.

"Brother Dom, we got the monastre's electric side-by-side parked right outside the Grouse Pharma door."

"That's the Key Deer people's one they gave us for emergencies, right?"

"Yeah. The one Master Kyle was the only person believed you'd need it. Extra-long bed that can hold this stretcher it came equipped with."

"Good."

"Good," Artie agrees.

"And the ambulance from town is on the way. It will meet us up at the school."

"Let's load him up." Brother Dom directs everyone. "Kiddo, you got the head and the head only: precious cargo. Keep it steady and even with the shoulders, no turning. Hands underneath, keep the head cradled with your forearms. You two each get by the shoulders. I got the knees." They lay the basket-stretcher next to Artie. The four position themselves around him.

Brother Dom says, "One, two, three, go." And they lift Artie just enough to clear the top of the basket-stretcher's rail, then over and gently down. "Straps across the top. Kiddo, check that closet. We gotta get something to cover him more and some stuff to put by his ears to stabilize his head."

–This all seems so nice of them. Glad you didn't bad-mouth them to Headmistress now. She'll hear about this. What will she think? What will Eggrett say? Will she find out?

Jorgie checks the closet but then leaves the room. He comes back in as the straps are snugged around Artie. "I got these towels and cowls. I got one for you too, Brother Dom. I figured it's still real cold and we'll have to take it slow."

"Good thinking." They cover Artie, shape a rolled towel into a U and place it to secure the head.

"We'll do two at the head, two at the feet. Kiddo, come back with me. Ready slowly lift." They get Artie up, the two monks each hold the rails by Artie's shoulders, and Brother Dom and Jorgie are at the sides of his shins. "We're walkin'," Brother Dom says loudly as they exit the room.

Artie has to close his eyes as they exit into sunlight but gives another look at the door despite the discomfort. "Beautiful door."

The bearers can't coordinate their steps on the stairway, and Artie's body is rocked as they descend to ground level. "Steady, steady," Brother Dom says. The snow crunches and slops as they go. Then they slide him headfirst into the bed of the side-by-side with the Key Deer Energy logo on each side.

After they secure the stretcher to the vehicle, the two assistants bow to Artie and say, "Namaste." They stay there patiently, to see them off.

"Thank you, thank all of you."

—Good fellows.

Artie, with difficulty, turns his head slightly up and sees Jorgie's back, in the driver's seat, Brother Dom next to him, elbow thrown over the seat back, body turned, checking on Artie. "This is no smooth road. You been on it, right? It's steep. This may be more than uncomfortable when your blood rushes out of your head down toward your feet. But you got the best driver around."

"Yes."

"This is the inaugural ride up the hill for this electric buggy, and it's gotta do it in the snow. If it can't make it, we gotta get Doc Washington's six-wheel and throw you in the back of that. Take her away, kiddo. Slow."

The side-by-side moves along quietly, slowly. "You probably want to close your eyes," Brother Dom says. "It's a bright day."

"The sun through the trees is beautiful."

—It really is.

The side-by-side inclines, and Artie can see the monastery building surrounded by slushy snow before it slips away behind the thick weave of branches. His head throbs. He closes his eyes.

"There's a lesson for you, Jorgie. I hope you appreciate me telling you to carry the stretcher by the feet. The head and torso end is much heavier. Remember that."

"I like helpin' people. I don't mind the heavy end."

—He's a good one, that Jorgie.

"How's she handling?" Brother Dom asks Jorgie.

"Fine. Steady as always."

"It's very quiet."

"Sure is."

"First time driving an electric? I know you told me Doc Washington didn't have you driving them, wasn't convinced these electrics could handle the difficult terrain."

"They handle it just fine. Quiet and smooth like always."

—Good, glad Washington's wrong about the clean-energy technology. He's old-fashioned. But heartened to learn he has continued looking for Swaine.

"So you drove the electric before? Or didn't?" Brother Dom asks, not facing Jorgie, his arm still slung over the seat back. Jorgie readjusts his seating position. "I thought you said you didn't drive one 'cause Doc Washington didn't trust them."

—What's he picking on Jorgie for?

"The day they came with the donation. I drove it that day. I meant I didn't drive one up and back to the monastre. You know? The rough terrain. Only that day across a fairly level field."

—He must have liked giving Veronica that ride.

"Yeah. I didn't notice that day. It wasn't steep like this."

"I got a pretty good sense of them. The quiet engine is what you notice mostly. Drive is almost the same. No low gears to feel out."

They continue their slow ascent. Artie's pain lessens, though he keeps his eyes closed.

"Did you hear the rumor?" Brother Dom asks Jorgie as he faces forward and puts a foot up on the dashboard. "About them finding a body in the woods. People are saying it's Terri."

"No, I didn't hear that."

Artie wants to respond but just winds up grimacing.

"I sure am glad we didn't go adventuring that night, the last night she was seen. The cops would have locked me up. I got that kinda face. Plus, I'm in the system. I was never indicted, convicted or nothing. Did I ever tell you that one?"

"No, Brother Dom."

"Don't know if I'm supposed to, but between you me and the trees, the company I worked for did consulting work. I was mostly a marketing guy. We found ways to save companies money, which to them was profit. I had this idea about foam containers for takeout food. They were cheaper, wider, and lighter and could separate your hot and cold items until you got home. Well, these things were like paper airplanes that never degraded. All with company logos on 'em. They were being blown out of landfills into parks and natural land. People went crazy, and not only the greenies. It was in the news. The companies were sued by fifteen states. The producers, designers, retailers, even individual franchisees—well, they had people bringing in full garbage bags and dumping 'em out on the floor of their restaurants. You know what a franchise is, right?"

"Sure."

"Well, it all circled back, and each one of them pointed the finger at this one guy: me. We took a bath. Me too, because I had a piece of the manufacturer, you know, on the side that I should have—maybe legally required—declared. And that's how I got signed up at the monastery, a victim of my own optimism. I didn't know I had to do aerodynamic studies on food containers. So long story short, career over, I wind up at this place."

"Things happen for a reason," Jorgie says. "If you didn't make them flyin' containers, Mister would be dead."

"There's too many what-ifs involved there to make that correlation, kiddo. It was hubris, thinking I was gonna make it big. You know what hubris is?"

"Yeah, it's that dip for pita bread."

"Whuh?" Brother Dom says and then laughs. "You almost had me there, kiddo. Master Kyle, he had some problems as the numbers guy for some big casino's sports-betting app. That's how he got signed up. Odds were too good. Even the house is only allowed to win so much."

"Here we are at the top of the trail, Mister," Jorgie says, glancing back. "Remember? Gonna be a bit of a lurch when we get over."

Artie groans as the side-by-side pitches and then roughly lands flat.

"Sorry, Mister. I guess this one, being a longer machine than I'm used to, it rocked a bit more and a bit harder."

"That's okay. You're doing a great job."

–Good lad.

"It's gotta be done, like rippin' off a bandage dried into the scab. There's the ambulance, by that house," Brother Dom says.

The side-by-side turns, and Artie's skull throbs as they head downhill and blood moves to his head.

–Are we going toward the chancellor's lodgings?

"Looks like they're all set up waiting for us, Art. You brought out a little crowd. These people ain't used to this excitement."

The side-by-side comes to a stop.

"Oh, Artie. I am so troubled this happened."

Artie opens his eyes and sees Headmistress, wearing sunglasses, bent, face hovering over him.

"I never should have let you go out in the snowstorm. I should have insisted you stay over. Here."

–Her place?

Artie smiles. "I'll be okay. Jorgie and this Brother Dom, they saved me."

–Still all made-up, showing cleavage.

"Yes, you will be okay. Hang in there. And I will make sure you get home if I have to drive you myself. I will."

"Jorgie did a great job," Brother Dom says loudly to Headmistress as he steps back.

"That'd be nice."

–Did a door open for you and her?

"Can we get in there, ma'am?" an EMT that Artie can't see says timidly.

Artie, with his face stuck pointing up, can only see those who move close to him. He can hear a group of people talking nearby.

"Soon as I see you off, I am going to the chapel to pray." Headmistress steps aside saying, "Go right ahead, young lady. Take good care of Artie."

"He's concussed," Brother Dom says.

The EMT appears over Artie.

–Looks so young.

"Sir, do you know your name?"

"It's Artie," Headmistress says.

"Ma'am, we need him to answer these questions. It's part of patient assessment."

"Artie Alston," Artie says.

"Where are you?"

"The orphanage."

"What day is it?"

"Wednesday."

She palpates Artie's arms, legs and ribs. "Good. We are going to get you in the ambulance. First, we have to get you out of this rescue basket and onto the backboard that's on our stretcher and secure you.

Then we'll slide you in the back, check vitals and head to county. You seem pretty good for all you went through."

"They took good care of me. Getting cold."

"We'll have you inside the ambulance in a minute."

The two EMTs move around Artie and get ready to lift him.

"I'll help," Jorgie says. He climbs onto the side-by-side's bed adjacent to Artie's shoulders and helps lift Artie over to the EMT's stretcher.

–Good, kiddo. Don't listen to Brother Dom. Taking the easy way is not always best. Kiddo?

The EMTs secure Artie's head with the immobilizer blocking and strap him down. Coach Irma comes over to Artie's side.

–How many people are watching?

"You should have worn your helmet," Coach Irma tells Artie.

–Is she still in a softball uniform?

"I was in my car."

"Practice how you play. Practice makes your whole game better."

"Coach," Doc Washington calls. "Let the EMTs do what they need to do."

The EMTs start rolling Artie away, past Coach Irma's face. She smiles, takes off her cap and waves goodbye to Artie with it.

The stretcher stops moving and starts to tip. "Hold up," the EMT at Artie's feet says. "Snow's too much for the wheels. We'll lower and carry the last few yards."

"Ten-four," the other EMT at Artie's head says. "Ready, down."

A click and Artie is lowered. He can see more faces now. Some familiar, some not.

"I'll help," Jorgie says and appears next to Artie. The EMT by his head moves opposite Jorgie.

"Up on one, two, three," the EMT at the feet says, and they easily lift him, walk a few wobbly feet and then smoothly slide Artie into the back of the ambulance. The EMTs climb in and start checking Artie's blood pressure.

"Thanks, Jorgie, and good luck to you," Artie says to Jorgie, whose face he can see just beyond his feet, standing outside the ambulance watching the EMTs work.

"I believe it's ultimate, you two helpin' like this," Jorgie says. "Is it hard to be an ambulance driver?"

"It takes some doing," one of them says while she keeps working. "Worth it. Give it a shot. They give a class at the community college."

"Maybe when I graduate."

"You'd be a great EMT," Artie says to encourage Jorgie.

"Thank you, Mister," Jorgie says and slips away.

Doc Washington appears at the ambulance doors. "The police said if they don't make it here with the ambulance, they'll meet you at the hospital to talk reports and if you need anything."

"Sure," Artie replies.

"Also, Jorgie and Brother Dom want to come to the hospital and check on you once you're settled, if that's all right."

"That'd be nice."

"I'd have to drive them."

"Okay." Artie's head is starting to hurt behind his eyes from straining to look past his feet.

"Jorgie's gotta bring the side-by-side back down to the club and get himself settled. Then we'll be over. You'll be plenty busy over there anyway."

Artie closes his eyes and tries to relax. He hears Headmistress say, "Doc Washington, meet me at the office after the ambulance gets off campus."

"We have to get moving," an EMT tells Doc Washington. She shuts the ambulance doors. One EMT goes up front to the driver's seat, and the other sits by Artie's head and buckles in. She knocks two times above her head on the bulkhead. The ambulance drives away.

–Everyone's so nice to you when you need them.

26

My intonation will be broken. I will hear the mop cadet calling as he draws closer in, driving the machine.

"We got Mister in the ambulance, Master Kyle. He'll be okay."

I will bow as he continues to the recently built Key Deer Energy Garage that houses the vehicles and charges them from solar panels, freeing our earth a little.

His opening of the garage door, situating the charging cable and adjusting the equipment—each in their precise place—will distract me from my course of prayer for the injured and prayer for the monastery that the incident will not bring bad karma to it and those who reside within it. Though my place at the top of the stair, surrounded by the melting snow, in front of the Grouse Pharma door will be the perfect place for contemplation, the silence will be abated by him.

The mop cadet will return, back in front, on the bottom step, calling my name. I will look down at him. His boots and lower pant legs will be soaked from sloshing through the wet snow.

"Master Kyle?"

I will bow to him, attempting to convey the importance of peace, of quiet.

"I ain't gonna be able to shovel the snow from the steps and such. Gotta head back up in a minute. Goin' to the hospital to visit. I could give you an update, though Brother Dom, he's comin'. I guess you can get the info from him."

I will bow to him again.

"Can I ask you a question?"

"I thought you were called to the hospital?"

"I got a minute. Do you believe confession can help a soul?"

"We do not believe in structured confession. I have imparted this wisdom to you before."

"I remember. But do you believe it helps people? Like takes a load off people, even if it doesn't help them in the afterlife, heaven?"

"I suppose, if one believed that being confessed and forgiven freed one to enter their version of heaven, when their mortal life ended, then yes. It would unburden them in this world. But confession and forgiveness are different and distinct things."

"Yeah. So just because you confess doesn't mean God forgives you. Is that what you're sayin'?"

"It is not my place to say. Maybe you should return and dwell on it. Open your mind and find your peace."

"Sure. I have my own peace, as you say. You monks almost got me in trouble for stealin' food from the school. Do you have peace from that? This school is all I have."

"Stealing? Is that what you want to confess?"

"No. I feel like I was told to steal."

"The brothers and I are under no confessorial vow."

"One night, I decided I am going to be the cheetah and not the gazelle—like you told me."

"I never said that. You misunderstood—"

"So I sneak out of bed after everyone was sleepin'. I slip on my new, dark blue coveralls and put a cowl on over it—one I stole from Brother Dom's closet."

"You do not have to explain."

The mop cadet will go on anyway. "I get outside and unplug one of them new, quiet, battery-powered quads. Load up a tarp, garbage bags and rake. I got gloves on my hands because they can get real cold holding them handlebars. I drive away, behind the Butt, no helmet, just the cowl's hood. I can see all right by the dim landscape lights. Gotta go no headlights, until I get back into the woods on what Swaine used to call the deer trails. I loop uphill, back around, way in, beyond the Joes' buildings. The trail then brings you downhill from there and close to the clearing. Then it exits right up there, near onto campus where it meets the top of the trail leadin' down to the monastre. Like a big semicircle around the campus."

"Monastery."

"I ride that monastre trail for a bit. Had to kill the headlights again when I got close to the clearing but soon veered off onto a trail that took me back, going close to the open space by the Key Deer Energy Greenhouse. Then I am on my usual trail that winds close to the road, not too far from where Mister crashed. I go real slow, takin' my time. I don't want any cars seein' my lights from the road.

"Cross the road, further down than usual, past the bar. The OBI. First, I took a good long time makin' sure the road was quiet."

"We all appreciate quiet," I will say, trying to get him to truncate his petty tale.

"Quiet. The electric quad's sure quiet. You were sure right to want that side-by-side."

I will bow to him, but he continues.

"Almost no vibration. I don't get an erection like I sometimes do when I'm alone on the gas-powered quads, and the one-seater handles better than the two-seater I usually ride down here. Anyways, the streetlight by the road and the parkin' lot are a good bit away. OBI's fairly dead. I cross the road unseen and make my way to the far back of the OBI property, quite a bit off, with the quad hidden in the nature.

"I wait in a dark spot where I can see people if they come out. I am off to the side in case Manny—Manny's the cook there, nice to me—well, in case Manny came out the back door to the dumpster or something. No activity. I've waited there plenty, but you probably know that. Someone comes out and gets in their little car and starts it. He lingers. Then Terri comes out and goes to the car. Terri's the one that drove Zoie away. Zoie's the waitress that worked there. We got along.

"Anyways, Terri's out, no jacket, at the car window of this fellow, bent over, shufflin' her backside. Oh, I should tell you she's supposed to have given me a ride, as some call it, for compensation. Seems like that's what she's arrangin' with this other guy, tryin' to sell a car stop or something. I move more into the light and catch her eye. She stands up and looks back at me. I wave a wad of bills at her. That's the money I stole from Doc Washington's wallet at the Home Center USA. That's like a big hardware store with everything. You could build a house with all they have there. The whole thing.

"She sees what she wants and starts back toward me, and I move behind the OBI, staying in the shadows so that fellow she was workin' on, or anyone else, can't spot me. I stay a bit ahead of Terri and work my way back to near the quad. She gets over to me and asks where I got all the money. I made somethin' up about workin' at the school part-time for pay. I tell her I want my ride, and she tells me to come on up to her room. She got a room above the OBI. I tell her I can't be seen, and I'm embarrassed. Besides, I like nature. I want my first time to be outdoors, under the stars. She really believes it is my first time doin' this. I give her some of the money, and she agrees. She asks me about the cowl, somethin' like, 'Is that my Dommie's robe?' I tell her he lent it to me to try out.

"I walk back to the quad, grab the tarp and rake, and start headin' deeper into the woods. She hesitates, lookin' at me. I tell her the rake and tarp are to make her more comfortable, that I'll smooth out a spot and put the tarp down. Now she's smilin' like I'm unscary and follows me some more. I ask who the car was. She tells me some jerk she wasted her time with, and that I'm on the clock, so it'll have to be a quickie with all this walkin'.

"I stop and shuffle the rake around like I'm tryin' to find a good spot. We're at a break in the tree canopy. She's trailin' me, rubbing her bare arms and shoulders—left her jacket in the OBI because she was not expectin' to be outside very long. Soon she comes to the small clearing. Beautiful, still night. I look up at all the stars. She comes close and looks up too.

"I smash her in the neck with the rake handle, right in the wind-pipe. Then I'm on her as she goes down. I got both hands wrapped tight at the front of her throat, all my weight on her—over her. Big mistake she makes: she grabs each of my forearms with a hand, tryin' to dig her nails in 'em. But I got the long-sleeve coveralls and the cowl on. She messed up. Her eyes roll back and then close. She goes still. Her body is gettin' cold already. I was feelin' real stubborn over the whole thing with Zoie, so I keep my hands wrenched down to her neck even longer than necessary. I was ponderin' how Zoie might even come back now.

"I get up and lay out the tarp and roll her onto it. I rake around the area, make it look undisturbed. That's a part of golf course upkeep— makin' things look natural for the linksmen. I drag her, on the tarp, deeper in. It's mostly downhill. I considered using the quad. I could have gone a bunch further but would leave obvious signs. Anyways, I find this tree, long dead, that had tipped over, and the trunk fallin' had pulled all the roots up, like a giant divot. I got Terri in there and covered her with the debris of the forest floor. I make my way, walkin' backwards, usin' the rake to cover my tracks. Hard to see, but I had a good sense of it.

"I drive back the way I came, being just as cautious. I worried a little about the electric motor havin' enough juice to get up the steep part, but it was no problem. I get to the campus, put the cowl and tarp in a garbage bag, and I throw it all in the monastre's dumpster. You guys have your own dumpster, separate from the orphanary. That's how Doc Washington wants it. I sneak around the building, connect the quad back up to power, replace the rake where I got it, wash my hands good and hit the hay. I don't know how all this affects me coming here."

"Why did you tell me all this?" I will ask the mop cadet.

"I had to tell someone."

"I told you I am under no obligation to keep your secret."

"I believe you will. Everybody's got secrets."

27

Artie is sitting up in his hospital bed. He is in a double room but with no other patient. He has been scanned and told he has a concussion and should stay a night for observation. The surgeon decided not to stitch his head wound because of the time that had passed and his pre-hospital care providers did a good job with the Steri-Strips. He is on acetaminophen with codeine.

He can hear the TV going—some afternoon talk show with celebrity interviews. He fishes around his bedside table and finds his glasses. He wrangles them on even though one of the temples and the hinge are twisted. His pain lessens as soon as his eyes focus properly, like someone let the pressure out of his skull.

The room is nicely lit, with sunlight coming through the sheer outer curtains and the opaque, inner curtains open. The light-blue and aqua-green walls are pleasing. The white ceiling is unvaried and soothing. He finds the TV remote and turns it off.

–Who put that on? You've got to get your phone back.

He looks around through the top drawer of the table beside him.

–Not there. Nurse said no phone came in with you, that it wasn't on the list of personal belongings that came up from the ER. You have to get back to Albany about that promotion. Maybe if you are working in Manhattan, you can get an apartment in Westchester and still commute, and if things work out with Headmistress, you'll be significantly closer to her—to the orphanage. She did say she would drive you home. You would need a substantial raise or a car. It was nice having the state car: no tolls, insurance, gas. You could have a longer commute with a state car. Naturally you would need a place to park it in Manhattan. Need to ask. You need to get back to them before they reconsider. Working with Orange after his letdown might be difficult. This whole thing drove a wedge of sorts between you. What did that pretty doctor in the ER say about being discharged?

Brother Dom comes into the room, cracking the wide room door against the ajar bathroom door. "Hey, Crash. You lookin' better and better."

"Thank you so much."

"Nothing, part of the job of balancing out the universe."

"The ER doctor said you did a good job on the Steri-Strips. She didn't even believe stitches would be better after all the time that went by."

"I'll be sure to stop by and see him, get my cut of the bill." Brother Dom pulls the visitor's chair noisily over to the bed and flops down on it, his legs splayed out, covered in tight denim.

Artie smiles. "Doctor's a woman."

"As long as I get my cut."

"Did you come alone?"

"Doc Washington dropped kiddo—Jorgie—and me off. He'll pick us up later."

"He didn't want to come up?"

"Jorgie stopped at the vending machines. He's giving them all a look-over to see what he wants. They don't have anything like that at the school. I gave him a few bucks, said get whatever you want."

"I thought you monks weren't to carry money?"

"Just for incidentals."

"And Doc Washington?"

Jorgie comes in, eating a chocolate bar. "Hi, Mister." He holds out two chocolate bars for Artie and Brother Dom to take.

"No thank you. You have it. I have to wait a little while before I can eat. Nauseous."

Brother Dom takes one, rips it open, breaking the bar, and pops a piece in his mouth. "Doc Washington is driving around."

"He's still searchin' for Swaine," Jorgie says. "He figured he would drive the whole neighborhood around here lookin' while we visited. Killin' two birds with one stone. He figured you were safe now, Swaine's not."

"That's what he said," Brother Dom confirms.

–Washington seems a good man, protective of his students. Maybe you judged him harshly.

Hudson and Brewer enter the room.

"Hello, Mr. Alston. Sorry to see you like this," Brewer says. Hudson nods. Brother Dom stops eating.

"Artie, please."

"I heard these two did a great job on your head."

"Sure did," Jorgie says.

"Yes, getting better."

"As for the car, we located it, and we got our local tow truck guy, Mary, going to tow it today. She's gotten plenty of cars out of rough spots before. She's having a busy day."

"Big money day," Hudson says. "Quite a few winchings were needed for people going off the roadway. None as bad as you."

"I really need my phone. It's state property," Artie says.

–You gotta call about that promotion.

Hudson steps closer, up against the bed, eyeing Artie's bandaged head. "We told the tow guy the car was state property and nothing better disappear from it. We were pretty clear."

"I'll bet," Brother Dom says.

"It'll still be in there if it stayed in there through the crash. She has to keep on our good side. If it got ejected, though, you're going to have to do some looking. Hopefully you're all backed up and they get you a new one."

"We spoke to Orange, your supervisor," Brewer says from behind his partner. "He is going to take care of the car end of things. We gave him the tow info. That's one thing you don't have to worry about. Just do the MV-104 when you're feeling up to it. You grab the form at the DMV website."

–Paperwork.

"Thank you. Any report on the missing student, Swaine?"

"No, unfortunately," Brewer says.

"Did you hear anything from Swaine," Hudson asks Jorgie.

"No, sir, Officer. I mean Detective."

"We have other news," Brewer says. "We found the girl, Terri Dover."

"We found the body," Hudson says, looking around the room at the three civilians' facial expressions.

"Oh," Artie says.

–So sad.

"Three days ago," Brewer explains. "Cadaver dogs found her. Off the main road between the school and town, pretty far into the woods. Sort of behind the OBI, but well off their property. She probably went with the killer willingly. It was too far to drag a body from the OBI or the road. The medical examiner confirmed the ID today. It will be in the news tonight. She was straight murdered. No rape."

–A small consolation.

"I can't say much more. We have to hold details for interviews with suspects."

"Of course," Brother Dom says.

"We got her phone," Hudson says. "She left it in her jacket, in the bar, when she went outside. A lot of johns' numbers."

"Johns?" Jorgie asks.

"She was a sex worker," Brewer says, taking over the storyline. "All the suspicious contacts in the phone are aliases. We tracked a few down and questioned them. That was before we found the body."

"They alibied up," Hudson adds.

"Figures," Brother Dom says.

"So far, it looks like no DNA under the nails or anywhere. No fingerprints or weapon. She was hidden well for about two weeks. Decay accelerated because of the moist environment."

"Most of this stuff, the transactions," Hudson says, "are done on hidden accounts. Any perv could have found her online and transacted."

"Hard to trace," Brewer says. "All sorts of delivery, truckers, even exec types go on these websites and find a girl. They could be at their million-dollar, ski-vacation home."

"Or lakeside," Hudson says. "Going to be tough."

"She got with the wrong one."

"Sex work is a tough business," Brother Dom says. Both detectives look at him for a moment. "I'm just saying."

–Awkward.

"We wanted, before we go, to tie up some loose ends on your two parts," Brewer says. "We cleared you two from the murder investigation. We have no suspect in mind, but there's no longer any reason to contact you about this again."

"We'll probably never find who did it," Hudson states, and the room stays quiet.

–Sad. Not sure how you should feel after being told you're not a homicide suspect.

"Well, you have our number if you need anything else. Police report for the moving vehicle accident will be available in a day or two. If Mary, the tow guy, gets a hold of your phone, we'll have her bring it to you."

"Thank you."

–Headmistress will be impressed if you get that promotion. You gotta get that phone or hope the voicemail is still accessible. Can't remember that guy's name. Yancy? Can't ask Orange.

"And if Mary starts talking about how she gave you a tow job, do not engage. You don't want to get involved with her." Hudson, open-mouthed smiling, gets blank stares from everyone in the room. "Feel better," he says to Artie and walks out without waiting for a reply.

"We are busy," Brewer says and shrugs.

"Better get to it," Brother Dom says.

They all say goodbye. Brewer shakes Artie's hand and leaves the room.

–That hurt. Your hand is all bruised too.

"I guess that's sort of behind us," Artie says.

"Yeah." Brother Dom stands, goes and looks out the window. He takes the last bite of his chocolate before turning back to Artie and rests his butt and hands on the sill. He has a smear on his chin.

Jorgie opens the last bar. "Murder suspects. Those two detectives were wasting their time. I could've told them you two weren't killers." Jorgie snorts and then laughs.

Brother Dom first and then Artie join him laughing. The agitation of his head brings Artie fresh pain.

–Don't know why you think this is funny.

THE END

Acknowledgments

I would like to thank a lot of people. Please excuse my brevity. My wife and children, my parents and siblings. My extended family. My friends. All the many people who did so much for me to get me to the point where I could publish this book—you know who you are. Thank you all.

Thank you to everyone who read my first novel, *The Outcast Missing Someone*, especially those who took the time to rate and review it.

Thanks to Kathleen Biesty, James Dennis and Maureen Biesty for reading an early draft and giving me great notes.

Thank you, Lisa Gilliam, for the great job copyediting and designing this book.

About the Author

David Biesty was born and raised in Brooklyn, New York. He is a graduate of Hofstra University. He retired from the New York City Fire Department with the rank of Battalion Chief. He lives in Staten Island, NY, with his wife and two children. His first novel, *The Outcast Missing Someone*, was published in 2020.

CPSIA information can be obtained
at www.ICGtesting.com
Printed in the USA
JSHW041542260822
29715JS00001B/75